The **SEX**pert

HUSSMcCLAIN

The SEXPERT

HUSSMcCLAIN

DEDICATION

To the "journey".
Because the "destination" is never the goal.

JA HUSS and JOHNATHAN McCLAIN

HOW TO PLAY
WITH HER DONUT

Yes, kids. Today's Sexpert video is all about butt plugs!
How to get her sweet donut ready for some delicious fun!
By the end of this lesson you will learn how to put it in,
take it out, and make her want to do it again!

CHAPTER ONE

*Zoey: **Turn your radio on***. 93.3 is talking about us!

That's the text that just dinged on my phone. I stare at that message for a few seconds, forcing it to make sense, then have this exact thought process:

First of all—do people still listen to the radio?

Second—why the hell would 93.3 be talking about us? That must be a typo.

Third—why is it so fucking hot out this morning? I mean, Jesus Christ, it's not even eight AM and the Kenny Rogers temperature-gauge bobble head on the dash is telling me it's already eighty-five degrees.

The last one is really the only thing I care about right now because I've been sitting in standstill bumper-to-bumper traffic for the better part of ten minutes and this old truck has no AC, which means I have all the windows down and the hot July wind is making everything a million times worse than it needs to be. Plus, I forgot my hair tie, so my hair is sticking to my neck sweat because I can't pull it back into my professional pony-tail. Which is just gross.

My phone dings another text.

Zoey: Are you listening?

I love that Zoey uses proper punctuation in her texts. It's so cute.

Me: WTF you thinking abt I tink your lats tit was typo

I tell everyone I'm hip and cool and don't use proper punctuation but the truth is I'm just a really bad texter. My fingers just don't work the little keyboard right. I've tried the two-thumb technique and found it just takes too long because I always press two letters at the same time and it's rarely true that you're aiming for two letters right next to each other on the keyboard. So I use the tried-and-true pecking method when I text and… well, example A above. (I can't take all the credit because autocorrect helps me make that magic.)

Me: Do you tink the sun shitting my bobbled makes it red the wrong tampon

Then I add:

Me: Temp. ?

To make it clear.
My phone rings in my hand.

Incoming Call
Zoey

"Hey," I say. "Sorry, autocorrect turned 'temp' into 'tampon.' I wasn't really asking about a tampon."

"Are you listening to the fuckin' radio?"

"I thought that was a typo."

"It's not! They're talking about us! Turn on 93.3 quick!"

"Hold on," I whine. "You know I have one of those pushbutton radios from the Sixties, right?"

"Just turn it on."

So I turn the knob on the radio to the right until it clicks, get nothing but static because I wasn't even aware this thing worked until right this moment, and then start pushing those little placeholder buttons to see if it's been magically programmed to 93.3.

It hasn't.

"Hurry! They're gonna go to break!"

"I'm trying, dammit. I'm not really sure how to find an analog radio station, OK?" I turn the other knob down towards 93.3 and get a station playing *I Can See Clearly Now* by… someone I don't know. But I do know the words. "'I can see clearly now the rain is gone…'" I sing to Zoey. "Is this the right one?"

I can hear her taking deep breaths on the other end of the phone.

"What?"

"No," she snaps. "That's the Rock. 93.7."

"Well, excuse me if I'm not precise. OK, hold on." I sigh, nudging the dial to the left just an eensy bit more…

"And did you see the one about the butt plugs?" is followed by hysterical male laughter.

But that's when I notice the pickup truck next to me must be listening to the same thing because I hear it coming from the open window.

When I look over I see a guy with light brown hair and a scruffy chin—also talking on the phone. Our eyes meet for a brief second and I look away real fast, but then look back just as quickly because damn. The guy is cute.

He smiles and I roll my window up. It protests with a sickening squeak noise that makes my teeth hurt, but I soldier on because I don't need some cute stranger hearing this conversation.

"What is this?" I ask Zoey. "What the hell are they talking about?"

"Us, you dipshit! Us! The Sexpert!"

"Oh, my God," one of the radio guys says as he tries to breathe through his laughing fit. "Where did she come up with this stuff?"

"Wait," I say, holding up a finger. "Is he saying my lesson was inaccurate? Because I did a lot of research on proper butt-plug technique. And," I add, stressing the word, "that *is* our most popular video. It's got like twenty-seven thumbs up and only three thumbs down. So people must find it helpful."

"Eden," Zoey says in her stern mom voice. "Who cares what they think about the video? They're talking about us! We're going viral, baby! We're going viral!"

She's literally talking to her baby. I think. Then he coos back at her on the other end of the phone, and yes. She was talking to him.

"We have to find out who she is," says the other morning radio DJ. "I mean, she's local, yeah?"

"Has to be. All the stuff she said comparing the TDH to a collection of dildos was classic. Hey, if any of you out there know who she is, give us a call!"

"Can internet videos be nominated for Pulitzers?"

"Webby Awards, I think."

"Well, then let's get this chick a Webby!"

"Viral," I say. "Well, that's awesome, right?"

"Yes!" Zoey screams. "Yes! Do you know we've already gotten eight emails since these guys started talking about us fifteen minutes ago?"

"Eight emails," I say. Damn. We've been putting these Sexpert videos out for a year now and never got a single inquiry. We get plenty of comments, but those are mostly rude and talk about how men want to do things to my vagina. (Or butthole—that's a pretty popular comment on the butt plug video.) So eight emails... in fifteen minutes. "That's fantastic!"

"And we have fifty-five—no, fifty-six thousand views now! We've gotten a thousand more since I first texted you!"

"Jesus. This might be serious, huh?" I turn the radio down again because it's gone to commercial. "How'd they hear about us?"

11

"Who cares? It's the break we've been waiting for!" Zoey says. "Oh, my God. I gotta get back to editing the next video. We shouldn't wait until Friday for this one. We should put it up tomorrow! Bye!"

I get hang-up beeps as the call drops. And for a few seconds I can only stare at the screen wondering if all that really just happened.

When I came up with the idea for the Sexpert it was out of desperation. I hate being broke. And I hate living at home. And since I work in the Tall, Dark, and Handsome neighborhood just south of the Denver Tech Center and live all the way over in the crappy part of Lakewood, sleeping in my childhood canopy bed since I graduated college four years ago has really sucked. The commute is horrible.

Example A of horrible commutes is the bumper-to-bumper traffic I'm currently stuck in. Though it usually isn't this bad. Something must be happening over that next hill.

A knock on my window makes me jump. And when I turn my head cute-scruffy-jaw stranger is standing there—outside of his truck—motioning for me to roll my window back down.

I do that automatically, even though he might be a serial killer, because he's very nice to look at.

"Can I help you?" I ask, squirming in my seat because I'm so hot now since I had the window rolled up for that phone conversation, sweat is literally pooling between my boobs.

"Do you have a charger I can borrow?" He holds up his phone like this explains everything.

"You shouldn't be out of your truck," I say, looking over my shoulder to see if he's holding anyone up.

"We haven't moved in eleven minutes. I think it's OK just this once to get out of my truck on the freeway."

"It could start moving any second," I say, looking around because you just don't get out of your car on the freeway. Even in stopped traffic.

"No, really. There's a cow giving birth up over that hill. I heard it on the radio."

"Stop it!" I laugh, slapping his hand. Which is gripping my half-open window. "There is not!"

"Seriously. Some cow got out of that pasture over there"—he points to a rolling pasture where dozens of cows are trotting up the hill like they're late for an event or something—"and got onto the freeway and now she's giving birth in the fast lane."

I snort. It's something I'm not proud of, but do often. "That's crazy."

He holds his phone again. "I was on a call and my phone died. Since we're gonna be stuck here for the unforeseeable future, do you happen to have a charger I could borrow?"

We both glance down at my radio. Or, more accurately, the cassette player. Which is how I charge my phone in this old-ass truck my dad gave me when my college car died a horrible death during an impromptu trip to Vegas last fall.

"Oh," he says.

"I have a real one," I say quickly. Because he's even cuter up close than he was from ten feet away and I want to be helpful. "But you gotta give it back. It's the only good one I have."

I don't add, *And I can't afford to buy another one*, because everyone knows they sell them for ten bucks at Wal-Mart. But even ten bucks is a lot of money to me today. I'm dead broke until payday and that's not until the end of the week. I need that ten bucks for gas.

"Cross my heart," he says, crossing his heart.

God, that's adorable.

So I say, "One sec. Let me find it," and start digging into my purse.

"You moving or something?" he asks.

I glance out the back window at the boxes I'm hauling in the bed and say, "Yeah. Finally. I scored a cool studio in the TDH so today is my move-in."

"TDH," he says, like he's trying out the acronym. "That's the Tall, Dark, and Handsome neighborhood, right? Named for, presumably, all the hot dudes living there?" He rolls his eyes when he says "hot dudes."

"Yup." I beam. "Hottest place to live in Colorado right now and I'm there!"

What I don't say is that I've been saving for two years to be able to afford my own apartment. I'm overly cautious that way. I have a year's worth of rent tucked away in a savings account as my safety net that will not be touched under any circumstances. I might not look like one of those practical girls, but I am. Just thinking about spending my savings gives me a little sick feeling in my stomach.

"That's funny," he says.

"What is?"

"I'm moving in there today too."

Holy shit. "Really?"

"Yup. Just drove in from Moab." Then he leans in and says, "Don't tell anybody, though. I'm not sure I'm tall, dark, or handsome enough to be there. Don't wanna get booted out on my first day." He winks. He's clearly making a joke. He could probably be the damn mayor of the TDH.

"Maybe we'll be neighbors?" I say, then immediately blush. Because I think I just used my secret Sexpert voice on him.

"So… that charger? Sorry, I don't mean to be rude but I was on a call with my friend, and he's in some kind of crisis and needs someone to vent to. Sorry. Can I borrow it? Please?" He smiles again.

"Ah," I say, finding the charger cord in my purse. "Here you go. But you gotta give it back," I remind him.

"Already crossed my heart…"

"Eden," I say, catching his unsaid question about my name.

"Eden," he says. "Good name. Suits you." Then he winks again, says, "Thanks!" and turns away.

I watch him walk around the front of his truck and get in the driver's side, then continue to watch as he plugs my charger in and starts tapping on his phone.

"Sorry, dude," I can hear him say into the phone over the din of the stopped traffic. "My phone died. What? Oh, I had to beg a charger off…" But before I hear any more, he rolls up the window and shuts me out.

"Hmmmph," I huff.

Well, those were two completely unexpected and exciting things to happen on the way to work. And it's my move-in day. So that makes three exciting things to happen today.

I can tell my life is gonna be great from now on. It's like things are finally falling into place. Things are finally going my way. Things are finally gonna get better.

But that's when I notice traffic is moving again.

I look over at cute guy—hey, he didn't give me his name back—and I'm about to yell out the window about my charger, but he just waves and pulls away.

I beep my horn, but he doesn't even bother looking over his shoulder. Just butts his way between two cars and disappears over the hill.

I turn on my blinker to signal I want to get over so I can go after him, but a guy driving a BMW gives me the finger and scoots past me.

Assholes. Both of those stupid men are assholes.

And cue the irony. Because now I really do have to spend my last ten bucks on a new phone charger just because I fell for a handsome stranger on the freeway.

CHAPTER TWO

"Shit," I say, watching my new friend Eden disappear in my rearview.

"What? What's wrong?" That's Pierce on speakerphone.

"The chick I borrowed the charger from. Traffic started moving and this dude honked at me and I had to take off. I tried to wave to her to follow me so that I can pull over and give it back but I don't think she saw me."

"Fuck her. Her own stupid fault for giving her shit to a stranger on the freeway."

Sometimes I can forget that Pierce is an unapologetic asshole. Occasionally I even wonder why I continue being friends with the guy. Normally I try to make it a rule to avoid being friends with assholes, but... Pierce and I go back, and I love him like a brother, so he gets a pass.

Also, he's French. So it's kind of to be expected.

"Nice, dude," I say. "You're a real treat."

"Fuck everybody," he shouts.

"Slow down, K? Start over. I'm not sure I have a handle on what's twisting your croissant."

He makes a sound like an engine revving down and says, "Someone is stealing my IP. OK? Someone has stolen *my* fucking intellectual property. And when I find out who it is... woe be unto them. Woe be unto them, I say!"

"Very biblical. What makes you think that someone *stole* it? Couldn't someone simply have had a similar idea?"

"A similar idea *called* the Sexpert? Are you fucking kidding me? That shit is gold. And it was my idea! And where are you? I went down to your office and they said you were in fucking Utah. What the fuck's in Utah?"

"Rocks. I was bouldering."

"Rocks? There are rocks all over the place! It's Colorado!"

"Dude, relax. It was my last weekend of freedom before I start being Johnny Corporate and I wanted to just ... y'know ... commune with the universe."

"What the fuck did they do to you at Berkeley?" He asks it with a dire sincerity.

As timing would have it, I'm pulling up to the roundabout driveway in front of Pierce's building. Which is now, I guess, also my building.

I didn't want a big, sprawling, conventional-type workspace for the Aureality offices, but I also didn't particularly want to take the company public and have all the pressure that comes with an IPO and the burdens of running a newly billion-dollar-valued company. Hell, I didn't want to have a company and a career and have to do any of the things I'm doing in the first place. But these are, to say the least, first-world problems of the silliest order, so really... I shouldn't complain. And I'm not. We're doing all kinds of cool stuff with the company. Stuff I can't even talk about, but it's kind of badass and I'm pretty stoked, to be honest. I've left all the drama and bullshit in California behind me and I'm ready for a new start. I'm gonna be working just two floors below my best friend and it's gonna be like old times. Just instead of talking shit about professors, we'll be talking shit about shareholders. It's gonna be awesome.

"Dude," I say into the phone, "I'm just pulling up. Give me two minutes, I'll come up to your office."

"And also—!" But that's all I let him get out before I tap End and hop out of the cab. I grab the charger as I step out of my pickup. I have this notion that I should just carry it with me wherever I go until I run into my new friend Eden again. If she's moving into the TDH—which I can't even say to myself without making fun of—today, then I have to assume we'll run into each other at some point. Maybe a restaurant somewhere. Or a coffee shop. Or someplace. Denver feels like that kind of town, and this neighborhood, from what I've seen, feels like that kind of burg.

She was cute. More than cute, if I'm being honest. It's been a while since I've been with a girl. More than a while, actually. Which hasn't been by accident. It's been a choice. I've been careful not to wind up in another situation like my last one, but that's taken me out of the game for a long minute, so there is a slim chance that I'm just, like, super horny.

But even if that's true, it doesn't change the fact that she was objectively comfortable to look at for an extended period of time. And if I see her again and get a chance to give her back her charger—even if nothing else ever happens—I can sleep easy knowing I did the right thing by a cute girl called Eden.

When I hand him the key, the valet looks at me like he's not sure what to do with my busted-ass truck. "Oh, uh, I'm Andrew Hawthorne. CEO of Aureality Enterprises? I probably have a parking place somewhere?"

The valet looks to his left where a row of Bentleys and Porsches and Mercedes and other dick-size-compensating cars are parked. And there, in the middle, is an empty space with a sign that reads "A. Hawthorne. Aureality." Probably make more sense if it said, "A. Hawthorne. Surreality." But, hey, is what it is. The valet takes my key, smiles, and tries to avoid getting mud and dust all over his black pants as he opens the door and plops down inside.

"Don't scratch it!" I call to him. He doesn't seem amused.

There's a distinct difference between me and all the other people I see running around in the lobby. They look like successful businesspeople, dressed for work. I look like I was just bouldering in the grimy heat and took a break to smoke some of that sweet, sticky Colorado weed.

Ironic, since I don't smoke. Or drink. Or even take aspirin if I don't have to. Whereas I'm pretty sure the three guys in three-thousand-dollar suits who are walking past me right now are already coked up at nine in the morning.

I swipe my glossy new key card on the security turnstile and it goes from red to green. I breeze through and jog toward the elevator doors that are closing just as I get there. A hand reaches out and the doors spring open again, allowing me to step on. I notice that it's a woman's hand. Long fingers and red nails.

Landing in the vertical people mover, I confirm that I was right. It is a woman. Pencil skirt, blouse open one button too far down, shoes that make her seem deceptively taller than she is. The kind of woman who reminds me of my ex-fiancée. Not personality-wise or anything. Sex itself is baked into this person's DNA, and that was definitely not true of my Alice. But this woman is gorgeous in a harsh way and is looking at me like there's something wrong with me, so in that regard, they're twins. And so, by no fault of hers, I'm wishing she had just let the doors close on me.

"Thanks," I say as we start moving up.

"Which floor?"

"Sorry?"

"Which floor?" she repeats, nodding to the panel of numbered buttons.

"Oh, uh..." I look and see the floor she's pressed. "Oh. That one. Yeah, that's me."

She eyes me—in my opinion—oddly. "You have business at *Le Man?*"

"Huh? Oh. Uh, not really. Just seeing a friend."

"Oh? Who's that?"

Trapped in a closed space with this dominatrix-looking dame is making me feel much more uneasy than I normally like to start my mornings. Again, I think it's because she reminds me so much of my ex. The exact opposite of what I'm looking for in my life. Why couldn't I be stuck in here with that Eden girl? I still have her charger and all. Speaking of... I can sense myself backing up and kind of gripping the charger like a bolo. I don't want to have to fight for my life in this elevator car right now, but I'll do it if it comes to it.

"Uh... Pierce Chevalier? He's the—"

"He's the editor-in-chief," she interrupts.

I nod. "Yep. Sure is." I smile a tight-lipped smile and raise my eyebrows in what I'm pretty certain conveys a "what-the-fuck?" vibe.

And now she smiles and says, "I'll take you to him. I'm Myrtle. His executive assistant." OK. So, in the spirit of not judging a book by its cover, there's no way I would've pegged this broad as a 'Myrtle.' "And I'm sorry... I didn't catch your name?"

"Um, me?" She nods and gives a tiny smile. The kind you offer to a slow-learning three-year-old when you want to encourage them. "My name's Andrew Hawthorne."

Her expression turns now to one of seeming surprise. "You're Andrew Hawthorne? Founder of Aureality? Creator of Voice Lift?"

She certainly seems to know a lot about me. Which makes me even more uncomfortable. Which I didn't think was possible in this moment. "Uh... Yup. I'm him."

"Well," she says, her gaze turning kinda bedroom-y. "You are not what I expected."

I don't know what the fuck she's talking about, but I do my best not to show my confusion and try to play it cool. So, I just hit her back with... "Sure. Nobody ever is."

CHAPTER THREE

The Tall, Dark, and Handsome is actually a building, not a neighborhood. Or, well, it started that way. The publishing empire I work for decided to put a corporate office in Denver about fifteen years ago and came up with the most ridiculous idea for a building.

At fifty-one floors and a little over a million square feet, it's the fourth tallest building in Colorado. Problem

25

was, there was no room in the actual city of Denver to build it. So, they bought a whole bunch of farm land down south of the Tech Center and put it there. When it was completed ten years ago it was a shining tower of black glass, chrome accents, and marble floors. So it got the nickname the Tall, Dark, and Handsome building.

At first the publishing company was just gonna make it a huge sprawling campus like all the other corporate offices down here. But then the property values shot up once the building was underway and they started selling off parcels.

And today we have this.

It comes into view like the Rock of Gibraltar. (I stole that analogy. People say that all the time about the TDH building and I never got it, so one day I decided to look it up. So apparently the Rock of Gibraltar was the edge of the known world back in ancient times. And since the TDH is the edge of the Denver Tech Center, it sorta makes sense.)

A perfectly planned walkable urban neighborhood smack in the middle of cows.

Which explains the emergency birth on the freeway this morning.

There's like ten tall buildings now. And a whole bunch of low ones. And then, of course, there are the inevitable townhouses and condos for all the people who work here, and further east there are sprawling mansions for the CEO's.

It's nice.

No, it's cool as fuck. It's like living in New York with a view of Pikes Peak. You can walk everywhere because the Towne Centre is pedestrian only. So there's tons of parking garages, and little stores, and places to shop, and lunch trucks.

It's my dream neighborhood. And today I'm moving in.

Not even the cute serial killer who stole my phone charger can put a damper on my good mood today.

I park my truck in the garage, pretending I don't see the stink eye the garage attendant is giving me. He does that every day. Every. Day. Like it's the first time he's seen my shitty truck. Like I haven't been pulling in at eight AM every workday for the past two years. Like he's holding out hope that one morning I will show up in a Mercedes like everyone else and when I don't, he's disappointed all over again.

For a moment when I get out I have a second of hesitation about leaving all my boxes here in the bed while I'm inside. But then I decide—hell, if anyone wants my ten-year-old pink comforter and boxes of thrift-store clothes, they can have them. It would give me a reason to go buy new stuff.

I haven't been able to justify that expense. My savings account is off limits. And I refuse to break into it. Refuse. Because the truth is, I don't make enough money to afford a studio apartment in the TDH Towne Centre. The only reason they rented me this one was because I paid three months' rent in advance as well as my security deposit and last month's rent too.

I pull on my work shirt. I'm wearing a white t-shirt for the ride in because it's so damn hot today. But I like to look professional for work and a light blue button-down shirt with a wrinkle-free collar is how I do that. And my glasses. And my hair tie. I find people take you seriously if you look a little nerdy and I *am* a little nerdy. I'm a Star

Wars freak, for one. And regardless of my lack of texting skills, I'm pretty smart.

Smart enough to come up with that whole Sexpert idea on YouTube. Which makes me snort.

Because I have to admit, it was starting to feel like a time suck. But since Zoey is a web designer with access to a private server she already pays for (not to mention her mad video editing skills), I figure why not?

It's sorta fun. And no one can see my face. It's boob-shot all the way, bitches. If you're gonna be a video sexpert, you gotta show the goods. And I've got goods, let me tell you. They are spectacular.

So as I walk to the elevator I decide to let the whole phone charger setback become good luck. Because if cute serial killer had stolen it *last* week, I really would have to buy a new one with my gas money and then I'd be out gas money. But because that happened today, and today is the day I'm moving in to my new place in the TDH, I don't need gas money. I can walk to work tomorrow.

I smile as I flash my badge and push the call button for the elevator.

It's a very lucky day.

When the doors open I walk inside with a crowd of other people and push the button for the fiftieth floor.

I get a little sense of pride every time I do that. Maybe even feel a little smug. Because fifty-one is the top floor and I'm only one down. I don't even mind that it takes forever to get up there. Because when I step out of the elevators after almost everyone else is gone, I see nothing but mountains for hundreds of miles out every floor-to-ceiling window. Pikes Peak, and Mount Evans, and sometimes, on a very clear day, I can see the Spanish Peaks down south and Longs Peak up north too.

"Hey, Charlotte!" I say, passing the reception desk in the lobby. "Hi, Lynne!" I call out to the other receptionist.

They're both on the phone, but they simultaneously cover the handsets and say, "Hey, Eden!" in their brightest and cheeriest voices.

I flash my badge again, enter the west side of the offices, and say, "Good morning, Sylvia!" as I pass the printer. And then do that again as I walk by each person on my way to my cubicle.

They all say "Hi," back. I'm just one of those girls who likes to be friendly. I've found that if you're friendly you make people happy. Happy people who say hello to you every day are far less likely to confront you when you mess up. I hate confrontation and I regularly make mistakes, so it's a necessary precaution.

Plus, I like them. And being friendly is free. So why not?

"Eden!" my boss, Gretchen, calls from her corner glass-enclosed office on this end of the building. "Get in here! We're having a crisis!"

"Coming," I call, still using my friendly voice. I don't actually like being friendly to Gretchen. She's stiff, and pouty, and a little mean if I'm being honest. But she is the boss, and I'm a girl who respects the hierarchy.

So I set my purse down, find a hair tie in my desk drawer and tame my blonde mane, then fish out my tablet and go into her office, ready to deal with today's social media nightmare.

"Good morning, Gretchen! Happy Monday!"

She glares at me. I know she hates it when I say that every week, but I say it anyway. Not to piss her off, either. It's because Mondays already suck, right? So why not make them better? Sometimes, when there's not a cow

29

giving birth on the freeway, making me late, I bring her donuts from the donut truck parked outside in the Towne Centre on Mondays. She always complains I'm trying to sabotage her diet, but when I brought her grapefruit to show her I was considerate of her struggle, she didn't eat it.

She always eats the donuts.

And she's not even a little bit chubby, so... really? Come on, Gretch. Live a little.

"We have a crisis on our hands."

"Did someone hack our Facebook again?"

"No," Gretchen says. "Worse."

"Jesus. What's going on?"

"Pierce"—he's the big boss upstairs on fifty-one— "is raging about some little twat who stole *Le Man*'s intellectual property."

"No shit?" I say. "Well, that totally sucks. Did he call the lawyers?"

"Oh, you betcha."

"Phew," I say, wiping sweat off my brow. "Well, what can I do to help? Just tell me what you guys need and I'm there. Should I make a post on Facebook and start a trending hashtag on Twitter? Oh, I know! I can call it #StopTheStealing!"

That's my job. I'm the social media expert here. I even have an assistant. Well, I share an intern with the advertising department and they monopolize him most of the time, but still. He's one-tenth mine.

Gretchen chews her lip for a second like she's nervous. It's not something she normally does. In fact, she's not normally nervous. She's a little bit overconfident at all times. Zoey says it's just a show to make up for her inferiority complex, but I actually think Gretchen is quite competent, even if she is a little bit mean.

"No," she finally says. "No, you see… the problem is… we don't have much of a claim to this IP."

"What do you mean?"

"Well, it was in the planning stages, so it hasn't been published yet."

"Oh. So… what do we do, then?"

She sighs. "Here's the main problem, Eden. We don't know who she is."

"Oh." I'm confused. "Then how do you know she stole something from us?"

"She has faceless videos on YouTube."

I open my mouth to say, *No way! So do I!* but stop myself just in time because that's my secret life.

"So Pierce wants to soft-launch this new content today. Like immediately."

"OK," I say, tapping notes on my tablet. "Cool. Just point me to the articles and I will blast that stuff all over the place."

"No, see, we haven't… written anything yet. We don't have it yet."

I stop tapping and look up at her. "O-*kay*. So what should I blast?"

She chews her lip again. "Eden."

"Gretchen?"

"Eden, I need an idea. I need an idea of how to do this soft launch when we don't have content. Help me. I need you to come up with something by lunchtime and—"

"Why don't we just pull together all related articles from the past… oh, two years? And I can blast those?"

She goes still for a moment. I'm almost afraid she's having a seizure or something. "Gretchen?"

She blinks at me. Three times real fast. "You're a genius."

I beam a smile at her. Gretchen isn't one to hand out compliments, so my lucky day just keeps going. I might get a raise out of this. "Oh, I have a million more where that came from. This is just my off-the-top-of-the-head idea."

"Mmmm-hmmm," Gretchen says, pressing her lips together. "Perfect. Then I want twenty articles, ready to go. We'll feature one a day. And Eden—"

"Yes?" I say. And for some reason my lucky feeling fades as I stare at her sour face staring intently back at me.

"Give them all the same hashtag so we can collate them later. Maybe rebrand them. Yes, that's what we'll do. We should do that first. Take all those old articles and rebrand them with new graphics."

I'm tapping on my tablet again. "New graphics, got it. But I'll have to take this up to the art department. I don't know how quick—"

"I'll run my idea past Pierce and get his approval. He'll want to make this first priority, so just go pull the articles and tell them to get started."

She does this little wave thing with her hand. It's one of those you're-dismissed gestures. So I nod, gather myself by straightening my back and turn to leave.

"Oh, and Eden?"

"Yes?" I say, turning back again.

"#StopTheStealing is stupid. Don't use it."

"Sure," I say. "OK. I'll brainstorm with my intern and we'll come up with something—"

But she's already pressing text buttons on her phone. "I have to tell Pierce I have an idea how to save this."

I leave because that's what I'm supposed to do. But... she? She has an idea?

No. That was my idea.

I'm totally a team player. I'm not a credit whore at all. But...

She's *stealing* my idea.

CHAPTER FOUR

"*Pierce? Mr. Hawthorne* is here."

Pierce nods at Myrtle and waves me into his private office. Pierce's office looks like someone took a French castle, whittled it down to fit into twenty-five hundred square feet, and then plopped it onto the top floor of this glass and steel monolith in the middle of the Colorado mountains. The artist in me wants to believe that he did this as an artistic choice. Like, he was making some conscious commentary on the contrast between the man-made and the nature-made. The glory of the natural world versus the grandeur of human design. The contradicting aesthetic between the new, the old, and the ancient.

But the realist in me knows that he just likes having nicer, cooler shit than everyone else.

Myrtle holds the door open for me, and as I pass by her into the space, I'm pretty sure she lets her hand graze my dick when she turns away. She's kind of the perfect assistant for Pierce, I decide.

"Derek, I'm telling you, we are going to find out who this bitch is, and we're going to sue her until she dies!"

He's marching around the space, swinging a golf club in circles like it's a weapon. Which I suppose it could be. I hate golf, so it's torture for me either way.

"Pierce, calm down," comes the voice from the speaker phone. The voice I assume belongs to Derek.

"Fuck you, Derek!" he yells at Derek and hangs up on him.

"Who was that?" I ask, plopping down on the Victorian-era loveseat that my friend, the editor-in-chief of *Le Man* magazine, keeps in his office. (Asshole. You gotta love him.)

"Goddamn attorney," he kind of growls, still swinging his golf club around.

"Mon ami? Could you put that down before you hit something with it? Notably, me?" He throws the club to the ground, flopping down in the throne (literally—a *throne*) across from the loveseat. "Dude... What's going on? Why are you so upset?"

"You heard the bitch on the radio."

"I did."

"Someone is trying to sabotage me!"

"Sabotage you? You don't think that's a little...looking for the word...hold on...oh, got it...fucking paranoid and insane? Realize that's four words, but..."

"I'll bet it's one of my enemies," he says, ignoring my question. Which is fine. It was rhetorical anyway.

"Your enemies, huh? OK, man. I'll play. Let's assume for a second that you're right, and that this woman on the radio is trying to undermine your grand Sexpert idea by doing it first. What makes you think it's one of your enemies?"

There's a long pause as he looks out the window. Finally, he says, "Our quarterly reports came in today."

Doesn't feel like an answer to my question, but I go with it anyway. "Yeah?"

"Yeah. Do you know how much money this magazine lost last quarter?"

"I very much do not know."

"Seventeen percent over the same quarter last year."

"Wow, that's—"

"Yeah, it's a fucking lot."

"K. That sucks. So?"

"Man, all of our publications are taking a hit. Everything. All the newspapers. The magazines. Even the goddamn TV stations. Everything. Know why?"

"Because people don't read or watch TV anymore?"

"Give Andrew a gold star!" He leaps to his feet, grabs up the discarded golf club, and once again, I feel like it's only a matter of moments before I catch a nine-iron to the dome.

"So..." I start. Cautiously. "And I just want to make sure I'm tracking this... So, you're assuming that someone who's got a grudge against your publishing *empire*—"

"It's my dad's empire. I only run this part of the kingdom."

"Fine. So, you think someone who's got a grudge against your fiefdom is trying to take it down by launching a—from what I heard this morning—lightly viewed vlog about sex that happens to share the same name as an idea you had for some branded online content about sex tips. Is that what I'm hearing you say? Because that *is* what I'm hearing you say."

He points the golf club at me in a way that says, *J'accuse!* "You got it, man."

"OK," I say. I don't say the other things that are in my head. Things like, *You've gone round the bend.* Or, *Not to be a dick, but it's possible you're just kind of bad at running a magazine and looking for reasons to explain why it's coming undone.* Or, *What do you want me to do about it?* Instead, I just listen.

He goes running behind his desk. "Have you seen her?"

"Seen her? No. I didn't even know about her until you told me to turn the radio on."

"C'mere." He hits some keys on his computer and waves me over. "Check this shit out."

I swing around behind his desk, pushing the golf club away from my head as I do. What I see, looking at his monitor, are two of the—and I don't think this casually—most perfect-looking breasts I have ever seen. They're not even naked. They're covered by a V-neck tank-top kind of a thing. But even so. They. Are. Perfect. Holy shit. I don't know if it's possible for tits to have a personality, but these do. So I guess it is possible. They seem to say, *Hi. We're friendly but dangerous. And we will fucking end you, dude.* I'm momentarily transported somewhere, imagining what the rest of the human who is attached to these breasts might look like.

And then I hear the *voice*.

"Hi, everybody, and welcome to another installment of *The Sexpert.*"

There's this momentary jolt of déjà vu that hits me at hearing the sound coming from the speakers. Which isn't all that weird. It happens a lot these days, since the little app I invented that has started this avalanche of tech success currently chasing me down the mountain is a thing that alters and masks your voice virtually into one of a couple dozen or so pre-programmed vocal IDs and has— for reasons passing understanding—caught the public's imagination and gone global.

There's the husky setting. Tweety Bird, which actually drives me insane. Darth Vader is a super-popular one (better be for what we had to pay George Lucas to get the rights), and so forth.

It's just kind of a silly thing I stumbled on in my bedroom while I was frustrated with the progress I was making on an art project that I have since abandoned. And then wham, bam, thank you, augmented voice reality... Next thing you know, I'm a friggin' tech billionaire and titan of industry.

Life's weird that way.

The fabulous breasts on Pierce's monitor are using the Sultry Siren setting.

"Are you listening?" Pierce's voice is now the one doing to my thoughts exactly what his first name implies.

"No. I wasn't, actually. What?"

"How do we figure out who this is?"

"What do you mean?"

"Can't we use your app to ID this fucking harlot?"

"Harlot? Dude... No. That's not what the app does."

"Jesus Christ!" He thrusts his hands into his suit pants' pockets and kicks at the ground. It almost looks like a Gene Kelly imitation.

"I don't get it. Can't you just send a cease-and-desist order to the website? I presume you have Sexpert trademarked."

I have only once in my life seen Pierce Chevalier appear shamed or embarrassed. Junior year of college, I slept with a girl he had a crush on. Not my fault. It was at a party, I was drunk, and I didn't know it was the girl he had been crushing on. She and I wound up dating for almost a year. A year in which I stayed drunk most of the time. Because she was the first in a series of relationships I had with fairly unpleasant and kind of—what's the word? Oh—*mean* women over the next several years.

Pierce never said anything though until it was all over. And then, finally, after we broke up, he admitted to me that he was jealous and had been since that first night we got together.

I said, "Why? She's awful."

And he said, "I know. For you. But I think she and I were made for each other."

I have to give him credit. Guy knows what kind of an asshole he is.

Anyway, the sheepish, lost-little-boy expression he had when he admitted that to me is one I'll never forget. It really got to me. It exposed a side of Pierce that he doesn't show many people. Or maybe any people. And it's the one that caused me to say, "Hey, I'm sorry. I will never let something like that happen again. For both our sakes." And I quit drinking and after that started making all my bad relationship decisions stone-cold sober.

40

But the point is, that it was the only time I ever saw that fragile, almost weirdly untethered look on his face. Until now, when I make the relatively simple assumption that he put a protection in place for his idea that he thinks will save his magazine.

"Dude," I say, slowly.

"Just don't. OK? I was going to get to it!"

Jesus.

"OK," I offer up. "So. What's your plan?"

"I've got Derek, et. al. looking into fast-tracking this trademark thing. I assume that whoever this chick is, she hasn't yet. I'm hoping."

"And?"

"And we're going to roll out our own content. Our reach is broader. Our microphone is bigger. And we're going to drown her out."

"But she..."

"And that's why I need to know who she is. I need to know who the hell we're dealing with here. She has to be someone with access to what we're doing."

"You mean... like a spy?"

"Exactement, mon frère! A spy!" He spins around in a circle as he says it. It's odd. Pierce is sober too. But to see him now, you wouldn't know it. "Isn't there anything you can do to help? You make voice software, for fuck's sake!"

I sigh. Long. Hard. And then allow words I know I'll regret to start slipping out of my mouth. "We are..."

"What?" he asks. "What? You are what?"

"We are working on this voice tracker ID thing that..."

"That what? That you can find out who this is?"

"Yeah? I mean the reason we're developing it is…" I take a long pause because Pierce is my brother and always will be, but it may be best if…

"Is what? What's it for?"

"Nothing. Just… I'm happy to help, but again, man, it feels like maybe you're just having a bad morning."

"Oh, I am definitely having a bad fucking morning. But one thing's got nothing to do with the other."

"Really? 'Cause it feels like maybe it does."

"Can you help me find out who this person is or can't you?" He points over at his computer screen.

I sigh the sigh of a friend. A friend who swore a private oath to his brother that he would always have his back. "Yes. I can help you."

He grabs me and kisses me on both cheeks. I always think of the French thing as kind of a joke because he came to America when he was, like, four, and has only even been to Paris for visits and stuff, but Pierce takes it all very seriously. Just like he takes everything.

"Stop kissing me now, thanks." He does. I back up and look him in the eye. "Can I ask you something?"

"Does it matter if I say no?"

"No," I tell him, then continue, "Is the magazine going under?"

He looks at me like I asked him if he's really Aquaman or something. "*Le Man* is my baby. I don't want to be too dramatic—"

"Since when?"

"—but I don't think it's a stretch to say that this is my life's work. This is something that I told my father was important. Even with the death of the publishing industry, even with other, more established men's publications closing shop, there was a place in the world for a sophisticated and sexy magazine for men. That men would buy. That men would care about. That would compete with the likes of *Vogue*, and *GQ*, and *Vanity Fair*, and..." He pauses. His eyes drift off to the mountains somewhere and he looks lost for a second. Sad, maybe. "*Le Man* is not gonna go under. K? It's not. So..."

I press my lips together and slap him on the shoulder. "OK, man. Good deal. I'll help you. I'll find your mystery saboteur. K? I'm on it." I'm not sure that I actually can. At least not yet. And I'm less sure that'll it'll matter all that much if I do. But I said I would and my man clearly needs to feel like there's something hopeful about the view he's facing. And if I can help grant him that for a little while, so be it.

I start to leave, and he asks, "You excited?"

"About what?"

"All of it. Being here. Running things. Living in the TDH. All of it."

"Yeah. Yeah, I am. I feel like..."

"Like what?"

"Like I'm making a fresh start. I feel... I dunno. Invigorated or something."

"Yeah? That mean you're finally gonna start getting laid again?"

"Dude..."

"Because if not, I heard there's an order of Franciscans that might be recruiting."

"Goodbye." I start to leave.

"Hey, wait, I'm just fucking around. I think it's good that you took some time off. Even if it was a total overreaction in my opinion."

"Think you're the guy to lecture someone about overreaction?"

"No, I mean it. I like that you went out and got in touch with you. Or whatever the fuck you do in the desert. That is what you do, right? You touch yourself?"

"Goodbye."

"No! Wait. I'm sorry. I just... Seriously, I just worry about you dying alone. Like, literally. Like falling off a mountain or some shit and dying alone."

"Well, then you should come climbing with me."

"Fuck that. I look like a Sherpa to you?"

"Goodbye."

"Let me introduce you around. I know some hot chicks who're into all that outdoorsy shit."

"Let me just... get settled. K? Besides, I already met a girl, if it makes you feel better."

"Yeah? Who?"

"The girl who loaned me this." I hold up the charger.

"The dumb broad who let you steal her shit on the highway?"

"I didn't steal it."

"It was hers, and now you have it. Did you pay for it?"

"Dude—"

"I don't write the laws! Stealing is stealing. Speaking of... help me find this Sexpert bitch!"

And we're back to that.

"I will. Cross my heart. But I gotta go. I'm supposed to be giving some rousing speech to the troops or something."

"Rouse them into helping me bring this bitch down," he says.

"Sure. Should totally get 'em fired up. Launching an assault on a faceless internet person in order to save the rep of a men's magazine? Who wouldn't be stoked to hear that first thing in the morning? That's some real Saint Crispin's Day shit."

I don't wait for him to throw a golf club at me—I open the glass door and head out. I pass Myrtle, who somehow makes me reflexively cover my crotch with my hands as I walk by where she's bent over, adjusting her stockings and eyeing me with a look that's half-amusement, half-tiger-stalking-prey. And as I'm glancing back over my shoulder at her to make sure she's not going to follow me and drink my blood or something like that, I bump into someone and drop the charger I'm still holding onto the ground.

We both go to pick it up at the same time.

"Oh," I say, seeing her face.

"Oh!" she says back. She's holding the charger now.

"Oh, good," I say. "That's yours. Thanks."

Eden blinks at me a few times and tilts her head to the side. She sniffs and pushes her glasses up the bridge of her nose. She opens her mouth, squints at me, then closes her mouth again.

She is so goddamn cute.

"Why are you here?" she asks.

"Me? 'Cause. Why are *you*?"

"I work here."

"Oh, yeah? Cool. So do I."

"You do?"

"Uh-huh."

"At... *Le Man*?"

"Oh. No. Not *here*." I gesture around me. "I mean HERE. Like, here in this building. What do you do here?"

"Here in this building?"

"No, here at *Le Man*."

"Oh," she says. This is even more awkward than talking in traffic on the freeway. "Social media."

"Oh. Cool." A beat. No one says anything. And finally—"So. Anyway," I continue. "Thanks again for letting me borrow the charger. I think my friend would've done something silly if I hadn't been able to talk him off the ledge."

"Is he OK now? Your friend?"

"Not really. But that's not unusual."

Pierce sticks his head out of his office now and shouts in my direction, "What are you doing for dinner?"

I shout back, "Dunno. I've still got to get settled in my place, get some work done, somebody told me there's a good rock climbing gym I should check out..."

"Fuck that. We're going out. Myrtle, make a reservation for eight-thirty."

"For where?" Myrtle asks.

"Someplace not shitty," he says. And goes back into his office.

I turn back to face my new friend Eden, who says, stutteringly, "Your friend is Pierce Chevalier?"

I sigh again. "Yup."

We stare at each other for a second.

"You need something, Eden?" That's Myrtle, breaking the mood.

"Oh, yeah, I, uh... I wanted to ask you something, actually."

"OK," says Myrtle. Then she looks at Eden. Who raises her eyebrows at Myrtle. Who gives a look like, *What?* to Eden. Who looks back at Myrtle like, *Gimme a second.* And then Eden looks back to me.

And I can't help but grin as I say, "OK. Well. See ya!" And head off.

As I reach the elevator bank and press the button to summon a car, Eden calls out, "I... I thought you stole my charger!"

I stop and turn back. "Stole it? I'm shocked. Who do you think I am?"

She shrugs. "I dunno. Who are you?"

My grin spreads in such a way as to make my eyes close when I respond, "I'm just a guy who tries to do what he says he's gonna do."

"Yeah?" she asks, a flirty little grin on her lips that I'm now noticing are plumper and poutier than I realized before. Oh, boy...

"Yeah," I say with a hint of a laugh. Then I add, "Cross my heart," as the elevator doors open, and I step inside and out of sight.

CHAPTER FIVE

I sigh as the elevator doors close and he disappears, then call out, "Hey! Your name!"

But he's gone.

"It's Andrew," Myrtle purrs in my ear.

"Jesus," I say, swatting her away. She was so close to me when she said that, she gave me a chill. "Why do you have to do that to me? You know it's weird."

49

She laughs. And Myrtle laughing is a beautiful thing because she doesn't do it often. She's one of those women who takes her role in life seriously and her role in life seems to be making people uncomfortable in every way imaginable. So she purrs into my ear a lot and every time I get this chill up my spine. Not like a creepy chill either. And I swear to God, I'm not bisexual, but Myrtle purring into my ear makes me want to reconsider that decision sometimes.

I rub the back of my neck to make that feeling go away. "Andrew, huh?"

She nods, winking at me. "Andrew Hawthorne. CEO of Aureality and creator of that app, Voice Lift."

"Voice Lift, no shit?" That's what I use to disguise my voice for the Sexpert videos. And just as that thought manifests in my head I get a weird feeling. Like...

"Yes, he's got the empty offices down on forty-nine."

"That big ol' space that used to house all our creative people?"

"Yup," Myrtle says, peeling a banana and taking a bite. She never eats the donuts I bring on Mondays. Ever. And I'm pretty sure she only eats the bananas to drive all the men up here crazy because Josh Washburn is watching her chew from the open doorway of his office right now. "He's Pierce's best friend or something. So we're going to be seeing a lot of him."

"He stole my charger on the freeway this morning." I hold up the charger as evidence. "But he gave it back, so I guess he didn't really steal it."

Myrtle laughs again, but this time it's the normal kind. Where she only tips up the corners of her mouth as she lets out a small huff. "Did you come up here for something? Or are you just making your good-morning rounds?"

Sometimes, if I bring donuts, I come up to fifty-one to say hello as well. I figure you can't be too friendly with the upper management, right? And almost all of them appreciate the gesture. I was voted Most Likely To Brighten Your Day two years in a row at the company picnic we have every summer.

But I am here for a reason. "So listen," I say. "Apparently something big is happening because Gretchen has me on an assignment to thwart a twat's takeover of some intellectual property we don't actually have. Do you know anything about this? I'd go back and ask Gretchen, but she's in a pissy mood right now and I figured you'd know better than anyone. So what's going on?"

"Oh." Myrtle waves her hand in the air. Then she leans in to whisper at me, but this time she's not trying to turn me on by purring. She's just being quiet so Pierce can't hear her. "If you think Gretchen is in a mood…" She huffs again. "He's going out of his mind about this shit."

"What shit?" I ask.

She takes my arm and pulls me down the hallway, looking over her shoulder as we walk. "Some girl is on YouTube with a video series Pierce thought up."

"Yeah, I got that much from Gretchen. I'm supposed to grab related articles from the past two years and start blasting them all over social media. My problem is that Gretchen never told me what the videos are about."

"Sex," Myrtle says. "She's calling herself the Sexpert. And Pierce is pissed off because…"

I stop hearing Myrtle and just stare at her glossy red lips as she continues talking because the word Sexpert is echoing through my head.

She didn't just say that. I made it up. There's no way all this stress and angst is about me. I just have the Sexpert on my mind because we were on the radio and we're getting hits, and...

I snap out of my momentary shock just in time to hear Myrtle say, "And she's gone viral, Eden. Oh, Pierce is livid. He thinks it's someone he knows."

"What?"

"Like an enemy of his father's. But I think it's probably someone here at the company."

"Why would you say that?" I ask.

"It only makes sense. It was a super-secret project. He only has a small group in on it and they've been twiddling their dicks about it for almost a year, so one of them probably decided, *Hey, if he's not gonna do it, I will.*" Myrtle shrugs, like this really does make all the sense.

"Oh, my God," I say. He's gonna think I stole that idea. And I didn't! So I say, "I had no idea he was working on something like this."

And then I realize I should really shut the fuck up, because Myrtle doesn't even know I'm the Sexpert.

No one does.

And it needs to stay that way forever, and ever, and ever.

"Of course you didn't," Myrtle says. "But that's what this is all about. So you should grab all the sex advice articles. That's what you needed to know, right?"

I nod. Still in shock.

"Oh, and that Andrew guy you were swooning over?"

"Yeah?" I say.

"Well, Pierce got him to agree to find this Sexpert using some new voice app. I guess he can do that. So…"

"He what? I mean… How do you know?"

"Same way I know Pierce has a foot fetish. Myrtle hears everything, sweetie." She winks and pats my shoulder. "This will all blow over soon. Don't worry too much about it."

I take a deep breath. Hold it. Let it out. Swallow. Smile. Then pull on the hem of my shirt to help mentally straighten myself out, and say, "Well, I have work to do. Gotta get the art department to make new sexy graphics! Byeeee!"

So I wave my usual cheerful wave and scoot past her.

I head straight to the stairs and immediately get out my phone and start texting Zoey as I pass through the door.

Me: bitch we got problems pierce is sexpert

I didn't mean it to come out like that but I can't be bothered with punctuation right now. And anyway, two seconds later my phone buzzes an incoming call from Zoey. I tab accept and whisper, "I'm gonna get fired today."

"What the hell are you talking about? What's that mean? Pierce is Sexpert?"

"I stole his idea and then he found out and I didn't mean to do it and now the cute freeway guy is on the case and he's gonna out me and get me fired! I'm fucked!" I whisper-scream that last part into the phone while I hold it at arm's length.

"Eden!" Zoey snaps. "Calm the fuck down and explain! I didn't understand any of that."

53

But then the stairwell door opens on fifty and two girls—Sara from accounting and Leslie from data entry—start walking up to fifty-one towards me.

"Hey, girls!" I wave and smile at them, trying to act normal.

"Hey, Eden!" they chime back together. "Happy Monday!" they say.

"Happy Monday," I say back.

Now I get it. I totally get why people hate it when I say that.

When they disappear onto fifty-one I go back to the phone. "How… when… Zoey! I think I might've stolen this idea from Pierce!"

"Don't be ridiculous. I was there when you came up with it. Remember? It was Valentine's Day two years ago and I was pregnant, and sad, and poor because business was bad and you said, 'We should be strippers.' And then I said, 'I can't be a stripper because I'm fat.' And you said, 'You're not fat, you're beautiful.' And then I said, 'We need a stupid YouTube series like that dumbass seventeen-year-old who got famous on *Ellen!* after she made stop-motion movies of Barbie and Ken having sex.' And you said, 'We should totally make a ridiculous sex advice channel and we should call ourselves the Sexperts!' Remember all that?"

That *was* how it went down. "I was drunk though, remember? That asshole Matthew dumped me after I put out and I was pissed off. So maybe I accidentally heard Pierce say something about the Sexpert and then I only thought it was my idea?"

"That's stupid. Don't be stupid, Eden. You're not stupid. You came up with the name! I was there!"

"Yeah, but we've been using Voice Lift to disguise my voice and the goddamned Voice Lift inventor is the cute freeway guy and now Myrtle says he's on the case and he's gonna figure out who I am!"

"Ridiculous!" Zoey yells. "No one is gonna find out who you are, Eden. We don't even show your face."

True.

I take a deep breath. Maybe I'm just overreacting?

"Besides, this was our idea so fuck-face Pierce can just fuck off. We're viral, I've got the next video ready to post for tomorrow. We're gonna ride this wave, baby! All the fucking way into shore and all the hard work we've put into it over the last year will finally pay off."

"How many hits do we have now? Like sixty thousand?"

"Sixty!" She laughs. "Bitch, we're at almost one hundred thirty thousand hits. And that's just for *How to Play With Her Donut! Licking His Sour Apple Pucker* is a close second with almost a hundred thousand. All of them, Eden. All of them are going crazy right now. I just got an invitation from YouTube to monetize. We hit the threshold like ten minutes ago! So we're gonna start getting paid!"

"Really?" I say. "For real?"

"Yes! We're in, Eden. We paid our dues. We created this content. We put in all the sweat equity and now we're going to get paid. We did not steal this idea. We invented this idea! OK? So just calm down and relax. I know it's a lot to take in. I mean, just yesterday we were nobodies and today everyone in Denver is talking about us. But we can lose it all if we make the wrong moves. So don't say anything to anyone about what you just told me, got it?"

I nod. "Yeah, OK. Got it."

"We did this," she repeats. "*We*. Did this. Pierce needs to just fuck off."

"OK," I say. "OK."

"So... tell me about the cute freeway guy."

"Later," I say. "I have to pull together a campaign to fight the Sexpert first." And then I end the call and force myself to walk down to my floor, open the door, and pretend I'm not the real reason why Pierce Chevalier is having a very bad Monday.

When I get back to my desk I get back to work trying to calm myself down. I make a list of all the sex advice articles we've run over the past two years, rank them in order of popularity, then send the entire list up to the art department so they can come up with new graphics. Then I email my intern and tell him we need a meeting today to come up with hashtag ideas.

When all that's done, it's lunchtime. And while usually I just go sit outside in the Towne Centre and eat something from one of the many lunch trucks, today I actually have an appointment to sign my rental agreement in the hottest residential building in the entire TDH neighborhood.

The place is called Sunset Towers. It's not as tall as the TDH building, but it's got thirty-seven floors. My place is on the second floor, and there's no view of the sunset. Or the mountains. But I did manage to get a view of the Towne Centre from my small terrace. So all summer I'll have a front-row seat for the free concerts in the square. And I can walk to work, and walk to the dry cleaners, and walk to bars... it's fabulous. And even though I have to pay an extra two hundred bucks a month for these privileges, it's worth it.

I might just have the very best studio apartment in the entire world.

So I walk across the square, my checkbook ready to commit, and make my way into the leasing office with a smile on my face, the whole horrible morning behind me and my whole lucky day feeling back in place.

"Eden!"

The greeting makes me turn, just as I'm about to approach the receptionist and tell her I'm here. And there he is. Andrew Hawthorne. The man I now know Pierce has charged with spilling my secrets and ruining my life.

"Hey! Looks like we're going to be for-real neighbors," he says. "You don't have a cup of sugar I can borrow, do you?"

CHAPTER SIX

She doesn't look happy to see me. She did look happy. Just, like, a second ago when she walked in. And now she looks unhappy.

I'm sure it's just a coincidence.

"What are you doing here?" she asks. With some definite snark.

"I'm signing my rental agreement. Just like you, I assume."

"*You're* renting?"

"Yeah, I'm renting. Whattayou mean '*you're* renting?'"

"Whattayou mean what do I mean?"

"I dunno. You said 'you're' like I have scabies or something."

"No, I didn't."

"You totally did. You said it like a mean sorority girl."

I know I'm pushing her buttons. Every word that comes out of my mouth seems to make her more and more upset. And the more upset she gets, somehow, the cuter she gets. Which is why I'm deliberately fucking with her. Which some might call mean, but I would counter that it's her fault for being so dadgum cute. The sorority girl crack is making her especially flustered.

"I... Wha...? Sorority?" she stammers out.

A piece of her hair falls down in her face as she shakes her head. Her breathing has sped up, which is causing me to notice something that I somehow completely overlooked before. Her breasts are... well, they're something. Holy shit.

"Um, did I do something wrong? Why are you so upset?" I ask.

"I'm not upset!"

"You're not?"

"No! I'm not! You're upset!"

I can feel my brow furrow. I look quizzically from side to side. I take a breath to respond, stop, then try again, "Yeah, I'm really not."

"Whatever. You stole my charger."

"That's what Pierce... I thought we went through this. No, I didn't."

"You so did!"

"I gave it back. That's, I think, by definition, borrowing. Which is what I asked. If I could *borrow* your charger."

"You drove off."

"What did you want me to do? Traffic started moving. I waved for you to follow me, so I could pull over and give it back."

She starts to protest but stops. "You... That's what you were waving for?"

"That's what I was waving for."

"So I would follow you?"

"So you would follow me."

"So you could give me back my charger?"

"Affirmative."

She presses her lips together and pouts. Which is maddeningly adorable. "I totally misread that," she finally says. And I break up laughing. Oh, my God. This girl is a little weirdo.

I think I love it.

"Well, somebody's in a good mood." That's the leasing agent who has just swooped in with the awkward grace of a herd of ostriches. She's wearing a grey business suit thing. Like a skirt and jacket-type deal. The jacket has a nametag on it that reads "Cheryl." "I'm Cheryl," she says, extending her hand. The nametag didn't lie.

"Hi, Cheryl, I'm Andrew. This is Eden," I say, gesturing to Eden.

"Oh." She looks down at a binder she's carrying. "Eden...Presley, yes?" Eden nods. "And Andrew... Oh." Her tone changes and she swallows a little. "Oh, Mr. Hawthorne, yes. Hello. Such a pleasure. I'm Cheryl." She extends her hand. Again.

I shake this time. "Uh, yeah. Hi." I look over at Eden, who cocks her head to the side. I shrug and bounce my eyebrows.

"But you're..." says Cheryl. "You're not... together? Are you?"

"Oh, no. No. No way," blurts Eden. Both Cheryl and I stare at her somewhat emphatic denial. "I mean... No. We're not."

Sighing, I say, "Yeah. That's for sure. We're definitely not. Together. We're just...y'know...old friends." I wink at Eden, who scrunches up her face and pushes her glasses up the bridge of her nose. Oh, man. Oh, man. Oh, man.

"Oh, well, that's lovely!" proclaims Cheryl. "Well, then, how about we get your rental agreements signed and I can show you both the property."

"Sounds great," I say, brightly, matching Cheryl. I don't even do it mockingly. Cheryl's just one of those people who is so unnaturally cheery, they drag you along with them.

I encourage Eden to sign her paperwork first. There's only three places to sign. And I have to assume she's signed a rental agreement before. But it takes her, like, half an hour because she reads every. Single. Word. Of the agreement. Twice she asks questions of Cheryl. I just stand off to the side and watch her.

Huh. I was kind of joking with Pierce about meeting a girl on the freeway, but...

I've been waiting. Waiting because I have this really bad habit of winding up with women who are... less than a good fit for me. I had this serial monogamy thing going for a long time and somehow managed to just go from one shitty relationship to another. I'm good at a few things in this world but finding the right partner to...uh...partner with does not seem to be one. And after the last one...

OK.

Here's what happened:

I had been living in California, the Bay Area. I went to grad school at Berkeley. Art history. I was pretty convinced that I wanted to get a PhD and maybe one day curate a museum, or teach or... y'know, the two things you can do with a PhD in art history. But, I dunno if it's the hippie vibe that still kind of exists in Northern California, or if it's just the way things went, but I started getting more and more into sort of avant-garde stuff.

Like, I met this group of guys who were really into peyote, and I started hanging out with them, and we'd go out into the desert and spend the weekend rock climbing, and talking about crazy ideas for these out-there art installations. I tried the peyote once and it didn't take—I just got really freaked out and hid in a cave for a couple days—but the experience of being out there with these free-thinking, super-creative dudes wound up being inspiring enough for me.

One of the ideas we came up with was something we called AVATAR. Which stands for Audio Visual Assisted Talk and Robotics. Which isn't even exactly accurate to what it was we wanted to make, but the acronym was too cool, so we ran with it. In a nutshell, what we wanted to do was build this massive, epic art installation that would be, like, the size of a small city and would be inhabited by these, like, highly sophisticated robots, but doing insanely mundane shit.

We were trying to make a commentary on the progression of innovation in the twenty-first century against a backdrop of commonality that unifies all people across all cultures and all times. Or something. I dunno. There's probably a reason it didn't work.

But in order to even attempt to pull it off, we had to draw in help from some of the students in the Berkeley Robotics and Intelligent Machines Lab. And that was where I met my ex-fiancée.

Now, I don't like to brag, but I'm pretty charming. Maybe it's just the Southern boy in me, but I can almost always charm my way into or out of any situation. With anyone. Always been like that.

Not with her.

Alice was the first person I met in my life who could give a fuck about how clever or charming I was. The robots that she built were easier to make laugh than she was.

And we were together for almost three years. We never really had much fun. She was cold. She really was. The sex was never even that great. I don't know why we stayed together. And then one day she turned to me and said, "You wanna get married?"

Honestly, it took me so off guard that I think that's why I said yes. I have no other logical explanation for why I would have done such a thing. But I did. And then we started planning a wedding. Which was ridiculous.

And this whole time, I'm still working on AVATAR. The other guys had sort of fallen off. A couple of them graduated and moved onto other stuff, one got busted for drug trafficking, and I'm not sure what happened to Todd. Anyway.

But I still believed in it. I did. The more I dug in, the more I thought it could be special and say something really important. She who shall not be named hated it. She's very, very, *very* practical. Methodical. Pragmatic. She doesn't have a lot of patience for "art." If she can't see the end game, she won't do it. I mean... she's a scientist.

And what I came to realize is that the end game for her with me was... stability. Or so she thought. On paper, I suppose I'm the kind of guy she imagined would be a good husband. I'm not totally stupid. I have pretty good genes when it comes to physical attributes that most people see as important. And I don't need a lot from other people to feel all right most of the time.

But the one thing she hated is that I'm an artist. I mean, I can't help it. It's just what gets my motor going. But she *hated* it. She wanted me to take all the work and research I'd done with AVATAR and "apply it to something useful."

And one day, after having a conversation-less breakfast, she looked at me and said, "I've been fucking someone else." Just like that. Cold. Impersonal. Robotic.

And I have to be very honest with myself about something: I didn't care that she was. I really didn't. Frankly, I was relieved that it gave us an excuse to break up. Because I don't have a lot of quit in me. I will stick with something until the bitter end. Whether it makes sense or not. Character flaw.

What bothered me is that she lied. And not just lied about cheating, lied about who she was. If that makes sense. She presented herself as one thing to me and the world, but somehow, underneath that, it turns out she did have blood and passion and feelings.

Just not with me.

I can take a lot in this life, but betrayal I'm not great with. Hell, when I felt I had betrayed Pierce in college— even though it was a total accident—it caused me to make some fundamental, core changes to my life that I stand by to this day. So, yeah, I take that shit seriously.

Anyhoo... Three days after our fateful breakfast, Alice moved out.

After that, I just worked on my project all the time. I got possessed. It was like a fever. And in the course of playing with some software that I didn't really know how to use, I accidentally stumbled onto what became Voice Lift.

The rest of the story is pretty boring and covers way more patent law than I ever thought I would learn, but being that close to Palo Alto at the time, it wasn't hard to find people who could take my little discovery and turn it into a billion-dollar company.

Ironically, it turns out that my art and my experimentation is what led directly to the success I'm having now. Also, it turns out that what I *really* love is making stuff. Figuring stuff out. Solving problems. Solving puzzles. So the company is kind of a perfect fit. It allows me to scratch my artistic itch while still doing something new and cool every day. And lately I've been thinking about how far I've come in this crazy journey and how...yeah...it might be cool to share it with someone. I'm not worried about falling to my death alone, as Pierce said (although belaying with someone else is almost as much fun as "laying" with someone else. I just made that up), but it just would be fun to, I dunno, share the adventure with someone, I suppose.

And the thing that's making me think about all this now is how one-hundred-and-eighty-degrees different this girl, Eden, is from all the other women I've known in my adult life. It's really that simple. She seems like the kind of girl who'd be up for...adventure.

I also happen to be thinking this while watching Eden's ass twitch in her skirt as she nibbles on the pen she's holding, sniffing and rubbing the back of her hand across her runny nose, which is probably all stuffed up from the air-conditioned coolness in here compared to the torrid heat outside.

She's a goddamn dirty trick.

"Yes, it's the same parking spot always," says Cheryl, fatigue setting into her once-chipper voice, the energy she had not so very long ago starting to fade.

"Hey, gang! Let's see the digs, shall we?" I bellow out. It's almost like I startled them both out of a deep sleep, the way they jump.

"I just have one more question," says Eden, but I grab her by the wrist and pull her along before she can ask it.

She looks shocked for a second that I would seize her like that, but I just smile and say, "Sorry, pumpkin, but see this five o'clock shadow?" She nods, still looking surprised. "Yeah... I didn't have that when you started talking. Let's go."

"Is this the pool?" Eden asks, as we are standing at the edge of what is very clearly a pool on the ground floor, just beyond the leasing office.

"Um... Yes," Cheryl says.

"Good eye," I lean in and whisper.

Eden ignores me and says, "Oh, that's nice. I think my apartment is right up there, so I'll be close." I feel like I can sense a hint of pride in her voice.

Cheryl glances at her file again, "Yes, yes, your unit is right by the elevator that comes here to the pool."

That causes Eden to gnaw at her lip. "Elevator to... Hm. Does it get very crowded? The pool, I mean?"

"Well, sure. It can. When it's hot out like this," Cheryl offers.

"Hm. How crowded?" Eden asks, nervously.

"Yeah, how crowded?" I ask too. I don't really care all that much. I'm just trying to make it appear like I'm interested in the crap Cheryl's telling us about the building and not just in hanging around Eden. Which, despite all my instincts telling me not to... I am.

"Oh, well, *you* don't really have to worry about that," Cheryl tells me.

"I don't?" I ask. She shakes her head at me. "Why don't I?"

She gets a smirk and says, "You haven't seen your unit yet?"

"Uh, no. Somebody from the company set it all up. I just got into town. I've barely even been to the office yet. Spent a couple days bouldering in Moab and drove straight here at three this morning."

"How rustic," Cheryl says. I can't tell if "rustic" means "charming" or "disgusting" to her. "Well, come along and let me show you."

She ostrich-galumphs toward the elevator she was just referencing, and I follow. Eden doesn't. I turn back. "Are you coming?"

"What? Where? To see your apartment? Why do I wanna see your apartment?"

I shrug. "Dunno. Cheryl's making it sound very mysterious. You're not curious?"

"Not really."

"Really?"

"Yeah. Really. Not really."

I walk over to her now, because... because I want her to not be mad at me for whatever thing it is that she's decided to be mad at me about. "Hey, listen. I don't know if it's really because I took your charger, but whatever I've done to rub you the wrong way... I'm sorry. OK? Really. I am. Do you wanna grab dinner with me tonight?"

What did I just say?

"What did you just say?"

"Um... It would appear that I asked if you want to... grab dinner with me tonight." *What am I doing right now?*

"I thought you were having dinner with Pierce. He told Myrtle to make a reservation."

"Yeah, and he said someplace not shitty. What? You don't wanna have dinner with me and your boss at someplace not shitty? Not-shitty dinners are usually the best kind."

She pushes her glasses up her nose again and eyes me. "What's your deal?"

"What do you mean?"

"I know who you are. Myrtle told me."

"Oh. Did she?"

"Yeah. So, I mean, what's your deal? You drive a crappy pickup, you steal chargers—"

"Borrow."

"Fine. *Borrow* chargers from strange women in traffic—"

"You are strange. That's true."

"You're renting an apartment instead of, I dunno, buying a ranch or whatever you could do, and for some reason you're hitting on me now. What's your deal?"

What is my deal? It's a reasonable question.

69

My deal? My deal, Eden, is that I've bided my time and re-centered myself in search of what I need in my life. And now that I feel like I'm close, I'm ready to get back into the business of sharing that with someone. And even though we've only known each other for about twenty minutes, I think you're fascinating and cute and funny and I'm sort of imagining what you'd look like spread out horizontally. So how about we go check out my place and maybe, if you're up for it, we do a little something my granddaddy used to call the "belly-bumping bed boogie...?"

"Yeah. I dunno. Shall we?"

I stare at her and gesture with my hand in the direction Cheryl just went. Eden stares back at me for another second, rubs her runny nose with the back of her hand once again, and then, finally, she walks past me toward the elevator.

Shit, man. What *is* my deal?

CHAPTER SEVEN

Am I hallucinating? Did I slip into an alternate reality after hearing those guys on that ridiculous morning show talk about the Sexpert? Because my life has suddenly turned into... not my life.

But I'm on autopilot right now as I follow Cheryl into the elevator. Andrew slips in next to me just as Cheryl presses the button for the penthouse, and I'm just about to make a run for it and get out of this hallucination when the elevators door close and force me to see it through.

Why? Why the hell did I agree to go see his apartment?

Well, I *am* a teeny-tiny bit curious at what a guy like him rents in this building, so I just fake-smile the whole ride up as Cheryl talks about the summer concert series down in the Towne Centre and how the TDH is sponsoring a rodeo this weekend.

"Rodeo?" I ask. "I've never heard of that and I've worked here for two years." Personally, I think Cheryl has the hots for Andrew and she's hinting around that he might like to take her to these events.

"It's new this year," Cheryl explains. "*Le Man* opened up the new event center last fall and there was a lot of controversy about land use and protests about stewardship from the local ranchers before it was built. So *Le Man* said they'd sponsor one of the local rodeos and bill it as a main event." Then she turns to Andrew. "It's going to be great fun. You should go."

I roll my eyes and realize Andrew is watching me, not looking at Cheryl or paying any attention to her obvious flirting.

"Are you going to the rodeo, Eden?" he asks.

Which makes me snort, it's that funny. To me, anyway. No one else laughs. "No," I say, serious again. "I'm deathly afraid of bulls."

"Really?" he asks, his eyebrows high up on his forehead like this is the most surprising thing he's heard today. "Why? Did you have a bad encounter with one as a child?"

I can't tell if he's joking because my fear of bulls is weird, or if he's really asking, but I don't have to worry about it, because the elevator doors open and Cheryl sings, "Here we are!"

Cheryl exits and Andrew waves a hand at me that says, *After you*, so I follow her out and stand in front of the massive, polished, hardwood double doors that have a little bronze plaque off to the side that says, *Penthouse*.

As if we didn't already figure that out.

"We can have your name engraved on that, Andrew," Cheryl says, pointing to the plaque. "Just tell me what you'd like it to say." She beams a smile at him and when I look over my shoulder at Andrew again, he's looking at me, not her.

"What?" I snap. "Why are you staring at me?"

It's like he knows. Like he's got some sixth sense that I am the target Pierce aimed him at. Like he's putting two and two together and any minute now he's gonna realize—

"Sorry," he says, eyes averting to Cheryl. "They're just eyeballs. Everybody calm down."

"Let's get inside," Cheryl says. "There's a lot to go over."

Cheryl passes a key card over the security panel and it flashes green as the locking mechanism disengages. Then she opens the double doors with one of those *ta-da* gestures with arms outstretched. Like she's a game-show girl presenting a brand-new car.

"Here we are! Notice the floor-to-ceiling windows highlighting the views. Come with me and I'll point out all the landmarks for you."

She hooks her hand into the crook of Andrew's arm and practically drags him over to the windows. He's looking over his shoulder at me. I'm still standing outside the apartment. He says, "Come on. She's gonna show us the views."

I consider turning around and leaving before I get caught in some trap I can't get out of, but... the views. They're like the ones from the fiftieth floor of the TDH building and I'm drawn to them.

So I push my glasses up my nose, sniffle from the overabundance of air conditioning, and walk forward with them.

His place, like mine, comes furnished. But this building is ultra-modern, so it has a sparse feeling to it. The couches and chairs are all a little bit retro-feeling. Those crisp geometric edges and skinny tapering peg legs. And they are brightly colored, but tasteful at the same time. Light blue and muted yellow.

"See, that's Pikes Peak," Cheryl says, drawing my attention away from the design. "The tallest mountain in Colorado."

"No, it's not," I say.

"Yes," Cheryl insists. "That *is* Pikes Peak."

I look at Andrew, sick of Cheryl's blatant flirting. "No. I mean Mount Elbert is the tallest mountain. Pikes Peak is the most famous, that's all. It's only fourteen thousand one hundred and fifteen feet. Mount Elbert is fourteen thousand four hundred forty feet." And then I snort again, and say, "Pikes Peak isn't even the second highest mountain in Colorado."

"Well—" Cheryl starts to say, but I continue.

"It's the twentieth."

Andrew laughs. Cheryl looks annoyed.

"You into mountains?" he asks.

"Not particularly. But I grew up here. We had to memorize all the Fourteeners in sixth grade because *that's* useful information every kid should know." And then I almost snort again but catch myself just in time. "Didn't you have to do that? Cheryl?" I look at her expectantly.

"I… I grew up in Nebraska."

I nod at her, smiling. My smile says, *I thought so*. Not that I thought she grew up in Nebraska. Just not here. I'm suddenly weirdly competitive with the Nebraska-born leasing agent. Which is… unexpected.

"OK, well, there's a lot more to see," Cheryl says. "I'm sure no one here wants an impromptu lesson in the Colorado mountains."

"I do. I love mountains," Andrew says. Which catches Cheryl off guard because she makes a face that totally says, *What?* "Really. What else can you teach me? Eden?"

"I… Uh…" *Was that innuendo?*

I look over at Cheryl, who, I think, is asking herself the very same question, because she says, "OK. So, that's the tour. How about we go back down and sign your lease, Andrew? You didn't sign yet."

"What about the pool?" he asks.

"The pool?" she says.

"Yeah, you said something about the pool downstairs. Crowded? What's up with the pool?"

"Oh," she responds, still kind of flustered and annoyed. I don't know how I've wound up in some kind of odd jealousy triangle. I just wanted to sign my lease on my little studio and I now find myself standing awkwardly in a penthouse with a rich, cute guy who's apparently been asked to destroy my life even though he doesn't know it and a clearly ovulating leasing agent.

In fairness, I always feel awkward. I just rarely find myself in a situation like this.

"Oh, right," Cheryl mutters. "The pool. You have your own."

"What's that now?" Andrew asks, twisting his neck. I may twist mine too. "My *own*, you say?"

"Yes. On the roof. That stair there"—she points—"leads to your own private pool just above us. Shall we go down and sign now?" Holy shit, her bedside manner disappeared fast.

"Tell you what. How about," Andrew says, turning to face Cheryl for the first time since we started this tour, "you go on ahead and I'll be down in a little bit." He heads for the stair to the roof. "Eden and I wanna check out this pool."

"We do?" I ask.

And at the same time Cheryl deflates and says, "You do?"

Andrew nods, taking her by the arm and pulling her towards the open double doors the same way she pulled him away from them a few minutes ago. "Yeah, just go on down and I'll stop by the leasing office before I head back to work. Then we can talk all about the rodeo."

"We can?" Cheryl says, hope in her eyes.

"Most def," Andrew replies, almost pushing her out the doors. "See you in a few." And then he closes the penthouse doors right as Cheryl opens her mouth to protest, and the matter is settled.

"Jesus Christ," Andrew says, walking back over to me. "I thought she'd never leave."

"I didn't get my key yet," I say.

"No worries. We can go back down to the leasing office after we check out the pool. Maybe you can show me your place later, huh?" He waggles his eyebrows at me.

I squint at him. "No."

"Look," Andrew says, taking my arm and pulling me closer to the windows. "We got off on the wrong foot this morning. I'm sorry, OK? Totally my fault. I wanna make it up to you. K? Let's go check out the pool. You can use it any time you want. You shouldn't have to hang out at some crowded, sweaty meat market with creepy guys. Which I'm sure is what's going on downstairs. So, c'mon. Check out your semi-private pool. There'll only be one creepy guy hanging out there." He smiles like he thinks he's so charming. Which he unfortunately is.

"No," I say. "No, I just... I wanna go see my apartment, OK? Please?"

This morning has been like getting whiplash. I find out that my stupid little video channel is going unexpectedly viral, then I meet this cute guy in the unlikeliest way, then he steals my charger from me, then I find out that my boss's boss's boss is making it his mission to destroy my little video channel because I stole the idea from him, which I didn't, then I run into the cute guy who hands me back the thing he didn't actually steal, and then I find out he's the very person tasked by my boss's boss's boss with bringing down the little channel and thereby getting me fired, sued, and tossed out of my adorable studio apartment—which I haven't even seen yet!—and out onto the street.

Yeah. Whiplash.

"OK, I get it." Andrew interrupts my thoughts. "But just before you go... which mountain is your favorite?"

"What?"

"Which mountain is your favorite? I climb. I wanna know everything about your favorite mountain."

"I... I don't have a favorite mountain. I just like looking at them, that's all." I push my glasses up my nose again. "And I like facts. Cheryl was wrong about Pikes Peak, so I just needed to set the record straight. That's all. Now, if you don't mind, I'm gonna go. I have to grab my key and get back to work to manage a big crisis, anyway."

"Oh... Sexpert?"

"What?"

"The crisis. Is it the Sexpert thing? Or is Pierce having some other crisis too?"

"Oh, no. Yeah. That's... Yeah," I say. Jesus. For a second there I thought he was saying he already knows I'm the Sexpert. Which is stupid. No one knows. Not even the inventor of Voice Lift could figure out my secret that fast.

Right? Right?

"Yeah," he says. Then, "Hey! You wanna see the terrace, though?" He walks forward, completely ignoring everything I just said about my apartment and needing to get back to work, and grabs a handle on the window and pulls it open. The glass slides smoothly aside, folding in on itself. He does this again for the other window, and suddenly we are outside.

"Wow," I say, kinda gobsmacked.

Andrew looks at me and smiles. "Not terrible, yeah?"

I walk outside with him, in kind of a trance, looking at all of Colorado as we make our way across the massive terrace filled with outdoor furniture, and stop right at the nearly invisible frameless glass railing to take in the unobstructed views.

The wind is hot and dry just like it is down on the ground, but stronger, so that my hair, even though it's tied back into a ponytail, blows across my face. We can hear the sound of the lapping water from his private pool just above our heads.

"Hey." He turns to face me. "So you're not really afraid of bulls, right? Bulls are awesome."

"No, I really am. When I was in school up at Colorado State we had Ag Day every fall. I don't know where you're from or where you went to school—"

"Originally from Kentucky," he says. "Bennington for undergrad, then Berkeley for grad school. Art history."

I snort. I can't help it. That's all funny. "Well, anyway. Ag Day is a big deal up there and the school actually has like… a farm? So they bring out the bulls for Ag Day and I swear to God, I was just minding my own business eating my waffle cone as I watched the cowboys do their cowboy thing. And this bull just comes charging up to me. Apparently, it had gotten loose while they were walking it around the stadium. And even though everyone insisted I overreacted and it was tame, I sorta… overreacted and… I don't really think it was tame."

"Did it trample you?" Andrew says, aghast.

"No, it licked my ice cream."

His laugh is so loud I startle.

"It wasn't funny," I say. "Do you have any idea how big a bull actually is? That thing was a monster. Scarred me for life."

"OK," he says. "Forget the rodeo. But seriously, let's have dinner tonight. Please?"

"I dunno. I think…"

"What? You think what?"

"I just… Pierce is my boss and…" *And you two are probably going to talk about figuring out who this Sexpert chick from the internet is.*

"He made a reservation for eight-thirty. Which is a ridiculously European thing to do. I'll find out where and change it to six-thirty. Which is a very *American* time to eat.

79

We can meet up then, have dinner first, and then you can scram before he gets there, if it makes you feel weird to hang with your boss socially. I get it. It's like seeing your elementary school teacher at the grocery store or something." He looks at me with these puppy-dog eyes that are totally unfair. "Please? I feel like taking you out is the least I can do to make up for stealing your charger."

I smile at him and say, "Borrowing."

Which makes him light up with delight. "So, is that a yes?"

I look at him. Consider how I should back away from this. It would be the smart thing to do. I mean, Pierce did ask him to figure out who the Sexpert is, and the more time I spend with him, the more likely it becomes that he will actually do that.

But he's... he's cute freeway guy. And well... "OK," I say. "But I really gotta go now so—"

"Sure," he says. "Let's go get keys, I'll sign my lease and I can walk back to the TDH with you. I'm still new. Don't wanna get lost." He winks again.

OK. It's not *un*-charming.

So I let him do all that. We go back to the leasing office where Cheryl pouts because she can tell Andrew is interested in me, not her, and we do our thing and pick up our respective keys.

And then he walks me back to work. And it sorta feels like he's holding my hand, even though he isn't.

And I'm starting to get the sinking feeling that very soon I'm really, really going to regret ever having let this guy borrow my charger.

CHAPTER EIGHT

The restaurant is French. Because of course it is. I'm sure that after he gave Myrtle carte blanche (that's roughly all the French I speak) to make a reservation, he vetoed every one until she got to the French place. You gotta love him.

I approach the maître d'—realizing suddenly how much French works its way into the English language, especially where food is concerned—and she says, "Bon soir, monsieur, under what name is la reservation?" At least she's actually French, like from France, or at least Montreal, so it doesn't make me wince like it does when Pierce says stuff like that.

"Uh, Chevalier? Pierce Chevalier?"

"Ah, oui, Monsieur Chevalier. Pour deux. Your other party is already here."

I drove in from Moab fourteen hours ago expecting to see what my new office and apartment are like, and maybe ask someone if they can get a ping-pong table put into the break room of Aureality, for, y'know, team-building and stuff (I really have no idea how to run a company, but I don't plan on telling anyone that), and now I'm wearing a blazer and a pair of pants that aren't jeans, going on an impromptu date with a girl I met during a traffic jam on the freeway this morning.

Colorado seems pretty solid, so far.

The dining room itself is appointed with burnished wood and soft lighting. The bar area is bustling with all the TDH denizens coming together after work to hook up and hit on each other under the pretense of talking about whatever important business thing it is they're pretending to talk about, but the main room is still pretty sparsely populated this early in the evening. Which is partially why it makes it easy to spot...

Pierce.

Sitting at a small, romantic-looking two-top. His tie is loose, causing the vest of his three-piece suit to protrude outward slightly, making him look like he has a bit of a paunch which isn't normally there. He's on the phone, and as I approach from across the room I hear him talking with Derek. I don't know for sure that it's Derek. But I know.

"What do you mean six months?" He's sort of yelling. "Six months for a trademark? What the fuck, Derek?"

I knew it was Derek.

"Find a way to fast-track it." And he hangs up the phone. I wonder how long this Derek guy will continue lawyering for Pierce if he keeps getting hung up on all the time.

"Monsieur," the maître d' says, showing me to my seat.

"Merci," I say, sort of as a reflex, as I sit. I probably sound like an asshole. But. Then again. Comparatively...

"Merde!" Pierce lets out, slamming the phone down on the table, and downing his Shirley Temple with an aggressiveness that comes over as really cute, since it's a Shirley Temple and all. (I think he drinks them so that other business types who may be watching him won't know he's a teetotaler. Gotta keep up appearances in the cut-throat world of douche-baggery.)

"Hey, man," I say, adjusting myself into place. "Um... Why are you here?"

"What do you mean?" he says, annoyed, chewing on an ice-cube. "We're having dinner."

"I thought—"

"Turns out I need to get out of here early, because I'm hooking up with a flight attendant chick I hook up with when she's in town. She's on a turn-and-burn from London, so if we wanna get it on, I gotta snap up twenty minutes in the airport Westin."

"Charming."

"So I had Myrtle call to see about making the rez for earlier, but it had already been pushed up to six-thirty. I assume you did that. Gauche American that you are. So anyway. I'm here. How we doing on figuring out who this bitch is?"

I smile at him with tired eyes, both because I am tired from the day and because being Pierce's best friend can tucker a body out. I let out a puff of air through my nose and say, "What was that on the phone?"

"Good news and bad news. The good news is that Sexpert hasn't been trademarked yet. Ha! Dumb hussy."

"OK, let's all just—"

"The bad news is that the attorneys say it's gonna take at least six months for *us* to get a trademark on the name."

"OK. And?"

"And? And who knows if this chick already has a trademark in motion. But more importantly, she's out there *now*. She's gaining traction in the public's perception. So, even if we get it legally locked in six months, by that time her brand will be established in the Zeit. Geist"—I don't know why he breaks it up into two words. For effect, I guess—"and that's it. The brand will be hers. It'll be meaningless to own the name. And we'll look like the copycats." He chews on another ice cube.

"Dude, I don't get it. I mean, it's a fun idea. It's a clever idea. Hell, man, it might even be a genius idea, but it's not the *only* idea. I get that you're freaked out about the magazine losing money. I do. OK? But don't you think you're putting a lot on this one thing?"

He stares at me for a moment while he crunches his ice cube.

"No, you don't get it," he finally says. "It's not just the idea. It's that it was *my* idea. And somebody has stolen *my* idea. My dad never wanted me to be a part of his business. You know this."

84

"Yeah, I know."

"I don't wanna get all Freudian and shit, but fuck it. You know my first memory of my dad?"

"I don't."

"It was him turning his back on me and Mom and closing the door to the house in Marseilles when the car drove us to the airport. I was four, and he didn't hug me, or say goodbye, or whatever. Didn't even wave. Just turned his back. And closed the door. And that was it. And then we were on a plane to America. And I spent the next twenty-three years—twenty. Three—trying to connect with the guy and get him to ... well, not love me, that's ridiculous. But, hell... like me. Or trust me. Or let me be a part of his world. And finally, finally, he gave me a shot. I came to him with the magazine idea and he finally acquiesced and gave me a chance to do this thing. That was five years ago. And in these last five years, I've gotten closer to him and had a relationship that I've wanted my whole life. Well, not exactly. But as close to a relationship as we're gonna have."

He's been chomping the ice all through his soliloquy—because I kind of think he forgot I'm here and is just saying all this for himself—and now that he's masticated it all down, he swallows and says...

"And if I don't pull this magazine around and it fails, or worse, becomes some kind of embarrassment or scandal, he and I are *done*." He emphasizes the word.

"What? No way, man. Come on."

"You ever meet my dad?"

"No."

"Exactly. You're my best friend and you've never met my dad. What does that tell you?" He lets that land and I just nod, slowly. Then he adds, "We. Will. Be. Done."

I take it in and only nod. Because there's nothing worse than telling a person that something they know way more about than you do isn't true, just so you'll feel like you're helping *them* feel better. After a moment, I breathe in deeply and say, "You need another Shirley Temple?" I nod at the empty highball glass.

"Nah," he says, "I'm driving."

And that right there is why I love Pierce. It's because despite all his very best efforts to be an asshole—and they are, honest-to-God, valiant attempts—he won't ever be able to disguise the fact that under it all he's a funny, good, decent person.

After a moment, he adds, "Can you track her down, And?"

I shake my head. "I mean, yeah. Probably. Yes. But again, what do you think that's going to do? Let's say I can find her. What good do you think it'll do?"

"If she somehow got wind of my idea and stole it, I'll fucking bury her."

"K. And what if it's—and just hear me out on this—what if it's just a shitty coincidence, and somebody had a similar idea to yours and just happened to get it out there first? What then?"

His eyes narrow and he breathes in and out heavily through his nose. His jaw tightens. He closes his eyelids and throws his head back. Then he says, "I'm gonna hit the WC." He stands. "I went ahead and ordered a steak. You should get yourself something. Think of a funny story to tell me when I get back."

"What kind of...?"

"I dunno. Something with jokes and shit."

Then he pats me on the shoulder and heads off to the men's room. It's tough—really tough—to watch someone you love spiraling. You're stuck in between wanting to help and not wanting to enable their spin. Pierce knows what that's like. He went through it with me. Not just with my breakup, but throughout the whole damn relationship. He was there for me. He would show up at my door unannounced if we had a phone call that left him worried. Just jump on a plane from Denver and show up at my door to make sure I was OK. It's why I'm here. I could've put the offices for the company anywhere, but I'm here because Pierce asked me to be. And so, whatever he needs right now to keep himself from falling off the edge of the planet, I'll do it. I owe him. I owe him for a lot of things.

"Sorry I'm late!"

Oh. Right. I'm on a date. Or whatever. And she's here now.

And she's barreling toward me all adither.

I've never described anyone before as being "adither," but she is. She's waving her hands around like a butterfly flapping its wings, which is a clear indication that she's already about two sentences deep into a conversation with me that I've yet to be included on. She looks amazing. Her blonde hair is down around her shoulders. And I do mean her shoulders. Her bare shoulders. She's wearing a sleeveless... I dunno what you call it. Tube dress, I guess? It's kind of like a ribbed cotton thing that goes to just below her knees. And it has a plunging neck line. And holy shit...

"Sorry, sorry, sorry," she continues as she arrives at the table. "I had to stay at work longer than I thought because I'm trying to pull all these articles for... Whatever. Doesn't matter. But I had to stay and then I rushed home, but, and this is just classic, right? My key didn't work. My key didn't work. Can you believe that?"

She sits down on Pierce's side of the table, which I begin to tell her is Pierce's side of the table, but she's on a roll, so I just sit back and take it in.

"Cheryl or whatever her name is gave me the wrong key! Can you even...? Or maybe it just didn't work. Or, but whatever! So, yeah, so anyway, so I had to get management to come let me in, but they haven't met me, right? Of course, they haven't, so they wanted proof that it was really me who lived there, but I was like, 'Uh, to give you proof, you need to let me in,' right? But so, Catch-22, which... But so anyway, then I remembered that I still had the rental agreement in my purse, so I showed them that, and then finally they let me in, but then, like, y'know, I only saw the apartment for two seconds, so I don't know where anything is! Are the faucets in your shower weird? The faucets in my shower are weird. It's like, I couldn't figure out how to change it over from the tub to the shower. Did you have that problem? Probably not. You probably have a separate tub and shower. How many do you have, anyway? I dunno, but it was so stupid. I mean IT'S not stupid. It just is what it is, but I felt stupid. Anyway, but so then, finally I figured out that you just have to pull a little knob, but then I couldn't get the water temperature right, and... Oh! And, yeah, the pool gets crazy. I can totally hear it from my place. It's like, it's so hot today and everybody was just, y'know, at the pool, and so... That really has nothing to do with why I was running late, I just thought of it. And then I thought I should text you, but I don't have your number. And then as I was running over here, I realized I could probably just call your office and have them get you a message, but then I thought it'd take longer to do that than just come here, so I did, and hi. Sorry I'm late. I'm just... Ugh."

Throughout her monologue, she sits, stands, adjusts her dress (which I don't *think* she does because she notices me staring at her chest, but I can't be sure), sits again, starts to take a sip from the empty highball glass that's there, stops, realizing it's not hers and it's empty anyway, puts her bag over the left arm of the chair, takes it off, puts it over the right, pulls the chair forward, pushes it back, picks up a piece of baguette, puts it down, and then finally flops her head forward, letting her hair fall in front of her face.

Man, oh, man. I am so fucked.

"Hi," I say, and smile.

She laughs a little. "Hi. Hi. Sorry. I just, I feel... Do you ever feel overwhelmed?"

"Everybody feels overwhelmed sometimes."

"Do you?"

"Nah. Not particularly."

She stares for a beat and then she laughs. She's got a fantastic laugh. The waiter approaches.

"Monsieur. Mademoiselle. Shall I get another chair for the table?"

"Oh..." I start.

"Another chair?" asks Eden.

"Yeah," I say. "Yeah, for, uh..."

"Or," comes the voice from behind me, "You know what I could do? I could find her, fuck her, THEN sue her. I mean if the face is anything like the tits, then I should at least sample the wares. Apparently, she's chock-a-block full of *great* sex tips. Jesus. Anyway. Hi. Who's this?"

He looks at Eden. He looks at me. Eden smiles at him with a painful grin. Then Eden looks at me too. I look at them both. I start to speak. Then I stop. Then. Finally.

89

"You know what?" I say aloud to no one in particular. "I guess it's possible for me to feel kind of overwhelmed sometimes."

THE CHERRY
ON TOP

The cherry on top of the end of a first date is the first kiss. Don't mistake this for nibbling her Kit-Kat. The first kiss is just topping. Nibbling her Kit-Kat is more of a prelude to baking her cake. Let's start with the right amount of tongue.

CHAPTER NINE

Fast-forward forty-five minutes. Because I don't have it in me to describe this first-date disaster in minute detail. My boss is having a very bad day because some tart has stolen his idea, so just insert one long tirade about how anonymous me is ruining his life and there you have it.

It's talk about trademarks, and he takes a call from his lawyer and has a three-minute conversation about how he's going to sue the fucking pants off me once he figures out who I am, and then his steak comes while Andrew and I are ordering, so now that we're back in present time, he's throwing his napkin on the plate as he stands up.

I smile with relief. Because I have maybe thirty more seconds of this before he leaves.

"Eden," he says.

"Yes?" I say, almost choking on my wine.

"It was a pleasure. Weird. But an absolute pleasure. I don't know what's going on here." He pauses to do a back-and-forth finger wave at Andrew and me. "But it's a good look for Andrew. And I get the feeling that me showing up early wasn't in the plan, so I am acutely aware that I just ruined your date, and for that I apologize." And then he reaches for my hand, kisses it, and lets go as I look nervously over at Andrew. "I just needed his ear. It's the only ear I can count on. So thank you for indulging me."

And for a second I wonder if he's going to reach for Andrew's hand and kiss it as well. But he doesn't. He just points his finger at his friend and says, "Welcome to Colorado. Don't worry, I've got the check. So you two kids just enjoy yourselves."

We watch him leave, then our heads slowly turn and our eyes meet.

"Holy shit," I say. Because that was stressful.

"Yeah," Andrew says. "Um... So you run his social media?"

"Yeah. Why?"

"Because, uh, I don't know if you noticed but...it seems like he doesn't know who you are."

"Yeah. I fly under the radar." I smile and glance down at my plate.

"How's your food?"

French food isn't my thing but I got the coq au vin because it said chicken in parentheses. I just didn't realize it was an entire jumbo leg. So while Pierce was lamenting his bad fortune at being the target of some massive conspiracy to ruin his life, I got nervous and started cutting up my meat into little pieces a toddler would be able to chew so I didn't have to look at him.

Which is stupid. And ridiculous. But mostly embarrassing.

"It's good," I say, answering Andrew's question as I scoop up some mashed potatoes with my fork and put it in my mouth.

I pause like that. And not because I'm trying to seduce him as I eat, either. He's just... he's looking at me like... "God, you're kind of adorable." And then he glances at my plate of tiny, bite-sized pieces of chicken and laughs.

I blush. I can feel it. My cheeks get hot. "Mmm-hmmm," I say, swallowing my potatoes. I place my fork down and say, "Well..."

"Oh, are we done?" Andrew asks. "Because we're going to have to do this again, of course. Properly next time with no third wheel. Um. Can I walk you home?"

"Uh. OK," I say. Because we live in the same building. We work in the same building. I mean, it's inevitable.

He gets up and walks behind my chair so he can pull it out for me.

"Thank you," I say, surprised. I don't think I've ever been on a date with a man who did that. They might hold my chair and help me sit if they're really feeling chivalrous, but not help me get up.

It's weird. But nice. And kinda sweet.

"Shall we?" Andrew says, waving his hand at the front of the restaurant.

We walk out of the restaurant and into the warm July night. The Towne Centre is bustling with people walking around. Going to dinner, or bars, or wherever.

"This place is kinda cool. I don't think I hate it," Andrew says.

"Yeah?" I say, thankful we have the TDH small talk to fill the silence. "I mean, yeah. I've been wanting to move here ever since I got the job at *Le Man*. It just feels so... alive and vibrant. I love all the shops and how everything is walkable. I don't even have to get in my car to go to the dry cleaner. Did you know the TDH has a walkable score of ninety-seven?" I ask.

When I glance over at him he's just grinning.

"What?"

"No, I didn't know that. But yeah, it's a regular walker's paradise."

"Why are you looking at me like that?"

"Like what?"

Like he wants to eat me. But I don't say that. "Like... I amuse you."

"Didn't know I was."

"You are."

"Oh. Well... because you do. It's not often you meet a person that you like right away."

I snort. Then feel awkward. I don't have my glasses on tonight—I usually reserve them for work hours or night-time reading. So I can't even busy myself pushing them up my nose right now.

My phone buzzes in my purse and I say a silent *Thank you, Jesus*. Only I say Hey-Sus instead of Jesus because... well, it's a joke left over from some Latin class I took in fourth grade and just something I say. And thank God it's silent. Because I don't feel like explaining. I fish around in my purse and find my phone to check the screen.

Zoey: *I need you. We have to add a voiceover to the video you recorded. Get here now.*

"Everything OK?"

"Um…" I say, looking at Andrew.

"Is it?" He seems genuinely concerned. I try not to think about it too hard.

"Yup. Yup. Just fine. I just… one second." I clumsily text Zoey back: *I'm onnna dte cant just use itlike it is*

"Yeah? You sure?" Andrew asks as I slide my phone into my purse.

"Everything's fine—" But there's another ding. "One sec," I say, pulling my phone back out.

Zoey: *No! We have to respond to a statement about this accusation from your boss! It's all over the internet! His lawyer says they will be presenting evidence or some shit that we stole their idea!*

Me: *What??????*

Zoey: *We have to address it. This started off as the best day and now it's fucked. Call me when you get home. Maybe we can just record you on the phone.*

Me: *K*

I scowl at my phone. I mean, having dinner with my new accidental archenemy was bad enough, but now I have inside information about his plan to take me down. Am I breaking a law? And I work for him. Hey-Sus! Can he send me to prison over this? Do I need a lawyer?

"Are you sure you're sure everything's OK?" Andrew asks again.

"Yup," I say. And OMG. He's the man Pierce has hired to take me down! I start walking faster. I need to get away from him like… now. And this dinner stuff? First date equals last date as far as Andrew and Eden go. Nope. I can't do this.

"Hey." Andrew laughs. "Slow down." He jogs to catch up to me and then grabs my elbow. "Is there an emergency?"

"Nope," I say. But then I cringe. And my lie is blown.

"What? What is it?"

"Nothing." I sigh. "I just… that was work and…"

"Work? Like the magazine needs you to go in tonight or something? For what? It's a magazine."

"No." I laugh. "No, no, no. My other job." Shit! Why the hell did I say that?

"Other job?" Andrew asks, eyebrows arched. "What's that? Oh, God. You're a prostitute, aren't you?"

"What?"

"OK, call girl then. Whatever."

"No! No! God, no! It's not… it's just…" Holy shit. I'm dying here. "It's not a *job*. It's just a hobby, really. That's all. But it's kinda having a good day. Sort of. I'm not sure. I gotta go."

I pull my hand away and start power-walking towards Sunset Towers, eager to get away from him and call Zoey. I need to know exactly what's happening here.

"Whoa, whoa, whoa," Andrew says, catching up with me and placing a hand on my shoulder. Which sends tingles up my arm because the dress I'm wearing is sleeveless. "We're going to the same place, remember?"

"Oh, right. Sure. You can walk with me. I just need to hurry."

He takes my hand this time, and when I try to pull away, he holds it firm.

"Eden." He laughs, this time nervously. "What's wrong?"

98

"I told you, it's just work. You can walk me home. You want to stroll? We can stroll. But just faster than most people stroll, if that's not too much to ask."

I let him keep my hand, but I start walking again. He keeps up and starts talking about the concert this weekend. Trying to make small talk and be ... cool? I guess?

I nod absently, making sure I look at him every few paces and smile. And then we're at the building, getting in the elevator.

I press the button for two as I look for my key card in my purse. And then the doors open again, and I turn to face him. "Thanks for the good time! See ya!"

"Wait," he says.

He's still smiling at me. Like he finds my flustered-ness... is that word? That can't be a word. What's the word? "Ruffled!" I say, then realize I said that out loud.

"What?" This time his laugh is suspicious. I am acting strange and there's no way in hell he's not noticing.

OK. Eden. You're not very good at this covert shit. Never have been. And you warned Zoey about how stressful situations make you... ruffled... when she suggested the anonymous thing back when Sexpert started. But there are real consequences at stake here and you need to up your fucking game.

In my head I shout that last part so the awkward person inside me will take this seriously. I need to play this right. I need to get this guy off my trail. Because I am his target.

So be smooth, that inner voice says. *Be cool. Play it...*

"Do you wanna kiss?" I blurt out.

What?

"What?" he asks.

Oh, God. He's going to call Pierce after this is all over and tell him how weird I am. He's going to tell him something's going on. And then…

"Eden," Andrew says, holding up a finger and furrowing his brow. "I just wanna make sure I heard you right. Did you just ask me if I wanted to kiss you?"

"Did I?"

"You did."

"Huh. Weird. Well, do you?"

He smiles. "Uh, yeah. Yeah. I wouldn't mind that at all." He leans in.

OK. Decision time. Give him a peck goodbye and make an escape? Or try to explain?

I choose the peck. It's the only rational option. So I lean in, lips puckered, and plant one right on his cheek.

The elevator doors close and we start ascending, because of course we friggin' do. I've been standing here for almost five seconds having an internal monologue.

"Know what?" he says. "Let me try."

And then his hands are on both my shoulders sending tingles up my arms, and his lips are on mine and…

Hey-Sus. Save me. Because I kiss him back.

I can't *not* kiss him back. He smells good, and he's handsome, and funny, and he appreciated my impromptu lesson on the Colorado Fourteeners this afternoon, and even though I know this is a very bad idea, it's starting to feel like a very good one—which is my first clue that I should back away now and get off this elevator pronto, then take the stairs back down to my apartment and never speak to him again…

But his tongue sweeps against my mouth and I don't know what I'm thinking—well, I sorta do. Because this is no peck, that's for sure. But I open my mouth and my tongue tangles with his. It's... it's...

"Yeah," he says, pulling back and whispering next to my cheek. "That seems better." Then, because this evening has been perfectly timed since it started, the elevator doors open with a ding.

He turns and we both stare at the massive double doors leading to his penthouse. Then our eyes meet and I know... I know if I don't stop this now, it's all over. My entire life will be over.

So I back away as he turns towards me, and then I place both hands on his chest and push him as hard as I can until he stumbles backwards, out of the elevator, a surprised and half-confused look on his face as the elevator doors close, taking all other options away from me.

Hey-Sus comes through for me tonight.

CHAPTER TEN

"Game, bitch!" shouts Dev as he slams down the ping-pong paddle on the table in the break room.

"Dude, I'm your boss," I remind him.

"Sorry, Andrew. I just... I get competitive."

Dev is my guy. My lead developer at the company. He's young. Nineteen. A prodigy. Graduated from Stanford when he was sixteen years old. He joked when I hired him that I was only giving him a job in tech with such big responsibility because he's Indian. I joked back that it's because his middle initial and last name are "E. Loper." (They're not.)

But he got the Dev E. Loper joke right away, told me I was "pretty funny for an old dude," and that was it. I was hooked on this kid.

It doesn't hurt that he is, quite literally, the smartest person I have ever met.

"You wanna rematch?" he asks.

"Nah," I tell him, wandering over to the fridge to grab a water. "I'm good."

"You OK, man?"

"Why?"

"Dunno. You seem less... Andrew-y than usual."

"Yeah?"

"Yeah. I mean I know we don't know each other that well, but you just seem down. Tell Papa Dev what's up."

Precocious doesn't even begin to describe this child.

"Oh." I groan, flopping down over the Roman arm of one of the fluffy chairs with the cow hide motif our designer picked for the break room. Wouldn't have been my first choice, but it is very Denver-ish. "Everything's fine. I think I'm just tired. Didn't sleep so well last night."

"Why? New place?"

"Nah, it's not the place. It's... I dunno. It's everything. But you know what? You don't wanna hear my bullshit."

"No, man. I do. I find you fascinating."

"Yeah? Why?"

He shrugs. Not an answer, but OK. "Seriously, what's going on?" he asks.

I sigh out in puffs of breath. "Oh, I'm just adjusting to the newness of everything happening at once, I think. I don't always do well with change."

"Why not?"

"Not sure. Always been that way. My dad died when I was a kid, and then my mom sent me to boarding school, so I was always on the move, and you know, basic Psych 101 whatever. And then I sort of found the thing I love, the thing that makes me feel purposeful—which is art— and then that didn't go the way I thought it would and now..."

"Ooooohhhhhh," he says, like he just cracked a programming code.

"What, ooooohhhhhh? Ooooohhhhhh what?"

"The rock climbing thing. I get it now."

"Hell are you talking about?"

"Your rock climbing obsession. The one that kept you in the middle of Moab while we were opening the offices so that a nineteen-year-old working in his first job in the real world was left to rally the troops and give a rousing speech welcoming a hundred and fifty employees to THE FUTURE of the audio-visual revolution."

"I heard it was a great speech."

"It was OK. But the point is that it makes sense now why you're so addicted to it."

"Yeah? Why's that, Sigmund?"

He leans down to me. "The rocks don't move. The mountains are stationary. They're timeless. Impassive. Constant. And when you're scaling one—or whatever the hell it is you do—you can feel confident that it'll stay where it is. I mean, you know, unless there's a rock slide or avalanche or whatever. Then you're screwed."

I crack open my water, look at him, shake my head. "You always been like this?"

"Like what?"

"Like you."

He shrugs again. Again, not an answer, but...

"I met a girl." Was that me? Jesus. Wow. I was not expecting to blurt that out.

"Ooooooh." Again with the "ooooooh" from this guy. "Do tell."

"Tell what? Nothing to tell, really. I met this girl on the freeway. I borrowed her phone charger. Turns out she works in the building. I gave her her charger back. Turns out she also lives in my building. I asked her to dinner. She came out with me and my friend Pierce. I tried to walk her home. She got weird. I think she may be a prostitute on the side. She kissed me on the cheek. I kissed her on the mouth. She pushed me out of the elevator into my apartment. I thought all night about going downstairs to ask her what the fuck. But then I remembered I don't actually know which apartment she's in. So I jerked off to her a couple of times. Then the next thing I knew, it was morning. And I'm kind of out of sorts. That's all."

He chews at his bottom lip for a moment before saying, "Cool, man. OK. I got work to do. See ya," and starts off.

"Wait," I call. He stops and turns. "I need you to do something for me."

"What? Not some weird sex thing?"

"What? No! Why would you...? How are we coming along with IN-VERSE?"

"OK. Not bad. Why?"

Before I get a chance to answer him, my cell rings. I look. Holding up the phone, I say, "This is why. I'll tell you more later. Oh, and I'll probably be up for that rematch when I feel less cloudy."

"OK. But I wasn't even playing with my dominant hand, so—"

"Go work, man." He leaves. I answer the phone. "Bonjour."

"You see this shit?"

"Oh, not bad. You? How was the stewardess?"

"Flight attendant. Jesus, man. Join us in the twenty-first century." The guy is confusing sometimes. "Have. You. *Seen*. This?"

"I don't know what *this* is."

"Come to my office." And he hangs up. In turn, I hang my head. I draw myself up from my seat, and as I cross to head up to Pierce's office, I glance out through the huge picture windows at the unmoving and constant mountains outside.

"Go on in," says Myrtle, before she goes back to lovingly sucking on the straw in her iced whatever-it-is that she's drinking. I can't help noticing the red lipstick on the green straw. She smirks and again, my hands go to protect my crotch out of some weird instinct.

"It's slander!" Pierce is yelling into the speaker phone. I assume he's talking to... "It's fucking slander, Derek!" I knew it was Derek.

"It's not slander," says Derek. "It meets no legal definition of slander."

"Yeah? What's the legal definition?"

"Making a false spoken statement damaging to a person's reputation."

"And this isn't that?"

"No."

"WHY?"

"*Le Man* is not a person. And, as far as I can tell, she's not saying anything false."

"She's saying she didn't steal my concept."

"OK."

"She did."

"You know this how?"

"She must have!"

"Why?"

"Because she's saying she didn't!"

I pause where I'm standing to simply appreciate the display of circular logic.

"Sorry, Pierce," says Derek, "I don't think we have strong legal footing to pursue an action based on the equivalent of a 'he who smelt it dealt it' accusation. Look, we've baited her to come out into the open with the threat of legal action, and it's clearly working. So let's just keep on with the plan. Until we know who the woman is..."

"I'm on that," Pierce says, hanging up the call and looking at me like I'm his saving grace. Which makes me feel stressed and sad at once. The mountains outside his windows look different somehow than they did on my floor.

"What is it now?" I ask.

"This." He points at his monitor and once again, I swing around to see what there is to see. And once again, those breasts. Pierce hits the space bar and I hear the sound of Sultry Siren speaking to me.

"Well, hi, kids." I have to say, we did a really good job with Sultry Siren. It's sexy as hell. The breasts don't hurt. "It's been an unexpectedly exciting day. First, the Sexpert wants to thank all of you who have been here from the start, and for all of you new fans who are just discovering this channel... welcome," she purrs. At the use of the word "Sexpert," Pierce grabs up his golf club. I think he only has the one. I know I don't know much about golf, but I'm pretty sure you need more than one club to really make a go of it.

The faceless voice continues, "So, if you heard about me on 93.3 this morning, thanks for dropping by. And thanks to 93.3 for getting the word out there. The Sexpert owes everyone at the station there a big. Wet. Juicy. Thank you." I swear she actually fucks the microphone with her vocal cords when she says 'thank you.' Or, I guess, actually, they're *my* vocal cords. This whole thing is so strange.

"But unfortunately," she goes on, "what started as a great day turned into a not very nice day at all." She pouts that second part. "Because it seems that some very mean man is alllll over the internet saying that the Sexpert— me—is his creation. And that somehow, little old me *stole* his idea. And I'm here to tell you all that that is simply not true. Cross my heart."

I have this weird little moment of déjà vu when she says that last bit. It's curious to hear an expression I use a lot being spoken by a voice I created. It's surreal. What is very real is the way she accentuates crossing her heart so that her finger grazes her nipple though the fabric of her...

Sleeveless...

Dress.

109

I blink twice and kind of twist my neck. Suddenly Pierce hits the space bar again and stops the stream.

"That's not slander?" he asks.

"What? What are you talking about? Which part?"

"She called me mean!"

"Man, I—"

"Am I crazy?" He flops onto his throne.

"What?"

"Am I? I mean, this is nuts, yeah? You were right. I'm looking for something to blame my failure on. It's me. I'm to blame. It's all my fault. Shit."

He drops the golf club to the ground and slumps down, looking almost exactly like what he is. A broken boy prince. My heart goes out to him. I come over and kneel down.

"Highness..."

"Stop," he says.

"I'm sorry. Look, seriously, no. You are not a failure. Look around, man. This is not what failing looks like."

"I inherited all this shit."

"So? There are plenty of people who inherit more and do less with it. Look at me." He doesn't. "Look. At. Me." He does. "You are fiercely capable, and you have vision, and that is special and rare and should be celebrated. Are you hearing me?"

"I dunno," he mumbles, looking lost.

"Dig this. I was just talking with my lead developer, Dev—"

"Your lead developer is called Dev?"

"Not now. Stay focused." I snap my fingers at him. "He says we're in good shape on an app that we're developing that can..." I trail off. If I open this jar up, there's no putting back inside what could spill out.

"That can what?"

"Basically, that can grab the vocal signature of any voice in the world and then run it through a database that will match it to its owner. A vocal thumbprint."

"Really?"

"Really."

"Where do you get the database from?"

I shake my head from side to side and kind of hold my breath. "That's... Don't worry about it."

"Dude," he says, sitting up in his chair, "are you into some illegal shit now?"

"No! No, it's all completely legal. Hyper-legal, actually."

He narrows his eyes at me and I just stare at him and nod, watching him sort out the implications.

"Are you..." he whispers now. "Are you working on some spy shit?"

"Mmmmmm," I moan, resisting the words that want to leave my mouth, and then... "We all have to play our part to defend democracy."

There's a long, long moment where neither of us says anything. Then, finally, he says, matter-of-factly, "You went to art school."

"Yeah." I laugh, sorrowfully. "I know."

And after another long moment, he says, "But it's not her voice. She's using your thing to disguise it."

"Yeah. But that part's easy. The stripping-down component is built into the app itself."

"It is?"

I nod.

"Do people know this?"

"I do. And now you do. We're people."

He drops his head and closes his eyes. He starts, "You don't have to—"

"I got you, man. OK? I got you. Look, at the very least, I will bring you the source. After that, you can decide what to do with the info. If you wanna sue some chick sitting in her bedroom making videos, you can do that."

He looks sad for a second and says, "It's what my dad would do."

"I know, man. I know. Look, lemme go pretend I care about my company, OK? But, hey, I'm on this. I got you, mon frère."

He nods slowly at first, getting more vigorous as he goes. I pat him on the knee, stand, and head for the door. As I get there he says, "Oh. Who was that chick last night?"

"Seriously?"

"Yeah. I mean, I'm thrilled, obviously, but who is she?"

"Pierce, she... Eden. Eden Presley?" He looks at me with a blank stare. "She runs your social media department?" Still nothing. "She's friends with Myrtle? She was up here yesterday?" Nada. I raise my eyebrows and shake my head. "OK. I'll talk to you later, man."

"Andrew?" I turn back. It looks like he wants to say, 'thank you.' He opens his mouth to speak... "Bang her if you didn't. She has a great rack."

I smile and huff a breath. I want to tell him he's welcome. So I say, "I'll try, man. I'll try."

I walk out of the office, past Myrtle who says, "Bye, Andrew," in a syrupy way that freaks me out, and I arrive at the elevator bank. Something about that video is gnawing at me. It's not fair to say that I don't know what, because I do, but it's just too...

Nah.

The elevator doors open and there's no one else in the car. I half expected to see Eden, only because... I dunno. That's the relationship we seem to be forming. If we are forming a relationship. Hell, I dunno what you call it. I just know that I don't feel like I can be trapped in a box right now.

Last night we talked about this being a walking community. And right now I feel like walking. So I decide to take the stairs.

I open the stairwell door, step inside, and begin trotting back down to my floor when I hear, in a voice I know, "Are you kidding me right now?"

CHAPTER ELEVEN

My desk phone rings. But I'm in the middle of composing a tweet to thwart that harlot Sexpert and bring people over to *Le Man* website to read a repurposed article about how to… well, let me just give you the title.

How to Find Your Way Through the Vaginal Forest and Hit Her Button.

I swear to God, that was the title.

And there was a picture of a man lost in a forest as a graphic.

'Was' is the operative word here. Because holy shit, I don't know who they were targeting with that title, but it's bad. And I don't even have time to get into how spectacularly that graphic missed the mark.

So now it's called *How to Eat Her Like Dessert* and there's a picture of a pink cupcake with a cherry on top of pink frosting. And sprinkles. Because sprinkles and frosting are—

"No," Gretchen says, walking up to my desk. "And I just buzzed your phone and no one answered, which is why I'm now standing at your desk. Why do you try my patience, Eden?"

I push my glasses up my nose and squint at her. "Which part was a no?"

"The cupcake," she says. "This isn't *Cosmo*, Eden. No man wants to see a picture of a cupcake while he's learning to…" She does a little wiggle move with her finger, which I can only presume is her gesture for eating a girl out.

"Well, you're wrong," I say, looking up at her. "This is the perfect graphic."

"Get rid of it," she snaps. "No cupcakes."

I pout. Because that cupcake is so beautiful. And the cherry and the pink… "But it's so delicious-looking, Gretchen. It makes men want to think of…" I look up at her again. "Delicious lady bits."

Gretchen's face contorts into this horrible, grouchy frown. "We're not *Penthouse*, either, Eden. Find something appropriate for our customer base or I'll let Pierce know we need to get a new marketing team."

Team? I'm the only one on this team. But I don't say that. I just make a sad face and stare at my computer.

"And that title. Just keep the titles and make new graphics, Eden. I didn't tell you to rewrite anything. You're not a writer." And then she laughs.

But I kinda am. I've written most of the scripts for the Sexpert this past year and that's how I know this title and this cupcake are both perfect.

"OK," I say, putting on my fake cheer. Because I don't want to fight with my boss. "What did you need?"

"The art department just called me. They have a question about a graphic and need you up there now so they can get the next article on track for approval. And if that graphic is pink, has sprinkles, or is a picture of a dessert, find a new one."

With that she turns on her heel and walks away.

I sigh, tired of taking orders from her when I'm the one who's qualified. She doesn't have a booming YouTube channel. And holy shit, Sexpert Channel is going crazy. Zoey texted me six times this morning to update me on our subscribers. She was so excited when we reached two hundred and fifty thousand last night, she called me at four AM. Apparently she was up all night just hitting refresh, watching the numbers climb in real time.

She even opened her bottle of Moët Champagne she's been saving since her baby shower to celebrate when we got to half a million this morning.

It's pretty fun and a part of me wishes I wasn't stuck here at my job and was home with her celebrating instead.

I hate having to hide. I can't even tell Myrtle about our new success.

"Eden!" Gretchen barks from her office. "Why are you still here?"

"Going!" I sing out, then grab my tablet and phone and make my way to the elevator. Just as I push the button

117

my phone dings a text in my hand so I glance down at the screen.

Myrtle: Guess who's here?
Me: I'm on my wayup now for graphics c u ina sec
Myrtle: He's leaving right now. Better hurry.
Me: shit andrew?
Myrtle: Hurry! He's waiting for the elevator.

Oh, thank you for the heads up, Myrtle. Because now I'm definitely taking the stairs up to the art department. The last thing I need is to see Andrew again. Last night was a total disaster. I mean—how unlucky can one girl get? I feel like the universe is conspiring against me. And it's not fair because Zoey and I have been working so hard on this Sexpert thing trying to make a go at it and finally, the very day we actually have a chance to make some actual money and move up, the whole thing gets tainted with stupid accusations that aren't even true.

At least I don't think they're true.

There's this little part of me that has doubts. Like maybe I did overhear Pierce saying something about his idea for the Sexpert and just don't remember. I'm that kind of girl. I'm always… *ruffled*.

The elevator dings and I realize Andrew could be on the other side of those doors right this second. So I spin around, open the door to the stairs, and duck inside.

When I look up who do I see? "Are you kidding me right now?"

"How lucky can a guy get?" Andrew laughs.

"Funny." I sigh. "I was just thinking the exact opposite. But apparently a girl can always get more unlucky than she is already."

We are in the middle of the floor—him coming down, me going up—and I just want to get past him as quickly as possible, so I push forward, dodging left, but he dodges right—his right, which is my left—and I actually smack into his chest.

There is a flurry of uncoordinated movements, and swearing (that's me) and his hands on my arms sending that now familiar tingle through my body, and I compensate by dodging left, but he dodges right—that's right, his right—and we smack together again.

I place two hands on his chest to push him away but then I lose my balance and I'm about to fall backwards down the stairs when he reaches out to grab me—his fingers slipping, but he overcompensates this time, snatching at my shirt in desperation because I truly am about to fall ass-backwards down half a flight of stairs—

And that's when all the buttons on my sensible, professional button-down collared shirt go flying off in all directions.

"Oh, shit!" That's me.

"Oh, shit!" That's Andrew.

And then we're both looking at my breasts.

I'm wearing a tank top, so we're not actually looking at my breasts. But my girls are quite spectacular. Which is why I hide them underneath a professional shirt every day. And to top it all off, the tank is white, and my bra is pink, and… yeah. You can see it through the shirt.

"Um…" Andrew begins. And then he just smiles.

"Thanks a lot!" I say too loudly.

"I'm sorry," he says. "But you were going to fall and I just…" Then he's laughing.

"It's not funny! I have two more hours until lunch and I have to walk around like this until I can scoot home and change!"

I push him away. This time he's got his hands up in the air, letting me know he's not going to touch me. And I take a step up, determined to push my way past him this time, but then my cute little ballet flat that has absolutely no tread on the sole slips and I fall to my knees on the stairs, palms down to catch my fall.

And in that moment, somehow, some way, Andrew's fingers are tangled in my hair. Like he was gonna save me by the ponytail.

I look up, hot with embarrassment, and find myself eye to eye with—yes, you guessed it—his junk.

He laughs again.

"This is not funny," I say, scrambling to my feet then backing down a few steps to put some distance between us. "What are you doing here anyway? You're down on forty-nine. These two floors are for *Le Man*. Go back to your floor!"

I'm wagging my finger at him, which is dumb, so I stop doing that.

He bends down, eyes still on me, and we're like... way too close. Like his lips—those lips I kissed last night—are just mere inches from mine because even though he's crouching down on the step, I'm three steps down.

"What are you doing?" I ask.

"Grabbing your tablet," he says, his hand reaching out to pat the stairs to find it by touch, because his eyes have not strayed. They are locked on mine. "God, you're adorable," he whispers.

And now I'm looking at his lips. They are very nice lips. You don't often think about a man's lips until you're presented with a set of spectacular ones. Lips like his. Which are just a little bit plump, and look very soft.

They are soft, I recall from last night.

And then he says, "Eden."

And I swallow hard and say, "What?"

And then he kisses me. He barely has to move at all, that's how close we are. The universe really is conspiring against me because when I walked into this stairwell thirty seconds ago there was no scenario that ended with me kissing Andrew Hawthorne.

I know what I should do. Push him away. Or run away. Or… or… pretty much anything else but let him kiss me, but that's what I do.

I let him.

And then I take it one step further. Because I kiss him back.

What happens next is like… a choreographed dance or something. It has to be. There's no other plausible explanation for how he gets to his feet, steps down the stairs, backs me down the stairs until my back is pressed up against the landing wall, and threads his fingers into my falling-apart ponytail while never breaking lip contact.

And it is the most amazing kiss. I'm talking half-open mouth with just the right amount of tongue. And he tastes like cinnamon. Like he was chewing a stick of Big Red or crunching on a cinnamon Tic-Tac just seconds before this whole encounter happened. Or maybe I'm imagining that because I'm obsessed with sweets?

Who cares?

"Shit," he says, catching his breath and backing away.

I stare into his eyes. Which, like his lips, are very nice. "I gotta go," I whisper. "The art department is waiting…"

But I don't get to finish because he leans back in and kisses me again.

And this is when we get... hands-y.

I don't know what I'm thinking. Probably not thinking, which, I realize, is the problem here. But my hands are on his upper arms, feeling his muscles underneath his shirt. And his hands are on my arms, riding up my shoulders, gripping them tightly before they slide down and...

Holy shit.

I moan into his mouth as he grabs my breasts and squeezes.

Voices outside the stairs make us both pull away quickly and I get this feeling. Like... what a magnet must feel like when it disconnects from a piece of iron.

He smiles at me.

I'm too busy wondering how this all just happened in the span of ninety seconds to smile back. And then he turns away, just as Lydia from data entry enters the stairs, and disappears down below.

"Hi, Eden," Lydia quips, walking down the stairs towards the landing where I'm still pressed up against the wall. She gives me a funny look. "Everything OK?"

It's only then that I realize my hair is all aflutter. Strands of it have come loose from my ponytail and are covering my eyes. I reach behind my head, grab my hair to make the hair band tight again, then blow the stray strands out of my eyes and say, "Just fine, thanks!"

Two seconds later I'm up on fifty-one and making my way to Myrtle's desk, because even though I have no interest in seeing Pierce right now, I have to tell someone about what just happened in the stairs.

The second Myrtle spies me coming towards her desk she laughs.

"What?" I ask, looking around nervously.

"You just fucked him in the elevator!"

"What? No! I took the stairs. And why would you say that anyway?"

She holds a hand over her mouth, her mischievous eyes darting back and forth as she looks at me. "Well, you better go fix that just-fucked hair if you don't want everyone to think you're banging the boss' best friend."

The moment I step back into my office and close the door, I see, through the window, a lightning strike out in the distance, just past the mountains.

There's a storm brewing somewhere.

Once I make my way over to the glass, I stand and look out at the broad sweep of earth that lives just beyond my confinement and think, "What am I doing?" Or I say it aloud. Which I don't mean to do. But do.

None of this is me. I'm not a CEO. I'm an artist. I'm not a guy who sits in an office. I'm an adventurer. I'm not a dude who presses up impulsively on impossibly cute and unexpectedly hot women in stairwells. I'm a guy who stays in a bloodless engagement until my will breaks and I can't take it anymore.

Except I'm not any of the things I think I am and I'm all the things I didn't know I was. At least I am today.

Do you have a charger I can borrow? What the hell was I doing? Rhetorical question. I know exactly what the hell I was doing. I was staring ahead of me at this new part of my life, listening to Pierce freak out about intellectual property and trademarks and thinking about how this is all the kind of shit that I have to concern myself with all the time now, and then I looked over and saw this person sitting there.

This person I saw who looked excited, and nervous, and confused and so, so, so fucking easy to stare at, and I decided to follow my instincts. Which is what I've always tried to do. It's why I left Kentucky for "Yankee Country," as my mom calls it. And why I left Vermont for Berkeley, or "Hippie Country," as my mom calls it. And why I got engaged, and why I got un-engaged, and why I kept working on a project that nobody else still believed in, and why I've done almost everything in my life.

Until now.

I didn't mean to build a company. I'm not Pierce. And I sure as hell didn't mean to *run* a company. And my instincts told me to just say 'no.' There would have been plenty of financial reward if I had just sold the idea and moved on. And it's not like I needed the money anyway, so...

Maybe that's it? Maybe it's actually commitment? Maybe that's my hang-up? Why I jump from thing to thing, idea to idea? And maybe I'm stupid that I'm only seeing it now?

I've been here less than forty-eight goddamn hours. I missed my welcome speech to the team. I haven't unpacked my office. I've barely said hello to anyone. And yet I've seen Eden like five times, kissed her twice, groped her once, and yet I don't know anything about her.

Maybe that's what's turning me on?

Shit.

I dunno. But I do know that my phone keeps dinging. I hear another email ding now and look to see yet another message from someone at the US Department of Justice. I've already ignored three phone calls and two other emails from them.

Flopping down into my desk chair, I realize I may be a crazy person. Which makes me laugh. I wish I didn't laugh so goddamn much at things that aren't actually funny, but I suppose I can get away with it because I have nice-looking teeth.

Sometimes I wish I still drank.

I close my eyes and take a breath, and in my mind's eye what I see are breasts. Eden's. From just a minute ago in the stairwell. And from last night in her dress. And...

Her dress. Her sleeveless, clingy, cottony dress that she was wearing. The one that showcased her perfect body. Her perfect and unexpected body that could make it hard to focus on anything else.

Cross my heart.

I said that to her. The girl in the videos that has Pierce losing his fucking mind said that in her last post. The girl in the videos has perfect breasts. The girl in the videos was wearing a sleeveless, clingy, cottony thing. The Sexpert was Pierce's idea. Pierce thinks that whoever this woman is in the videos stole his idea. To steal his idea, she would have to have access to the idea. She would have had to have known what Pierce was cooking up. Like somebody who was working for him.

Why would someone who works for Pierce steal his idea? What would it gain them? What would be the benefit? Maybe Pierce is right, and they have an axe to grind against him. Maybe they want to see him fail. Or at least be embarrassed or...

Or maybe they just need a break. Maybe they've worked hard and don't have much to show for it besides a small studio apartment and a job where they maybe feel unappreciated. Maybe they...

I like figuring out puzzles.

I pop open my laptop and type in my password. I open a browser, go to YouTube, and type in "Sexpert." The channel has nearly half a million subscribers. Yeah, I know how things can go unexpectedly viral.

There are dozens of videos, dating back about a year. I scroll down to the very first one and click on it. It's different than the one Pierce showed me this morning. The lighting is different. The background is different. The confidence that I've seen in the couple that I've watched is less present.

But the tits are the same.

And so is the sound of the voice. Sultry Siren.

"Hi, everyone." The voice is halting. Not the purring that's come gliding out in the other videos I've seen. It's the voice of someone who seems .... not flustered. That's not quite right. Ruffled maybe. The voice of someone who isn't sure of what they're doing or if they should be doing it. The last twenty-four months have been all about me listening to voices and analyzing voices and understanding voices, but even if my time hadn't been spent doing that, it would be easy to pick out the hesitancy.

"So," Sexpert continues. "So, um, I dunno if anybody is ever even going to watch these, but, um, I am the Sexpert. Hi." I have to be honest, anyone discovering these early videos might think it was a joke. Her... sexpertise... doesn't feel awe-inspiring. But somehow that's part of the charm.

That and the boobs filling the screen.

"So, what I hope to do with these videos is to help people understand sex, talk about sex, appreciate sex, and maybe just make the whole thing a little less taboo. So, to start, I thought it would be fun to ease in with framing sex in a friendly way. Comparing it to something everyone loves. Dessert." She holds up a Twinkie directly in between her breasts. It's a sight to see. "So, there are many different ways to get the cream out—"

"Boss?"

Dev poking his head into my office causes me to slam down the laptop screen like I just got caught jerking it. And that's not far off. Because, to my chagrin, as I push back from my desk to stand up, I realize I can't. Stand up. At least not as long as I don't want Dev to know about the more private parts of... No. That's it. My more private parts.

I wave him in.

"Yeah?" I say, sliding my unexpected erection back under the safety of my desk. "What's up?"

"Um," he says, approaching carefully. Because I am acting weird. And I know it. "I just wanted to ask... Why were you asking about IN-VERSE earlier?"

"What do you mean? Why are you asking why I was asking?"

"Because I got a call from Carrie at Justice—"

"Carrie? At the Justice Department?"

"Yeah. Like I said. Carrie at Justice." He shakes his head a little. "And she says you haven't returned her calls or emails."

"Oh. Yeah. I gotta do that." I get a tight grin, raise my eyebrows, and ask, "Anything else?"

His brows furrow and he draws in his chin, twisting his head to the side. He looks like an otter, kinda. "Nah. I don't think so. Just... Are you OK, man?"

"Yeah. Yeah. I'm dynamite. What time is it?"

He looks at his watch. "Almost noon. Why don't you keep a clock in your office?"

"Time is a construct designed to keep us down."

"It's really not. It's science. I could explain it, but I'd need more hours than I have to spare, and you'd probably need a different brain."

"You think it's wise to insult your boss's intelligence?"

He shrugs. "Dunno. Never had a boss before."

"Okay," I say, waving him out.

"Yeah. OK. But seriously, what's going on with IN-VERSE? Is everything OK with it? We're not going to lose the contract or anything, are we? I've busted my ass working out all the bugs."

"No. No way. We're good. In fact, there's a real-world test we're going to be able to run pretty soon."

"Yeah? What is it?"

"Don't worry about it. Just let me know when we can sync with the database."

"OK..." He nods, turns to leave, then turns back and says, "We're not all going to go to jail or anything, are we?"

I laugh. Because it's what I do. "No. No, of course not."

"OK. Because I wouldn't do well in jail. I'm frail and I don't punch well with my right hand."

"You're not going to jail, Dev. At worst you'll just be deported."

"Comforting. Thanks."

And he leaves.

I take a breath and close my eyes tightly. When I open them again I look to see if my dick is still trying to escape through my jeans or if I'm good to stand up. All the talk of the Justice Department and people going to jail seems to have chilled everything out, so I feel like I'm good to go.

I need to pull myself together. I'm going to go back to my place, take a few minutes to get my head in the game, and then come back to work and be a boss. I'm gonna help Pierce, I'm gonna stop distracting myself, and I'm gonna drill down on the task at hand. Which is not this Eden girl. It's not.

Although...

Maybe it is. I mean, maybe I should just ask her some questions. Just stuff about herself. Stuff like, "Hey, are you trying to sabotage my friend's life's work? And why?" Like that. Fun stuff. Small talk.

Maybe.

When I stand up to leave there's another sudden crash of lightning, accompanied this time by a bone-shaking clap of thunder above the great, towering peaks outside.

Yeah.

Maybe.

CHAPTER THIRTEEN

I wear the button-down shirts over my tanks for a reason. My tits are just… wow. Spectacular. I mean, I've watched a lot of porn over the past year for Sexpert research so I've seen lots of tits. Like thousands, probably. And mine rank right up there in like the top one percent of spectacular tits.

It's truly my one… hmmm, what to call it. Body gift, I guess. Because my hair is too thick, and my ankles are too skinny, and my hips are a little bit bigger than they should be, and no matter how much I diet, I have this hint of an extra chin.

Lots of guys have said they find it cute, but they can fuck off. I hate it. I hate my skinny ankles, and my wide hips, and yes, when your hair is too thick you can't even put it up in a regular hair tie. You need those big jumbo scrunchies.

My tits are perfect. They're not too big, not too small, not too soft, and not too hard.

My point is—people look at them if I don't cover them up properly. They can't help but look.

That night that Zoey and I came up with the Sexpert we knew right away we'd have to exploit my biggest assets. But the way I see it… what good is an asset if you can't exploit it?

"Where are you going?"

I look up, startled by Myrtle's voice coming from the open door of the stairs. "I'm going home to change my shirt," I say quickly. "The buttons…" I look down at the missing buttons and think about the way Andrew just accidentally popped them all off. "I just need a new shirt. Why are you down here?"

"I was gonna ask if you'd like to go check out the new baloney sandwich lunch truck."

"Who the hell eats baloney sandwiches? I feel like this is a cartoon joke. Like Bugs Bunny talking about liverwurst."

"Liverwurst is delicious," Myrtle purrs.

"I don't even know what liverwurst is, Myrtle. And nothing with liver in the word is delicious. I'm gonna pass on the BS." She likes that. Because she grins. "But I'll take a rain check and we'll have lunch tomorrow if you want."

I'm crossing my fingers that she doesn't ask to come look at my apartment. Not that I don't want to show it off, I do. And I need to have a little party soon for that. But today I'm all kinds of flustered and I just want a moment alone to try to make sense of all the new things happening in my life.

"Oh," she says. "I'll ride down with you." And then the elevator doors open and by some fortuitous miracle, there's no one else on board when we get in. She flashes her employee badge at the card reader near the floor buttons and presses one. "What's that?" I ask.

"It's an override so the elevator goes straight down. Pierce gave it to me for Administrative Professionals Day last year."

"Huh," I say, momentarily confused. Because it's weird how you don't know things and you never knew you didn't know them. Like this perk she has. It's a tiny secret superpower people never knew existed.

"If you ever want to have elevator sex, it can stop the car without the alarm and turn the cameras off for three minutes."

"What?"

She does that sly grin that makes men stop in their tracks. "You heard me. I don't know why Pierce has that programmed in, but he does. And he told me about it." Which makes her pause and squint her eyes.

"Do you... fuck in the elevator?" I ask her. And then I kinda get lost in that visual. Tall, thin, serious Myrtle being pushed back against the wall by someone like tall, broad-shouldered Pierce, probably. His hand would slip up her leg and find its way under her skirt, lifting it up a little to reveal thigh-high stockings. And not the elastic kind, either. The kind with garters. And then—

"A girl doesn't talk," Myrtle says. "Now back to you. Why is your shirt missing all the buttons?" She raises an eyebrow at me. A serious one too. One that says she expects an answer. And I don't know what it is about Myrtle that makes you want to do as she tells you, but she does have that power.

My cheeks go hot. And then I start laughing. "I bumped into him in the stairs this morning and we did this push-past-each-other dance, and I almost fell backwards, and then he tried to save me by popping off all my buttons and grabbing my ponytail, and then we kissed."

I don't think I've ever seen Myrtle smile so big. And then she practically chuckles. "I'm going to need all these details."

But the trip down to the lobby is surprisingly quick when you don't have to stop and let people on and off.

"Later," I say, stepping out into a waiting crowd of people. "I gotta go! Enjoy your BS sandwich!"

It's raining when I step outside. But not too bad, and my building is only a couple blocks away. So I walk fast and don't run because it's hot today and the rain is more like one of those water-mister thingies they have on non-stop in the summer at the Las Vegas hotel pools.

I can see my building—I'm like two minutes away—when the sky opens up, washes away my gentle, refreshing mist and replaces it with spectacular sheets of falling rain. I'm talking torrential downpour.

So now I *have* to run because I'm getting soaked. I make a mad dash for the lobby door, and since this place is fancy, there's a doorman rushing towards me holding an umbrella, which slides over my head the exact moment that the rain stops.

"Figures," I mumble. "But thank you. That was a valiant attempt!"

There's people waiting at the elevator, and I'm soaked, so I take the stairs up to the second floor, more eager than ever to get out of these wet clothes.

All my best-laid plans come to a screeching halt when I exit the stairwell to find... yes, you guessed it. Andrew, waiting by the elevator.

He spins around when he hears the door open, blinks twice as he checks out my condition, and then loses the battle trying not to stare at my tits, because I look like I'm in a wet t-shirt contest.

"Wow," he says, forcing himself to look me in the eyes. "What happened?" And then he puts a hand over his mouth to try to hide his laugh.

"I got stuck in a downpour. What are you doing here?"

"I was checking out the pool."

"Why?" I ask him. "It's not like you'll ever need to use it. You have a private one upstairs."

"I want to check out the gym too," he counters.

"Are you spying on me?"

"What?" Andrew chuckles.

I don't know why I say it. I'm taken aback at his appearance here. Plus I'm still kinda ruffled about the kiss in the stairwell, not to mention the fact that Pierce has him looking for me—even though he doesn't *know* he's looking for me, he is. And it's actually weird. Like why is he on my floor?

"Why would I be spying on you?"

"Never mind," I say, pushing past him. "I just came home to change my shirt, so I'll see ya later."

But as I push past him he blocks me. Which makes me want to back up. In fact, I do back up. Until I run out of backing-up space because I bump into the stairwell door.

"Why are you so nervous?"

He's so close now I have to tilt my chin up to look at him. I'm breathing heavy from the run and my sprint up the stairs. And I'm wet. Like very wet.

He places one hand on the wall next to my head, half blocking me in.

"Ummm..." I duck under and start down the hallway. "I gotta go," I say.

Because I am very nervous for all those reasons already discussed. But I don't feel like talking about the kiss in the stairwell and I'm very much not going to tell him about me being his target, so my only option is to power-walk down my hallway, key card in hand, ready to flash it at my door and get the hell away from him until I can pull all these weird coincidences together into some kind of coherent sense.

I fight the urge to look over my shoulder to see if he's following, but I can hear soft footsteps on the carpet behind me, so I know he is.

I flash my card at my door and then turn the handle.

But it doesn't unlock and let me in.

I flash the card again and this time I watch the red light on the door flash until...

"No," I say, swiping the card a third time. But no luck. "My damn key won't work!"

And then I lose the battle, because I do look over my shoulder at him. He's standing just a couple feet behind me, grinning like the cutest boy in high school. I bite my lip because he's oh-my-God handsome.

That was a mistake. Looking at him, I mean. Because all I see is the kiss back in the stairwell. And all I'm thinking about is doing that again.

Pull yourself together, Eden!

And somehow I do. I slide right past him and head for the stairwell.

"Where are you going?"

"I'm gonna go get this key fixed so I can change. I'm soaked." As I'm sure he's noticed.

He follows me into the stairs and then out onto the lobby floor. And by the time we're heading towards the leasing office, we're walking together. Like a couple or something.

But then I notice the leasing office door is closed. "What the fuck?" I mutter under my breath as I try to turn the handle and find it locked.

"Look," Andrew says. He's pointing to a sign off to the side of the door that says, *Be back in thirty minutes.*

"Thirty minutes?" It's like the universe is conspiring against me. "I can't just sit around in wet clothes for thirty minutes!"

"I have an idea," Andrew says.

"What?" I say, turning to face him. Which is a mistake. Big mistake. He's way too handsome to look at right now. Not with the memory of that kiss still making my body hot and tingly.

"You can come up to my place and borrow one of my shirts."

"I need more than a shirt," I say. Then regret that too. Because now he's probably picturing me taking my pants off.

Which I have to admit is what I'm picturing. Only… he's taking them off me.

"Well?" he asks, leaning against the locked door of the leasing office.

I should say no. That is the responsible thing to do here. Just nip this little tryst in the bud because if I go up there and start taking off my clothes…

"Come on," Andrew says, taking my hand. "You need to change. And I want to help you. Come on."

I let him lead me because… because… well, I don't know what else to do. I have no good options. And today is a little overwhelming. In fact this whole week is overwhelming. A lot of things have happened in the past two days. More than enough to ruffle me.

And I'm actually cold now. The AC is on high in the building and I'm soaking wet, and my teeth are beginning to chatter, and then Andrew pulls me into the elevator—thankfully, it's empty except for us—and then we're ascending up to the penthouse.

When the doors open we get out and he's got his key card ready. Flashing it at the little panel. And of course, his key works. It flashes green, and then he's got the massive double doors open and he's waving me in.

"Come in," he says. "My bedroom's this way."

And he's got a hold of my hand again, so I follow and don't even put up a fight. I'm shaking now. Mostly because of the wet and the cold, but also because I'm super nervous. Like… I'm alone in this guy's apartment and there's this magical sexual chemistry between us. And we've kissed twice now and so this trip to his apartment is like the third date. And the third date is when you're supposed to, you know, fuck the guy. And then I'm thinking about that. Kinda dreaming about it as he leads me into his bedroom and straight past the bed until we're inside his closet. Which is all neat, and unpacked, and... "Holy shit," I say, taking in the room. Because it's almost as big as my entire apartment down on two. There's lots of custom built-in shelves, and drawers, and... yeah. "You have a delicious closet."

Which makes him chuckle.

And stare at me.

Like he's gonna lick all the frosting off my cupcakes.

"What should we do?" Andrew asks. "Hmm? Get you out of those wet clothes and put you into something dry?"

"What's my other option?" I whisper back, unable to take my eyes off his.

He shrugs, grips my hip with his other hand, and says, "Get you out of those wet clothes and not put any back on?" His eyebrows shoot up and do a little wiggle. Which makes me smile and let out the breath I was holding.

"Will you eat me like dessert?" I say. "Swirl your tongue around in my frosting and hit my cherry button?"

He laughs. "What?"

"Oh, my God! I'm sorry! I didn't mean to say that. I was working on an article for the magazine earlier and that just popped into my head! I'm so—"

But the rest of my words get cut off. Because his mouth covers mine in a kiss.

I kiss him back. We're just gonna jump right in, I guess. And I'm glad. No awkward small talk for us. His hands are on my cheeks, holding my face close to his as we tangle our tongues together. His mouth demanding and hard, but only in all the best ways.

My mouth is soft and pliant. Willing to give in and let him lead.

And then his hands are on my button-down shirt. Pulling it over my shoulders and down my arms. Peeling it off until he gets it free and tosses it across the room.

I stop kissing him. Look up into his half-mast eyes as he stares down at me.

And then he says, "Fuck, yes. I am more than happy to lick your frosting."

He pulls my wet t-shirt down, my bra going with it, so my tits bounce up and out as he sets them free.

I feel ridiculous. And I want to say, *Hold up a second. Let me take my shirt off so we can do this right.*

But I've done enough Sexpert research to know that contorting clothing—especially bras—to make a girl's tits pop up like this is considered HAF.

Hot. As. Fuck.

So I let it ride. In fact, I do something I would never have dreamed of last year. I flaunt it. I grab his hands and place them on my breasts. He squeezes automatically. And I say, "My cupcakes are waiting."

CHAPTER FOURTEEN

The erection I had back in my office was nothing compared to what I'm rocking now. Holy shit. It's not like I've never felt breasts before. And it's not like I've never felt nice breasts before. But these... these are something else. Other. They're like the Sistine Chapel of tits. Michelangelo's *The Creation of Adam* if instead of creating

Adam to be placed in Eden, God had created these breasts to be placed *on* Eden.

"How does this happen?" I whisper out, involuntarily, as I squeeze her wet, tender skin.

She swallows and whispers back, "How does what happen?"

I didn't realize I said it aloud. And it's kind of embarrassing. So I opt for obfuscation. In this case, the distraction comes in the form of my mouth on the delicate flesh around her nipple.

She moans, and her hands grab for the sides of my head, taking me by the ears and holding me there. And I'll be goddamned if she doesn't, in fact, taste like a cupcake. Not the sticky sweetness that comes from the adornment of the frosting, but the buttery richness that's baked in and radiates from every delicious morsel. And, like a cupcake, there's something delicate and playful about her. She is decadent and sinful, but at the same time she is joyful and giddy.

Her breasts have, if such a thing is possible, personality.

Wait. I feel like—

A clap of thunder outside causes her to jolt.

I laugh a small breath of air out of my nostrils as my lips draw back from her body. She is wet, and shy, and anxious-looking, for which I cannot blame her. Thirty-seven hours ago, we didn't know each other. We still don't know each other, but it looks like we're about to discover a lot in the next couple of minutes.

"You OK?"

"Uh-huh." She nods her head. "That's incredible."

For a second I think she's talking about the feeling of my mouth on her, but then I notice that she's staring just past my shoulder at the white sheets of rain teeming down outside my windows, the mountains in the background, out beyond the concrete and steel of the TDH. She's correct. It's something to see. Some sort of messy Ansel Adams photograph in real life. In real time.

"Come here," I say, and draw her topless and shivering body over to the windows. I pull the handle and they open and fold in on themselves just like they did yesterday when Eden and I saw my place together for the first time. The rain splatters against the terrace and ricochets up and into the apartment.

"What are you doing?" she asks.

"I wanna show you something."

"What?"

"That." I point.

"What? The rain?"

"No. That"—I point again—"is Pikes Peak. Did you know that?"

"What are you—?"

"And I don't know if you knew this or not, but while many people think that Pikes Peak is the tallest peak in Colorado, it's not. Common misconception."

She rolls her eyes.

"Don't roll your eyes at me! It's not! Hell, it's not even the second tallest. It's like... the twentieth! The tallest is Mount Elmo."

"Elbert," she corrects.

"My God, you know everything," I say, and pull her toward me, hard. We stumble out onto the terrace, the rain pounding our bodies. Perhaps it's the rain, the force of the natural world painting us with its brush, but I'm overcome with the same feeling of blood rushing through my veins that I get when I'm climbing or making art. The sensation of life happening in a very conscious way. It's my favorite feeling in the world, and I haven't felt it enough lately.

I rip my shirt off and fall to my knees, pulling down her t-shirt that's bunched around her waist, and dragging her pants partially down her hips as well. She starts a bit, and I lean back to look up at her. The rain is hammering, and I blink the water out of my eyes. Her hair is stuck to her shoulders and the sides of her face. The slick wetness on her chest along with the competing elements of the sticky humidity outside and cool air from the air conditioning blasting out from within is making her nipples hard.

Or maybe that's not why they're hard at all.

"Still good?"

She nods.

My mouth lands on her stomach, kissing and licking, as I grab her exposed ass—her pants just below the edge of her ass cheeks in the back and hanging on to barely cover her pussy in the front—and I gulp in rainwater as I tickle and kiss in the space below her belly button, causing her to tense up. Down on my knees, the rain battering my shoulders, it feels like the pressure in my jeans is going to make my balls explode, so I spring to my feet with a force like I'm leaping to grab a crag in a wall on a pitch, and I strip myself bare, tossing my own pants over the edge of the railing by accident.

"Oh, shit," I say as we both grab the rail and lean over to watch my jeans and underwear go cascading to the ground below along with the rain. They land on top of someone scurrying by to get into the building. Someone who I'm pretty sure is Cheryl, the leasing agent. It looks like she may have gotten caught unaware by the sudden storm. She's holding a newspaper over her head. When my pants hit her, she looks up with a "what-the-fuck-was-that?" expression. Eden and I duck our heads back, quickly. Laughing.

And then the laughter subsides. She gulps in wet breaths. Breaths flecked with rainwater. She looks down at my erection and she shivers again. Then she shimmies her clothes the rest of the way down her legs and stands in front of me, perfect and wet.

And wet.

I step to her and wrap my arms around her waist, letting my hard cock slip in between her thighs and rub against the lips of her pussy. When I press my mouth against hers and allow my tongue to find its way to hers, she mutters out, "Oh, my God," and her voice... It's... The beating rain absorbs some of the sound, causing it to be muffled, and the tensing muscles in her stomach as we kiss suggests that she's moaning in urgent need from the bottom of her very core, but it's just that she sounds like... She sounds like...

She sounds like big goddamn trouble in my world.

SHOW HIM WHAT
BAKES YOUR CAKE

This one's for you ladies! You can't expect him to read your
mind. So today we're talking about getting comfortable
telling him eactly what bakes your cake. Lesson One. You
gotta try this out on yourself first... amiright?

CHAPTER FIFTEEN

Oh. Shit.

I'm in so much trouble.

I think I just used my Sexpert voice on him. And it's not like that's the voice on the videos or anything because I use the Voice Lift app, but... but the inflection. The rough edges of it. The purring. It's all *her*.

And he's got a weird look on his face now. His brows a little bit scrunched up. His eyes slightly narrowed. And not the half-mast kind like he had back in the stairwell, either. Those were I'm-hot-for-you eyes.

These are… these are I'm-on-to-you eyes.

So I basically have no choice. I pull out every Sexpert video I've done in the past year and use my unused, but much-talked-about, skills on him.

I lightly drag my fingernails down his chest as I crouch down and open my legs. I feel myself blushing as I take his cock in both hands and begin to twist and pump him in my palms.

The cold rain hitting our hot skin makes us steam. His eyes are locked with mine as I stare up at him.

And I know what I have to do. I know that the only way to make him forget about who I might be and force him to think about what I'm doing instead is to…

Yeah.

I have given exactly two blow jobs in my entire life. Eden has no clue how to give a man the perfect blowjob.

But Sexpert… well, she's studied hundreds of porn movies searching for the perfect tips she promotes in her *Drawing Cream from a Ding-Dong* video.

And she knows just what to do. (Even if she doesn't quite execute it with one-hundred-percent accuracy.)

I blow on the tip of his cock (tip number three) with exaggerated puckered lips and his eyes go wide. Which is fabulous. Because now he's thinking about what I'm doing, not who I might sound like.

My tongue darts out and swipes over the small opening while my hands travel up and down his thick, hard shaft. Twisting just enough. Gripping with just the right amount of pressure. (Tips one, four, and seven.)

152

Rain is still falling down like a backdrop to the apocalypse. Which is perfect. I don't even have to bring out tip number two. Spitting on my hands to make everything slide a little smoother.

And then, just as lightning shoots through the sky above his head, I take him into my mouth and suck, a crack of thunder making the building shudder.

His hands go to my wet hair. Guiding me with just the right amount of encouragement.

I open wide, so ready to take him fully into my mouth. My tongue is eager, and things are going so well I'm actually making myself horny. And then he's inside me, the steady pressure of his hands on my head making me want to give him more.

So I do that. And it's all pretty hot, and I'm feeling very proud of myself, kinda picturing how many women I've helped give the perfect blow job since we put this video out and…

And then I gag.

Like I push him away and it takes every ounce of self-control I have not to just throw up.

"Sorry," I purr, looking up at him—never breaking eye contact, trying to stay in sexy mode. And then I dive back in, my hands still busy twisting and pumping with just a little more pressure, but this time the second his thick, round head enters my mouth, I gag again.

Oh, my God. I suck. I suck at blow jobs! Not in a good way.

And then I gag again just thinking about putting his cock in my mouth.

Quick, Eden. Quick, quick, quick! You need to improvise.

I lick his shaft. Yeah. That was tip number nine. Lick the shaft and cup the balls.

Andrew moans.

He likes it.

I do it again. Dragging my tongue up and down his cock, giving his balls a little squeeze this time.

Another moan!

Success!

The Sexpert says the blowjob should last between four and ten minutes. I'm on like minute two, which is unfortunate. Because I can't think of any more tips. I really need to take a refresher course.

Oh, tip ten! Lick his balls. Mmmhmmm. I dip my face underneath him and at the same time I lift his balls up and drag my tongue over them.

"Shit," he moans.

I pull away, still gripping him, but now I've got his cock again. I didn't make it to four minutes. I know that for sure. But hell, a girl knows her limits.

And besides, I've got another idea.

Sexpert video number six. *How to Fuck Him With Your Cupcakes.*

I smile up at him as I take his cock and push it in between my girls. It's a devious smile that I think makes him nervous. Because even though his grin is still in place, it's a little lopsided now.

Shit. Am I doing this wrong?

No. No. I'm the Sexpert. And I have the perfect tits for titty-fucking. All the comments on that video say so.

I place my hands on the outside of my breasts and push, squeezing against his cock. "Fuck," he says, looking down at me.

Yup. This is the winner. I'm good at this one. Like… if you've got the right props, there's almost no skill required.

I jiggle them a little, then a little harder. I'm trying to get that look on his face again. The one where he's not wondering about who I might be but getting lost in what I'm doing.

Hmmm. He still looks kinda distracted. So I do a little wink, make this clicking noise with my tongue, and stick my tongue out as I lower my head, licking the tip of his cock again.

I take him in my mouth as he begins to get into it. Rocking his hips just enough to make his cock slide up to my mouth, then withdraw and almost get lost in my bosom.

Yes! Success is mine once again!

He starts moving a little faster, his dick thrusting up, then disappearing in quick succession.

I seal my lips over his head, trying to get up with the new rhythm, but I can't quite dip my head low enough to keep him in my mouth for the whole cycle, and then the next time he comes up, he does it with a little more excitement, and I'm just thinking this is it. I've got him right where I want him… he's not putting two and two together… he's not thinking about anything other than what we're doing right now…

And then I miscalculate and the tip of his cock pokes me in the eye.

I lose my concentration for a moment, pulling back as my fingertips go to the stab of pain in my eye. Like I swear, it's a second or two. But it's enough. Because…

"Shit," he says, bending down. "Are you OK?"

"Fine! I'm fine!"

But I can tell. This isn't going well. I need to pull out all the stops. He's still thinking way too hard.

So I take his hand in mine and jump forward to Sexpert video number ten. *Show Him What Bakes Your Cake.*

I place his fingers between my legs and show him exactly where he can find the cherry on top.

CHAPTER SIXTEEN

The idea that I had percolating in the back of my mind that my new, and now very intimate friend Eden might somehow, coincidentally, be the one behind this whole Sexpert nonsense is being quickly dispelled. There is no way in hell this woman is giving anyone anonymous sex tips. But here, now, with me, the clumsy awkwardness is making me feel that much more into her. It is the sexual manifestation of everything I have seen in her to this point. Goddamn, she is fucking adorable. And... fun.

She's fun. This is fun. I'm having fun.

I haven't had fun in a minute.

"What? What is it?" she asks, nervously. I realize that I got distracted for half a second and my fingers are sitting on her clit but not moving. So I fix that.

I grab her by the hips, spin her around, and throw her kind of roughly down onto this big, round daybed thing that's out here. It's puddled up from the rain and when she lands, water goes splashing off of it and she yelps a tiny bit and then giggles.

I slide my knees in between her legs, holding them apart with the outside of my thighs, and put my index and middle finger back onto the spot she showed me.

"There?"

She nods, and I start circling her. Firm, small, massaging rotations that cause her to throw her head back. But when she does, her mouth opens, and she drinks in about a pint of rainwater and starts coughing orgiastically.

"Shit." I step back from her and let her roll to her side where she continues to hack. "What can I do? Can I help?"

She shakes her head, and then manages to cough out, "I think I just need some water."

I can't help it. I burst out laughing.

She continues coughing and says, "Why are you laughing? What's fun—?" And then she realizes what's funny, I guess, because she starts laughing too. In between the coughing and hacking. She buries her face into the rain-soaked fabric and I can kind of make out her saying, "I'm such a fucking dork."

I say nothing, just smile and stare down at her back. She twists her head and pushes her hair out of her face as she glances over her shoulder at me. She blinks away the rain and raises her eyebrows in a "what now" way.

I show her what now.

I spread her legs wide again, slide in between them once again, and once again I put my two fingers on the spot she showed me and let them do their job. I've worked in so many mediums over the years—paint, pencil, clay, acrylic, silicone, you name it—and the thing I'm good at... the thing I'm best at... is finesse. I know how to use my hands to sculpt a delicate form. I know how to carefully craft every angle. I'm not prideful. It's just what I do the best. I have strong hands which have just gotten stronger over the years from climbing, but I also have *feel* and *touch* and I know how to treat each special material I touch with the right kind of care.

I haven't created art in a long time. And I haven't been with a woman in a long time. And right now, Eden is the beneficiary of the fact that I am re-engaged with two things I've missed.

She whines out with want as I let a third finger find her soft flesh and I maneuver around the skin between her thighs. Her hips slide back, and she pushes her ass toward me. I use my thumb to press back into her and hold her in place. The rain batters us, its pulsing, staccato beating on our bodies fueling the energy that's between us. I feel alive.

With my other hand, I start stroking myself. When I jerked off last night, I kind of imagined Eden. I don't know her, so it was just the idea of her. The fantasy of what the cute girl from the freeway... and the building where I work... and the building where I live... and the restaurant... and the elevator... (wow, when I thought I might run into her again, I had no idea...) might be like. But the reality of her is so much better.

Pumping my cock with one hand and stroking her with the other as the rain pounds onto my terrace high above the street below, I feel like I feel when I'm climbing. And looking out at Pikes Peak, the twentieth tallest mountain peak in Colorado, it has the same quality I get when I'm reaching a summit.

And I realize... I'm just about to hit the summit. We both are.

"Mmm, mmmm, mmmmmmmmmmmmm." The sounds she's making are getting longer, louder, and higher pitched each time a new "mmm" escapes from her. And each long, loud, high pitched "mmm" has me pumping on myself harder. And right at the moment she comes, a huge clap of thunder, a crash of lightning, and a scream from deep in her lungs all come along with her.

And so do I. My cock spits out hot, steamy come all over her back. It mixes with the rain and disperses down the small of her back and onto her ass, sliding down the side of her hips and along her legs. I don't think she can tell because the rain is still pounding on her and she's still writhing with the force of her own orgasm, and I make the choice not to say anything. I just rub my hands all over her body, massaging her and simultaneously wiping away the evidence of the fact that I couldn't keep myself from spilling out all over her during a rainstorm.

In the middle of the day.

On my second day in town.

It is, as could have been predicted, awkward in my apartment.

We're back in the bedroom. She's standing in front of me, wrapped in a towel. I'm just wearing a pair of boxer shorts. We look at each other. I smile. And then she says...

"Clothes?"

"What's that?"

"Clo-thes," she says again, drawing out the word.

"Oh, yeah," I say, realizing that this was the whole pretense under which we came up to my place. Because she couldn't get into hers to change and I might have something she could wear. Yeah. That's plausible. "Umm, well," I say, rummaging through my closet. "See, these aren't, like, my things. I mean, they are, but I didn't buy them. There was just this stuff waiting for me when I got here and I tried on one of the shirts, and I think they must be European or something because what they're calling 'large' is no large I've ever heard of, so..." I fan through the inventory of button-downs as I'm talking, offering one after the other to her, and she just shakes her head.

"What's your deal?" she finally says.

"What?"

"Seriously, what's your deal?"

"That's now the second time you've asked me that."

"Technically the fourth. I asked you twice yesterday. Or maybe fifth, I'm not sure, but you never answered anyway. So, for the fifth or sixth time... What's your deal?"

I take a second to think, nod my head, take a breath, and sit on the edge of the bed. "Um, I mean, I'm from Kentucky. Grew up on a horse farm. My dad died when I was, like, four. My mom is kind of a crazy Southern Belle type. I got sent off to boarding school, discovered I loved art, went to Bennington for undergrad because, I dunno, because it's expensive and my mom likes spending money. Met Pierce, became best friends because we both have daddy issues and Oedipal complexes? Probably? Uh, went to grad school at Berkeley. Planned to be an artist-slash-museum curator or something. Wound up in a bloodless relationship and got engaged. Got unengaged because it was bloodless. Stumbled onto what became Voice Lift and accidentally started a billion-dollar company. And then yesterday morning I moved here. Oh... And I climb. Rocks and stuff. I always thought it was probably because I was trying to run away from something, but my lead developer, Dev, thinks it's because they're sturdy. But he's nineteen, so take that with a grain of salt."

I sniff at the end of that because the A/C is making me a little stuffy.

"You have a lead developer whose name is Dev?"

I find it interesting that that's what she chose to take from everything I just said.

"You and Pierce are super close, huh?"

"Uh, yeah. I know, he's a dick. But he's my brother. I love the guy. Love's weird that way. It just kind of finds you. You can't really pick and choose who you love, I don't think."

"Huh," she says.

"And it's fucked up that you work for him and that, hell, we had dinner together and he doesn't really even know who you are, but..." I wish I hadn't said that. Stupid. She gets very cold. "Sorry."

She presses her lips together and shakes her head. Not like she's shaking it at me, just like she's thinking.

"What's—?" I start to ask.

"I gotta go," she says.

"But you... You're in a towel. Here. Lemme—"

"No, no, it's fine," she says, clutching the towel around her and grabbing up the things of hers that are around the apartment. She heads out of the bedroom. I follow.

"Hey, listen," I say. "I don't know—" But that's all I get out before she has her hand on the door. "Where are you going?"

"I need to get someone to let me into my place. I have to get back to work. I have to continue pulling material to help your friend Pierce ward off the threat from this *Sexpert* person." She really leans into *Sexpert*.

"Oh, shit, yeah," I say. "That's so..."

"That's so what?" she asks, after I trail off.

"Nothing. It's just... funny. Because..."

"Because what?"

I take a long, long beat. We just stare at each other.

"Nothing," I finally say.

"OK. Well, um, thanks for the... sexy... time... stuff." She reaches out to shake my hand.

"Uh." I raise my hands awkwardly. "OK." I reach to shake as well, but she withdraws her hand.

"I... Ugh... Just... UGH!" she exclaims, and then she swings the door open, walks out, looks back, says, "Wha—?" and then she kind of knocks her fists against her forehead and she leaves.

After she's gone, I turn to face the windows and see that the rain has stopped. The hazy, post rain sun is glinting off the mountain in the distance. And arcing the sky over the peak of Pike... A rainbow. It's incredible. Roy G. Biv. Red, orange, yellow, green, blue, indigo, violet, tracing the sky.

And in a weird, optical illusion, it looks like it ends right at the spot where Eden and I were just a bit ago. And that's when I also see that she left her underwear. Her discarded panties are still on the terrace, drying in the afternoon sun.

And I'll be damned if it doesn't look like that's the exact spot where my rainbow ends.

CHAPTER SEVENTEEN

So.

Yeah.

That day was kinda fucked up.

I ducked into the stairs, dried myself off with the towel, then forced my soaking wet clothes back on my body, realizing—too late—that I left my underwear behind in Andrew's penthouse like a token of my appreciation.

Yup. I'm classy like that.

Then I went back down to the office, found Cheryl, who was ranting to her co-worker about people throwing clothes off the balcony and they were gonna need to send out a memo on that, to ask for my key to be remade.

And then I went home, changed, went back to work where I promptly bumped into Myrtle—who somehow knew I'd just had sex—and...

Yeah.

"I haven't seen him again."

"Holy shit," Zoey says.

I'm at her place. She lives in a one-bedroom apartment in the proper part of the Tech Center, just a bit north of me. Before she got pregnant she worked here in the TDH in the tech support department for Computer Solutions.

But daycare is so expensive for a newborn. There was no way she could afford to work after Stevie was born. And her baby daddy... well, she never told him she was pregnant because it was just a one-time thing. That's why we started the Sexpert and she decided to make a go of her own web design business.

She had originally planned to go back to work once Stevie turned one—which is coming up quick—and last month that was still the plan since her business is still struggling and the whole Sexpert thing wasn't panning out the way we'd hoped.

But now... well, everything has changed. We are actually making money off our crazy sexy plan.

She called me the day after all that nooner stuff went down with Andrew to discuss our future, so here I am.

Except she's way more interested in my nooner than she is our future.

"That's like… something out of a half-baked rom-com movie!" Zoey continues. Her eyes are bright with dreamy happiness. Then her smile drops. "Wait, didn't you say Andrew was—"

"Yes," I finish for her. "He invented Voice Lift and he's Pierce's BFF, so now he's trying to figure out who I am. And he's gonna, Zoey. He will."

"So you're for sure not going to see him again?"

"Nope," I say. With as much conviction as I can muster up. Because God, he's all I can think about since we hooked up. That afternoon *was* like something out of a movie. So ridiculous and hot, and fun, and… not real, I add silently. To force myself to believe it was just one of those meaningless sexy encounters.

"Did he call you?"

"Yes. And I don't even know how he got my number." I secretly think it was Myrtle, but I have no proof. "But I hung up and blocked him immediately. As soon as I heard his voice," I say quickly. "Don't worry, there's no chance of him getting through now."

"But he works in your building," she says.

"I know," I say. Sighing. Suddenly all pouty. Lips all pucker-y. "But I've avoided him successfully so far."

Or is he avoiding me? I mean, how weird that I bumped into him again and again those first two days and then sexy times ensue and now nothing. Ghost.

"So you like him?" Zoey asks.

I grab a fuzzy pink throw pillow off her couch and hug it to my chest, still puckering my lips in one of those sad faces I make.

"Oh, shit, Eden. You can't fall for this guy. He's too dangerous. What if he does find out who you are? What if *Le Man* really does sue us? We've worked so hard to build something of our own, something that might get us out of the corporate rat race, and this could—"

"I know!" I say, a little too loudly, because Stevie, who is sitting in the middle of a blanket chewing on a plastic block, startles. "Sorry, baby," I say. "I know that though," I say, putting on a serious face for Zoey so she'll believe me. "I'm not going to see him again. And besides, he's forgotten all about me anyway. Hasn't even tried to come down to my desk and..." I shrug. "You know. I dunno. Whatever."

She stares at me for a little bit longer and I do my best to avoid her gaze.

Because I really do like him. He's like Prince fucking Charming, right? Rich, funny, hot, and he really seemed to like me. He thought all my weird quirks were adorable.

Not too many people get me like that. Most people just write me off as a dumb, ridiculous blonde girl who kicks ass at social media and that's about it.

I really felt like Andrew and I made a love connection.

"Well," Zoey says. "Let's just talk about the business."

"Yes," I say. "Let's do that."

She hands me a printout with all our numbers on it. She's a data freak. Which is perfect because I'm not. I take the paper automatically and notice she's giving me one of her quirky Zoey smiles and I say, "What? Why are you looking at me that way?"

"You haven't even looked at our numbers, have you?"

"No, why?" I say, glancing down at the printout. I squint. She's circled something at the bottom in lime-green sharpie. I blink, because for a second I think I'm hallucinating. "What? Does this say—"

"ONE MILLION SUBSCRIBERS!" Zoey screams it and this makes Stevie burst out crying. "Sorry, sorry, sorry!" Zoey is saying as she rushes over to pick him up. She holds him close to her chest and rocks back and forth on her heels as she starts spilling out facts. "We hit one million last night!" she says. "And we've gotten insane click-through rates for our affiliate ads since we went to paid last week," she continues, her voice high with sweet excitement. "And I've estimated that we're going to make about fifteen thousand dollars this month!"

"What? Oh, my God!"

"Yeah, and look," she says, swinging her laptop around so I can see our channel. "We're way past a million subscribers now! If we put out another video tomorrow, we're going to hit one point five in another couple days! And that means next month—who knows! Maybe we hit thirty thousand dollars!"

"Holy shit! We did it!"

"We did it!" she yells, her whole body doing her adorable little happy dance that involves a lot of ridiculous wiggling. Stevie is laughing with us now, happy about our success.

"Wait," I say, holding up a hand. "I hate to be the Debbie Downer and all, but we don't have another video."

"We will," she says, holding up a finger to make me pause. "But come with me first. I have a surprise for you!" She sings that last part, which makes Stevie laugh.

I get up and follow her down the hall to the bedroom. Half of it is decorated like a nursery and half is her bedroom. She could never afford a two-bedroom apartment in this neighborhood, so she and Stevie share a room.

"What the hell?" I ask, looking at the mess of clothes and boxes all over the place. "What's going on in here?"

"I had to empty my closet," she says. "Forget about the mess. Look what I made!"

And then she pulls on the barn door that covers her master closet and reveals...

"A studio! For you! And look! All the freaking desserts are on the wall!"

The whole closet has been painted cotton-candy pink. And there's like scalloped trim on the walls painted white. And a fake painted window with white mosquito-netting curtains. The eight-by-eight former closet looks like she's been watching way too many shabby chic shows on Home TV.

"We need to up our game," Zoey says, words rushing out of her mouth. "We needed a proper sexy backdrop and props. Look!" Then she covers little Stevie's eyes and adds, "Not you, baby. Don't look at Mommy's naughty closet."

And there, all neatly lined up on her built-in shelves that used to hold shoes, are the sex toys I demonstrate for the videos.

"We have to keep up with the videos, Eden. We have to. This is our big break. If we slow down now we could lose all of it. And this is important. We will not get paid for two months, OK? There's a payment delay with this kind of work. So I've got six new topics and we're gonna do them all right now before you leave. And then every time our numbers start to dip, I'll upload a new one. We get such a boost when we put out a new one, ya know?

The monthly schedule was a good start but you've seen how much more we could make if we just up our game."

"Jesus," I say. "Six videos? Tonight?"

"Not all tonight," she amends. "Just three? Maybe?"

"I have so much going on at work right now, Zoey, I don't think I have time to—"

"We have to," she says, her face serious now. "We have to, Eden. This is too good. We *must* make the most of it. Our lives are about to change and... and... I'm so tired of worrying about money, ya know? About how I'm going to take care of Stevie. And I hate this stupid apartment. I need something bigger. Something that's kid-friendly. A place with a playground or something. I can't raise my son in a Tech Center one-bedroom. There are no kids around here, either. This neighborhood is for single people. I need more for him. It was my decision to have him and now I have to provide the best life I can. This isn't what he deserves."

"Hmmm." I pout. Because I get it. If I had a baby I'd want the best for him too. Her apartment is cute as fuck. It's not some run-down place at all. It's only a one-bed one-bath, but it's quite nice. And quite pricey.

"I want a house," Zoey says, her voice suddenly sad. "I don't need anything special, Eden. Just a two-bedroom rental with a back yard in a safe neighborhood. That's all I want. And the Sexpert can provide this. I could move to Parker, or... or... Centennial. Somewhere quiet and green, and not a third-floor walk up."

"Yeah," I say. "I get it."

"So I know it's a lot of work for you. But..."

"Say no more." I cut her off, walking over to pull her into a hug. "It's no big. We're gonna make this the best sex advice show on the freaking internet!"

So that's what we do. It takes hours just to give the topics proper Sexpert names. And by the time we finish shooting the third video of the night, *How to Whip Cream Her Fun Bags*, it's almost five in the morning.

By the time I get home it's nearly six-thirty and I have just enough time to take a quick shower, get dressed, and walk over to one of the breakfast trucks to pick up a chocolate éclair and some crème brûlée coffee before heading into work to repurpose more *Le Man* articles that could topple our burgeoning little sex empire. (Making Sexpert videos always makes me crave sugar—I wonder why?)

I am so tired I sink into my desk chair and sigh, hoping against hope that Gretchen will be too busy to bug me today.

And that's when I hear roaring laughter coming from another end of the large open cubicle area.

I stand up to look over the muted blue upholstered partition, trying to see what's going on, when I hear… my voice.

Well, my Voice Lift voice.

They're playing our newest Sexpert video, *A Sprinkle of Nuts*, in the break room. And yup, you guessed it. Pierce is in there watching it.

I slink back down into my chair and pull up my email, trying to ignore all the hubbub.

I have seven messages about employee benefits, book clubs, and upcoming birthdays. Two from Gretchen with ideas about hashtags she thinks are winners, but aren't.

And one... oh, what fresh hell is this? *Emergency Team-Building Day Tomorrow.*

Are they fucking with me right now? I have to give up a Saturday?

I reluctantly open it because every now and then we have these stupid things and they've always been mandatory.

And yup. There it is in bright red caps.

MANDATORY TEAM-BUILDING DAY AT THE TALLEST ROCK.

The Tallest Rock is, you guessed it, a rock climbing gym.

I'm pretty athletic. And I'm sure I could climb the hell out of a rock wall. But... but... didn't Andrew say he was into rock climbing?

No, he wouldn't come to *our* team building day. He's not a *Le Man* family member.

But there's a little part of me... this teeny, tiny part of me... that hopes he might be there.

I know it's dangerous. I know seeing him could be the beginning of our Sexpert downfall.

And I don't care.

CHAPTER EIGHTEEN

"Why am I here? I don't work for you."

"You don't have to be here," says Pierce, sliding on his rock climbing shoes.

"Yeah, but—"

"But nothing. You don't wanna be here, go. I figured you'd dig all this rock climbing nonsense, but split if you don't wanna stick around. You've got free will."

I'm not sure he's right. I'm not certain that I do have free will. Feels like right now my will is somehow bound explicitly to my dick. Because that is the reason that I'm here at *Le Man*'s Saturday team-building jamboree/hootenanny. I figure, since PC told me that it's mandatory for his employees, that Eden will have to be here too.

I haven't seen her since we acted out the porno version of *Singin' in the Rain* at my place. (*Swingin' in the Rain? Slingin' in the Rain?*) And I can't stop thinking about her.

There are a few reasons for that.

First, there's the fact that despite me trying to tell myself it's not true... I'm pretty sure she *is* the Sexpert girl.

I don't have definitive confirmation yet; Dev's a perfectionist and won't let me field-test the new app until he's happy with it. He says, "It works, but it's clumsy. I won't use an inelegant product with my name on it." (He's young. He'll have to learn that sometimes good enough is good enough.) But I've watched several of the videos at this point and the coincidences can't be coincidences. They just can't.

Add to that the fact that having seen Eden's breasts up close and personal... Well. There are no two people on the planet with boobs like that.

Unless she has a twin.

Huh.

I didn't even think about that.

That's hot.

Regardless...

The second reason I can't stop thinking about her is because she's the first woman I've been with in a long, long, *long* time. And though we didn't actually have intercourse... Well, that's the thing. I really, really want to. So, yeah, she's been on my mind.

And the last reason I can't stop thinking about her is... I like her.

I just really like her. She feels good. And she makes me feel good. And she's funny. And she's fun. And I like her.

But I'm so far out of the game at this point, I'm not sure what's right. By which, I mean I'm not sure what the correct way to proceed is. She took off out of my place so freaked out that I wanted to give her some space. Besides, I figured I'd just run into her again. Hell, I ran into her all over the place when I wasn't trying to. But, of course, as the laws of the universe would have it, as soon as I wanted to run into her, it stopped happening.

I even did some weird shit like hang out by the pool downstairs to see if she'd show up. Cheryl saw me there and asked why I was at the community pool when I have my own, private one on the roof. But she asked the question a little too loudly and this girl in what can only be charitably described as a "micro-bikini" came flouncing over to find out more about me.

And now I don't hang out by the community pool anymore. (I may be horny, but I also enjoy being disease-free.)

The thing I did that's the most unlike me is that I convinced Myrtle to give me Eden's phone number. It took some cajoling. And it was both uncomfortable and something I know I'm going to regret. Because now I think I might owe Myrtle a favor. And I'm sure that at some point, that will involve making certain a body is never found.

In any case, after I called Eden and she hung up on me, I decided the best thing I can do is just try to forget about the whole thing. I've attempted to focus on running a company for the last few days, but my mind starts wandering in meetings. It's weird. Even as discomfited as I've been having to admit to myself that I'm a CEO now and not Jasper Johns, like I wanted to be, I've been pretty good about compartmentalizing it. I can knuckle down and do my job when I have to. But since the Eden/rain/mid-day romance thing, my mind is wandering more. I find myself drifting off and thinking about, hell, whatever, painting murals on the sides of mountains and stuff.

I know that it's just dopamine and norepinephrine and stuff like that coursing through my bloodstream as a result of the exciting newness of being with a woman I find interesting. I totally get that. It's the same reason I like to climb. The same chemicals get released. But y'know what? Who cares? It feels good and there's nothing wrong with feeling good. And I just kind of want to keep feeling it as long as I can.

So I'm here. Because I might see her. And at worst, this climbing gym has a V15 pitch which will be a good workout and release some endorphins, but not kill me when I fall. Which is always my preference.

"You find her yet?" Pierce's voice.

"What? Who?"

"The thief. The violator. She who is without ethics."

"No, man. Not yet. I'd tell you if I had. I promise I'm not holding out on you." (I'm kind of holding out. Sort of.) "We're, I dunno, maybe days away from being able to run some tests on the app. Then all I have to do is cross-match what we come up with against the database and I'll be able to tell you what we find."

"Cross-match against your secret NSA database, you mean?"

"Please don't. Just, don't, please."

"OK. So, you staying or going?" Pierce asks, huffily, for some reason. He's being oddly passive-aggressive.

"I'm staying, OK? Why are you being weird?"

He smiles, grabs me by the arm, and says, "Come with me."

He drags me to the front of a climbing wall, stands me beside him, and says, "Everyone! Everyone, may I have your attention, s'il vous plaît!"

Pierce rented the place for the day, so the only people there are the couple hundred *Le Man* employees. They cease milling around and come to gather in a loose semi-circle around where Pierce and I are standing.

"What are you doing?" I one-third whisper, one-third sigh, and one-third weep.

"Yep, yep, that's it! Gather round!"

I scan the group to see if I can spy Eden, but I don't. I wonder if she may have come in while I wasn't looking, seen me and taken off. But then I decide that I'm just being paranoid. I do spot Myrtle. She's hard to miss. Everyone else is in shorts and t-shirts, or like me, cargo pants and tank tops or whatever, but she's clad in these yoga-pants/tights kinds of things that have strategic cut-outs where there's just transparent mesh running all along the inside and outside of the thighs, exposing her skin in a peek-a-boo way. And the top she has on... Well, I kind of thought tube tops were a thing of the past, but apparently they're making a comeback.

She winks at me and waves by fanning her fingers in my direction starting with her pinky. She looks like a mountain lion swiping at me with her claws. Except that I've encountered mountain lions before and they don't scare me nearly as much.

Then Myrtle winks just past me. At Pierce. And he gets this look on his face. I've seen it before. It's like—

"Everyone, let me take just a moment to say welcome, and thanks for coming out today!" There is some head nodding as Pierce speaks, a couple of people give polite yet awkward golf claps, and somebody sneezes, causing a collage of muttered "bless yous" and "gesundheits."

Pierce continues, "I'm sure that many of you, when you saw the subject line—Emergency Team-Building—wondered, 'Emergency? What could be so emergent that it would require a team-building day?'"

Oh, dear God, do I know where this is going?

"Well, my fair Le Manians"—(Le Manians?)—"we are under attack."

Yep. I did know where this was going. Fuck.

"How many of you have heard of this internet personality known as the Sexpert?"

Pretty much every hand shoots up in unison. There's one guy wearing a Cannibal Corpse t-shirt standing in the back who looks around like he doesn't know what the hell the Sexpert is. Maybe he works in the mail room. I dunno.

"Indeed," Pierce goes on. "And let me ask this. How many of you were aware that this was our idea? Meaning MY idea? Meaning *Le Man*'s idea? An idea that has been stolen from us?"

More muttering now. I may hear a gasp, but it's probably just my imagination.

"Dude, what are you—?" But that's all I get out.

"This man to my left"—to his left? Oh, Jesus, I'm to his left—"is my dear friend Andrew Hawthorne! Some of you may have seen Andrew around. Andrew is the founder and CEO of Aureality Enterprises."

Please don't, please don't, please don't...

"And Andrew is going to help us figure out who this person is who has pilfered OUR intellectual property and assist us in bringing them to justice!"

The golf claps are even more scattered and cautious, and it feels like a bright light is suddenly shining on me, although I know it's just the flush of blood pumping through me that makes it seem that way. I get a tight smile and raise my hand to the group.

"Hi. I'm Andrew." I then step back and kind of press against the rock wall, noticing it's only a V2 behind me. I could scale it, top out, and probably escape through the skylight in the ceiling in under a minute.

"But why we are here today," Pierce continues, "is because I believe"—he takes a dramatic pause—"that we shouldn't have to seek outside aid in uncovering this felon." Felon? I wonder if Derek knows about what's happening right now. "Because I believe that whoever is responsible for stealing this idea is an enemy within!"

No gasps, no golf claps, just blank stares.

"I believe that the *only* way someone could have known about our idea is if they already work ... HERE." He really lands "here" in a super-operatic way. "Or, at the least, they are in some way affiliated with *Le Man*."

Heads turn. People glance at each other. Not in a guilty-seeming way, in a "what the fuck is happening right now?" way.

181

"So we are here today to work on trust. We must learn to trust each other. To rely on each other. To help each other and not to tear each other down!"

I have to admit, Pierce gives one hell of a speech. Maybe I can get him to give mine from now on.

"So, as we spend today climbing these"—he pats one of the climbing holds—"uh... And, what are these? They're not rocks."

I glance over out of the side of my eye. "They're, uh... polyurethane."

"These polyurethane handholds! Let them be a symbol! A symbol for each other! Think of these not as polyurethane rocks, but as polyurethane hands! The polyurethane hand of the person next to you!"

He's really kind of blown this metaphor apart, but it hasn't dimmed his commitment. Which is its own special kind of leadership skill.

"And if one of you does, in fact, know who might be behind this scurrilous action, I hope you'll take my real-life, skin-and-blood hand at the end of today, and hold it, secure in the knowledge that if you are honest with me, I will be kind in return!"

Huh. I always kind of thought that Pierce felt like the whole "king/kingdom" thing was sort of a joke, but now, I'm—

He waves his hand with a regal flourish. "And now... Build. Grow. Trust!" He gestures to the wall behind us, and slowly, his slightly confused employees wander over and begin climbing up and mostly falling down.

He steps off the pads and back into the main area of the gym, turning around to see a bunch of magazine employees struggling to maneuver up the walls. Over to our right, something I can already tell is going to result in a human avalanche begins forming. Pierce nods his head, satisfied.

"Dude," I begin slowly, the way one does when approaching an unstable person. "Um, are you OK?"

"Fine. Why?"

I decide not to say anything and shake my head. "No reason."

We watch the struggling going on in front of us for another moment and then he says, "Talked to my dad a couple nights ago."

"Oh. You did?"

"I did."

"How was that?"

"He's not thrilled about our sales."

"Isn't he?"

"He isn't."

The human avalanche collapses as expected.

"So..." I start. "What're you—?"

"Look at that."

I look at where Pierce is looking. Myrtle is pulling herself to the top of the wall she attacked. And I do mean attacked. She tore up it like she's been doing this for years. And now she stands at the top, looking down at everyone struggling. She doesn't have chalk all over her like I do when I finish topping out. She doesn't even look like she's broken a sweat.

"She's something, isn't she?" Pierce says.

"Uh, yeah. I guess so." There's something in his eyes as he stares at her and suddenly it dawns on me to ask, "Dude, are you two—?"

"I think it's her."

A beat. I blink.

"Come again?"

"I think it's her."

"Her what? You think what's her? You think she's—?"

"I think she stole my idea. I think it's her. I think she's the Sexpert."

I look at Myrtle staring down at all the struggling Le Manians. She reaches over the edge to help one of them up and lifts him with a strength that surprises me.

"Really? You honestly think that?"

"Makes all the sense in the world. Doesn't it?"

Watching her, it does make some sense. I can see why he'd think that. And it would be way more plausible than my half-cooked idea. (Even if my half-cooked idea is based on at least circumstantial evidence, as opposed to a *feeling*, but still...)

"Why would she do something like that, do you think?" I ask.

"Why does anyone do anything?"

"I... That's not an answer."

He doesn't say anything more, just stares at her as she walks over to the hand ladder and begins to lower herself down.

"Really?" I ask once more. "You really think it's her?"

"Who else?"

"Sorry! Sorry I'm late!" comes the flustered, urgent, familiar voice from behind us. Both Pierce and I turn to look at the same time. The explanation for her lateness is suddenly squelched and she stops talking and stares at us. We stare back.

"Oh," she says.

"Hey there," I say.

And then we stare some more. And finally, after a moment of no one saying anything, the thudding of bodies landing on padded mats behind us the only sound, Pierce leans in and whispers, "Uh, that's that girl who works for me, right?"

CHAPTER NINETEEN

Oh. My. God.

They're talking about me.

What are they saying? Did Andrew figure something out? Does he know? Did he tell Pierce?

My heart is beating fast and my hands are starting to get grossly sticky.

He knows. They both know. I'm gonna get sued, and fired and… My life is over. Over. It's just…

Get a fucking grip, Eden. If ever there was a time to play things cool, it's now.

I turn my back to them and push my glasses up my nose. It's hard to play cool when my whole body is suddenly a pool of nervous sweat. I want to take off this stupid button-down shirt and just wear my tank top, but I have a strict no-sexy policy for all things work-related and my boobies in a tank are a definite no-no.

Calm down. They don't know. They can't know. If they knew they'd confront me for sure. I might not know Pierce well, but he's a loose cannon. You don't need to work for him to know that.

Be brave. Be bold. Be… I want another B word to inspire me in this moment because I like alliteration, but I can't think of one.

Bubbly. No, that's stupid.

Beautiful. No, I laugh to myself. That's absolutely the wrong direction. Beautiful is what got me into this whole Sexpert mess in the first place. I mean, I'm not anything special in the looks department. I'm no Myrtle, for fuck's sake. But I have… qualities.

Two of them, to be exact.

Which makes me snort to myself. And that calms me down a little.

And then I find another B word.

"What are you doing?"

I spin around and say, "Brazen!" loudly. Too loudly.

"What?" Myrtle laughs. "Why is your face all red?" But just as those words are coming out of her mouth I look past her and see Andrew and Pierce heading this way.

Straight for *me*. And yup, something is definitely up with those two.

"Oh, shit," I mumble. "I gotta go."

I whirl around just as I hear Andrew say, "Eden! Wait!"

Fuck that noise.

I spy the front door and I'm just about to make a run for it, but there's now a whole bunch of *Le Man* employees, having given up on the wall and making straight for the snack table, blocking my way.

"Eden!" Andrew calls again. "Wait up!"

I make a sharp right, frantic, my eyes darting back and forth trying to find an escape plan, but all I see are indoor rock walls with all those colored handholds. To make matters worse, every one of them is crowded with *Le Man* employees trying to get their team-building in.

Every one of them… except one.

I don't know what my feet are thinking because they don't wait around for a discussion with my brain. They just head towards the empty rock wall.

When I reach it, I grab onto the little plastic handhold thingy and pull myself up. My foot scratches against the fake rock, seeking a place to plant itself. Finds one, and then I'm reaching for another handhold.

"Eden!" Andrew calls again.

Shit! Climb faster!

So I do. I might not look it because I have this whole nerdy librarian thing going at work, but I'm sporty. Totally sporty. I was captain of the volleyball team in high school and college. And I did gymnastics for like seven years before my breasts threw off my center of balance when I was fifteen and I had to give up my dream of Olympic glory.

So goddammit, I'm gonna climb this wall.

I find another handhold, then my foot finds a hold, and I'm pulling myself up.

"Eden! What are you doing?"

"I'm climbing," I call back in my most cheerful voice. "Gonna have to catch you later!"

"But wait! You're not wearing climbing shoes! You're gonna—"

I don't know if he finishes his sentence. I don't have time to worry about him anymore because my foot slips. I'm at a weird angle or something and I feel like I'm bending backwards. Every time I reach for a handhold, my fucking boobs are in the way. I'm squished up against the wall and there's nowhere to go but...

I look down. And that's a huge mistake. Because somehow I got halfway up this stupid wall.

"Shit!" Andrew calls. His eyes are wide with worry as he stares up at me. "Don't move! I'm coming up to get you!"

Oh, no, you're not, buddy! Noooo. I'm not getting stuck on this wall with you. No, sir.

My fingers find another handhold. I contort my body, releasing the pressure on my chest, and swing my leg out—toe tapping, looking for a place to anchor myself...

But I miss it, and I slip.

"Oh, my God!" someone cries from down below. "Eden is gonna fall!"

Shit. I'm gonna fall. One foot is still searching for an anchor and my hands are sweating so bad now, they're barely hanging on.

How far is that? Fifteen feet? Twenty at the most. I won't die, right? There's mats down there. People fall off climbing walls all the time and live.

Right? Right?

And then my fingers slip and a whole crowd of people gasp in unison.

"I'm gonna die," I whisper. "Fall and break my neck in like two seconds."

"No, you're not," Andrew says.

Somehow, in the last five seconds, he's climbed all the way up to where I'm barely hanging on. His thigh behind me, pressing against my ass, like he's trying to pin me to the wall.

"I got you," he says. "Just relax." His breath is warm against my neck and his words are soft. "You're OK."

"Um... I don't think I am." I turn my head and look down and instantly regret it. Like all two hundred *Le Man* employees are down there, faces upturned, watching me make a fool of myself.

"Don't look down," he says, his hand slipping between my stomach and the wall. My shirt lifts up a little and his fingers brush against my bare skin for a brief moment. Then his other arm is reaching around behind me.

"I got you," he says again. "Just relax. We're gonna go down now."

"Nope!" I say. "Nope. I can't go down."

"O-kaaay," he says. "Then we'll go up."

I tilt my head up to the sheer wall in front of me and my heart sinks down into my stomach. "I don't think I can do that either," I whisper.

He chuckles a little behind me. His laugh cools the back of my sweaty neck and feels oddly comforting.

I take a deep breath. "Can someone just... lower me down?"

"No," Andrew says. "I have you so you probably won't break your neck if you fall."

"*Probably* won't?"

"But you don't have a harness on, so no. We cannot lower you."

"Get a harness!"

"It's a gym. Not the Alps."

And at that moment, as if the universe is striving to emphasize the point, someone's ten-year-old goes flying up the wall beside us.

"Coming through," he says in his snotty ten-year-old voice.

"Who brought their kid?" I say, loudly. "Fire that person!"

"Eden, hi, hey, over here," Andrew whispers and I turn my attention back to him. "Here's the deal. We climb up"—he points up—"or we climb down." He points...the other way. "You choose."

I think about that. For a little too long, I guess, because he says, "Listen to me. Either way is fine. I can help you up this wall and I will not let you fall. But every step down is one step closer to the ground. And if you do fall—"

"You just said I wasn't gonna fall!"

"You won't. But if you do, we're that much closer to the ground and you'll just land on the mat."

"What if I miss the mat and hit the concrete?"

"OK, well, physically impossible, but if somehow you manage to defy science, I bet someone would catch you."

"Catch me?" I'm suddenly mortified picturing myself falling on top of all my co-workers. Toppling them all over like a bowling ball. And his arm around me is tight. It's pressing up underneath my tits. Which should feel good but right now is just making me self-conscious.

Jesus. Fucking big tits. They are the bane of my existence.

"Eden—"

"Up," I say. Because I can't deal with down right now. If I make it to the top I can rest. Hide, even. Everyone down on the floor will go back to their team-building bullshit and forget about me. "Up," I say again. "I can do this. Let's go up."

"OK," he says. And is he maybe… a little bit impressed with me?

Oh, my God, I'm delusional. He's thinking, *This Sexpert bitch is crazy.* That's what he's thinking. Because I know he knows. And he did tell Pierce. And Pierce is probably down there right now hoping I'll fall. So much for my sexy new career. I'm gonna be stuck making stupid hashtags for eternity.

Oh, no. No I won't. Because the second I get off this stupid climbing wall he's gonna fire me.

"Look at my foot. See where it is?"

I glance down, see the toe of his shoe tapping at a foothold, and say, "Yeah, I see it."

"OK. You put your foot there."

"But what about you? Where will your foot go?"

"Don't worry," he says. "I'm gonna use this one so I can box you in with my body."

When he says that he rubs his chest against my back. Probably to let me know that he's here. To comfort me and make me feel safe.

But it actually kinda makes me hot for him.

I roll my eyes at myself. Because really? I'm thinking about sex as I'm about to fall to my death? Although that actually makes a lot of sense. I hear people think of crazy things before they die and there are worse things to think about than sex with this guy, so—

"OK, ready?" Andrew asks.

Oh, right. Still here on the wall.

I nod. Swallow hard. And then whisper, "OK. I'm ready."

"This wall has a forty-five-degree angle at the top, so we're gonna just scoot over a little to that wall."

I feel him nod his head to the right. I glance over and see a different colored wall—steel-gray instead of black, like this one is—and say, "I see it."

"OK, good. Now put your foot where I told you." I have to stretch. Like really stretch my leg to reach that foothold. But I get the tip of my toe on it and he says, "Good. Now put your right hand on the pink hold right up there."

I have to stretch my arm too. It's all the way straight, like no bend at all. "Andrew," I say, my breath betraying how scared I actually am now that I fully comprehend what I'll have to do to get to the top. "I won't be able to pull myself up."

"You don't need to pull yourself up. You're going to use your legs for lift, not your arms. Just grip it with the tips of your fingers and then lift your left foot off and swing your body to the right a little."

"I don't think I can," I say. And I'm serious. Totally serious.

"Listen to me. I know what I'm doing. When you lift that foot and swing your body, you're gonna change your center of balance immediately. And it's going to feel right. Trust me."

194

Center of balance makes sense to me. I know how that works from all those years in gymnastics. So I do as I'm told and... and he's right. He's actually right! The second I lift my left foot and swing my body over—his body pressing hard against me still—I am centered again and don't feel like I'm gonna fall backwards anymore.

He's quick to tell me what to do after that. Like he knows I've given in to him. That I trust him. And I follow every direction. I put my hands and my feet exactly where he tells me to. We angle over onto the steel-gray wall and then the climb gets easier. I actually start picking my own path and Andrew backs off a little, concentrating on his own climb.

It's like... we're climbing together now. As partners or something.

And then—too soon almost—we're there at the top.

I swing my leg up and pull myself over the edge and the whole fucking gym erupts with clapping and whistling. And people are shouting, "Go, Eden!" and "He saved her!" Which... I mean... Dramatic.

I roll onto my back, my button-down shirt almost wet with sweat, and smile at Andrew as he comes over the edge to join me.

"You did it," he says, grinning wide.

"Thank you," I say. "I don't know what I was thinking, but...Jesus. I'm so hot." He raises his eyebrows at me. Like he's about to make a comment about me being hot. Or maybe I'm just delusional with rock-climbing endorphins and I just made that up. Probably that last one. But my fingers are busy unbuttoning my shirt, and then I sit up and take it off, throwing it off to the side.

When I glance over at him again he's staring right at my tits.

His eyes lift up, big question marks in them. Question marks that make me remember why I tried to climb that stupid wall in the first place.

"Soooo..." he says, slowly. "Where you been?"

"What?" I say, fake-laughing the word. "What do you mean?"

"I haven't seen you since... And when I called you you hung up on me. What's up?"

"Nothing. Why? Why is something up? Why would you think something is up? What's up with you? You ever think about that?"

He closes his eyes and smiles. "Why'd you run?"

"What?" I say, fake-laughing harder and longer. "What are you talking about?"

"You saw Pierce and me and ran. Why?"

"I didn't run! You ran!" I'm not sure I'm making sense. But sometimes if you commit to something hard enough you can convince people they're wrong.

"I ran after you. After you got yourself stuck on a wall."

I laugh again. Louder this time. Trying to buy myself some time. "Well... I mean, we were here to climb the walls, right?"

"Sort of," he says. "I mean, this was constructed as a team-building exercise. Because... Oh, right. You missed Pierce's opening statement because you came in late—"

"I... I..." I stutter. Because I was gonna say I got caught in traffic. But this is the TDH where everyone walks. So that excuse doesn't work anymore. "I couldn't decide what to wear," I say.

"I don't care that you were late. You don't work for me. That's not my point. I'm trying to make a point."

"OK. So. Fine. Make your point. What's your point?"

And then I see he's looking at my tits again.

"My point is that Pierce's big speech was about everyone at *Le Man* working together to find the Sexpert."

"Oh," I say. "Was it? Wow, that's weird. He's really upset about that, isn't he?"

"Super upset." Andrew nods. "He thinks he knows who it is."

"Oh, does he?" I say, gulping out the words.

"He does. You know who he thinks it is?" He's really close now, looking at me with a knowing stare. Oh fuck.

I shake my head slowly.

"He thinks," Andrew says, his voice a low whisper, "it's Myrtle."

"He what? Myrtle? That's... No way."

He presses his lips together and nods. "Yeah. I hear you. I think he may be wrong too."

"Oh. You do?" I swallow.

"Yeaahhhh, just too obvious. I think." He nods, like he's waiting on me to say something. Which is weird. And I'm not gonna. So...

I stand up and brush off my ass out of habit, not because I actually have anything to brush off. "OK. Well, good talk, Andrew. Good talk. And thank you for saving my ass." *Nope. Stop talking, Presley. Don't wanna talk about your ass or boobs or any of your other naughty bits right now.* I laugh, uncomfortable. "But I gotta go and I see there's a handy-dandy ladder to get down once you're at the top, so—"

He grabs my hand. Gently. Not squeezing tight, but he does pull. He sighs and says, "Dammit, Eden." He looks down and shakes his head.

"What? What?" I say, growing ever more emphatic. "What is it?"

197

"Do you know what Myrtle said to me the first time she and I met?"

Wow. Non-sequitur much?

I shake my head slowly. I can feel my eyes getting bigger.

"She said, 'You are not what I expected.'"

He stares right through me. I try to stare back right through him to show him that I'm not going to break first, but my eyes are kind of sweaty and it's fogging up my glasses and I can't really see him that clearly all of a sudden. Crap.

"You know what I told her?" he asks.

I don't say anything. Not because I'm being badass, just because I'm trying not to rub my eyes, because he might mistake that for crying and I don't want him to think that. But then again, he might be the kind of guy who gets all protector-ish when a girl cries and that could be to my advantage and—

"I told her, 'Nobody ever is.'"

Fuck it. I pull my glasses off, rub my eyes so I can see, and I look dead into his face. He's looking back at me with a mix of accusation and maybe disappointment.

"So... the next time I talk to Pierce..."

A long, thick moment. I double down and keep staring. But damned if, despite my best efforts, I don't wind up blinking first when he says...

"Who do I tell him *you* are?"

CHAPTER TWENTY

She turns away from me, says, "OK! Well... Thanks for the lift," kind of snorts because I think she thinks she was making a joke, and then makes for the edge of the wall. Her feet close to the lip, she stares at the handholds to get down. Down below, the Le Maniacs, as I have just decided to call them, are milling around again. Over by the entrance, Pierce and Myrtle appear to have missed the

199

whole thing. Pierce has his arm against the wall in very much a, "Hey, babe, let me tell you about my Porsche" kind of a way, and Myrtle is sweeping her hands across her clavicle, swiping away imaginary strands of hair. My guess is that she thinks she's flirting with the boss and he thinks he's interrogating her.

Maybe he's right. Maybe it is Myrtle. Maybe I'm way off about what I'm thinking. Except he isn't. She isn't. And I'm not.

"Hey," I say, going to stop her. "Hey." I reach her and grab her arm. She spins on me, her hair smacking me in the face.

"What?"

"I need you to talk to me."

"And I need you to let go of my arm."

I put both hands up in a gesture of surrender and take a step back.

"Listen," I start to say, but at that moment am interrupted by a new body cresting the wall's top. It's the dude in the Cannibal Corpse t-shirt.

"'Sup?" He nods.

"Uhhhh. 'Sup?" I nod back.

"Yo, Eden, nice climb," he says, lifting his chin toward her in affirmation.

"Aw, thanks, Leo," says Eden.

He pulls out a vape pen and takes a hit. The smell of cannabidiol oil fills the air.

"Um, dude, can you—?" I start to say.

"Oh, my bad," he says, and then extends the vape pen in our direction.

"No, no, I'm good. Thanks. I just... Never mind." I decide it's not worth the conversation.

"Eden?" He extends it in her direction.

"Oh, no, thanks Leo. I'm good too," she says. "I'm already higher than I'd like to be." She snorts again, slightly.

Leo laughs a bit and then excuses himself past us, giving Eden a fist bump on his way down.

"Friend of yours?" I ask.

"Leo's in tech support. He's fixed my computer a bunch of times. I made him brownies and now we're friends. What do you care?"

I take a second to eye her. "You're pretty popular at *Le Man*, aren't you?" I ask.

She points at me in an accusing way. Which is ironic. "Why are you asking so many questions? Who are you supposed to be? Nancy Drew?"

And for whatever reason I feel myself getting hot. "Yeah. That's it. That's it, Eden. You nailed it. I'm Nancy friggin' Drew." I say it with a fair amount of snark. Having the girl I'm into both blow me off and be responsible for making my friend lose his mind is starting to catch up to me a little bit and my naturally relaxed Southern charm is eluding me just at present. "And I'm on the case of the Girl with the Concealed Identity. But you know what, cupcake?" She stiffens at the word. Good. "I feel like I'm pretty damn close to cracking it wide open."

"Well," she says, now turning and eyeing the handholds that lead back down, "good luck with that. Hope you don't get a magnifying glass stuck up your ass looking for clues."

"Why would I get a—?"

"Whatever!"

She steps toward the hand grips, but then stops. She sort of stutteringly edges forward, then steps back.

"You're afraid of heights, aren't you?" I ask.

"Wow! You are really are fuckin' Nancy Drew! Figure that one out all by yourself?"

"Then why would you try to run away by scaling a climbing wall?"

"I make bad choices!"

Two more people land where we're standing, and walk past.

"Nice climb, Eden."

"Thanks, Lucy. Thanks, Peter."

They high-five her and begin their descent. Jesus. Everybody really does like her.

She storms past me.

"Where do you think you're going?" I say.

"I dunno! To see if there's another way down!"

She marches to the back corner of the top of the wall where there's a small, enclosed space that has a sign reading, "Yoga Studio." I follow her. Obviously.

"Hey, I'm not kidding. I need you to talk to me," I say as I follow her in.

And she—turns isn't the right word. Whirls? Whips? Pounces?—around. Whatever it is, it gives off the distinct impression of a cornered animal ready to fight for survival.

"What?" she groans out. "What do you want?"

A couple thoughts run through my mind in response to that question, but I decide that right now's probably not the time to say them. Shit. I'm so fuckin' bummed. I was really into this girl. I think. No, I know I was. More than I've been into a girl in a long time. She seemed like somebody who would be...well...fun to be around. But when I considered that she might be into adventure, this wasn't what I was thinking of.

I decide to just ask the question.

"*Are* you the Sexpert? And don't say no because I know you are."

She gets a half-caught, half-righteously indignant look on her face and says, "I have no idea what you're talking about."

"No? Really? No idea?"

"No. I don't. And honestly, I'm offended by the accusation."

"Well, I'm sorry if you're offended, but my best and oldest friend is being fucked over by someone, and even if he's putting an *insanely* disproportionate amount of import on the thing... he's still my best and oldest friend. And y'know what? I like you. Like, I really like you. But even so, I can't let you fuck my friend over. So, please, just tell me. Just come clean and tell me... Is it you? Why'd you do it?"

She huffs and when she does, her chest lifts up and down. If she wants to convince me it's not her, a heaving bosom, thinly veiled by a sexy tank top, is not getting the job done.

"I had you all wrong," she says.

"What? Sorry? Come again?"

"Yeah. I bet you'd like that."

"What?" And then I realize... *Ooooh. 'Come again.' Got it.*

She goes on. "I thought you were a good guy. But you're not. You're just like every other rich, privileged asshole in the world who's out only for themselves and to get what they want."

"What are you...?"

"You think I'm the Sexpert? Like really?"

I take a breath and then nod.

"So why didn't you say something before? I mean, it couldn't have been just so you could coerce me up to your stupid penthouse so you could get off before you go running to your friend and try to ruin my life, could it? Oh, nooooo. No waaaayyyyy."

"I didn't—"

"What? Is that your thing? You come on girls' backs and then fuck them over? Is that, like, some weird, creepy fetish you have? Because it is. It's creepy, Andrew. It's creepy. You're a creep."

"I feel like you're changing the subject."

She starts walking toward me now. Going on the offense. "So, riddle me this, Batman—"

"I thought I was Nancy Drew."

"Shut up! Let me..."

But that's all she gets out before she trips over a discarded yoga block thing sitting in the middle of the room and goes collapsing to the floor.

"Ow!"

"Jesus," I say, starting for her. "Are you OK? Did you hurt yourself?"

"I'm fine!" she says, waving me off. She struggles up to her feet. Her hair is a mess and her glasses are askew. She wipes the hair out of her face and pushes her specs up the bridge of her nose.

She's so goddamn cute, I want to fuck her right here. Which is not my usual reaction to things that are adorable, but oh, well. The heart wants what it wants.

"OK," she says. "You're so sure that I'm this awful Sexpert person, but meanwhile your friend is *sure* it's Myrtle, yeah?"

"Yes. That is an accurate summary of the last five minutes."

"Fine, Mr. Smart Breeches." *So fuckin' adorable.* She goes on, "So how come *you're* right and *he's* wrong?"

"Because I am. Because Myrtle doesn't have..." I nod at her chest.

"What? What are you talking about? Myrtle has fabulous boobs."

"They're fine."

"Seriously? Men go crazy for her."

"Sure. She's OK. And her boobs are too. But they're not..." Again, I indicate her chestal area.

She draws her head back, confused. "Wait. You can't possibly be saying that *I'm* sexier than Myrtle?"

"No, I think I can. And I think that's exactly what I'm saying."

She blushes. "Oh my God. That's... I've never... That's so... Wait! Stop! You're trying to Jedi mind trick me into admitting something!"

"I'm honestly not." I put my hand on my heart to suggest my earnestness, or something. "I just know it's not Myrtle."

"How?"

I shake my head a little. "Because. It's not her voice."

Eden swallows. She takes a breath. She blinks. "Wh—Why... I mean... How do you know?"

"Because I know."

"*How?*"

"Hi, Andrew Hawthorne? CEO of Aureality? Have we met? This is what I do for a living."

"But the...person, whoever it is, is using your app, aren't they? To disguise their voice? I mean, I've heard her. It sounds like she is."

"Yeah. *She* is. But we can decrypt it."

"You can?"

205

I nod. "And once we do—"

"You mean you haven't yet?"

I hate this. I wish she'd just come clean. "No. Not yet. But we will. And when we do, we'll run it through a new app we have and I'll be able to make a definitive call."

There's a long pause while I wait for her to say anything. Finally, she does.

"OK. Super. Good for you. And then what? What will Pierce do when you guys find her?"

I shrug. "I dunno."

"I mean, he can't really sue somebody just for having a similar idea, can he? I mean what if they had the idea first?"

I take a deep breath. Blow it out. OK. So. Here we go. "I dunno, Eden. *Did* they have it first?"

Her eyes go saucer wide behind her glasses. "Why do you keep asking me? Why do you think this Sexpert person is me? Seriously. Why?"

I shake my head and say, "Dessert."

"Dessert? Hell does that mean? What about dessert?"

"You shook your cupcakes at me in my place. And apart from the fact that you have, and I mean this sincerely, the *most* gorgeous cupcakes I have ever seen"— I smile, still trying to be charming even as I'm accusing this girl of being my friend's nemesis—"all of the videos I've watched now in trying to help Pierce... all of them have been heavily confection-oriented."

Her eyes go yet even wider. "Seriously? That's it?"

I lean in to her even closer so that I can whisper in her ear, "Eden, everything you did with me on my terrace. It's all in the videos."

I pull back and the look of abject despair on her face breaks my heart a little.

"But... I..."

"Hey," I say, taking her hand, which she jerks away. "It's OK. It really is. Just... and I have to ask... you didn't actually *steal* the idea, did you?"

And almost before the question is out of my mouth, that same mouth is being slapped. Hard. Like, shit, like, really, really fucking hard.

"Ow!" That's me. Obviously. "What the fuck?"

"I'm sorry! I'm sorry!" she says. "I'm sorry! That's not like me! I don't know what came over me, I just—"

But that's all that she gets out of her mouth before my just-slapped and still-stinging lips are on hers. Kissing her. Also hard.

CHAPTER TWENTY-ONE

Holy shit. Perfect timing!

Because for a second there I felt a little like a top-heavy ice cream cone and one more lick was gonna send it crashing down onto the sidewalk.

Oh… ohhhhhh…. ohhhhhhhh… that feels nice. He's such a great kisser.

"Eden," he says, still kissing me.

"I'm not the Sexpert," I whisper back.

"But the other day…"

"Look," I say, breaking contact. "I'm gonna tell you something but you gotta promise not to tell anyone, OK?"

He cocks his head at me. Like, *OK, here we go. I've finally worn her down and she's gonna come clean.*

But they've got nothing on me. Yet. He said they're working on decryption, but they don't have it. Yet.

So I still have time. Time to… I dunno, make him like me enough to keep my secret? Maybe? I'm kinda grasping at straws.

"Andrew," I say, whispering still. I make my voice sexy. Not Sexpert sexy, but sweet sexy. A little high-pitched. A teeny bit pouty. It's very annoying but I don't care. I'm dying here. *Dying.* "I have to confess…"

"Yes," he says, eyes locked on mine. "Yes."

I take a deep, deep breath and when I let it out, I go, "I really suck at blow jobs, no pun intended, and well, pretty much everything else that goes with having noon-time sex with the boss's best friend. I'm no good. I'm a terrible sexifier. And the blow job, well. I just didn't know what to do. But like everyone else these days, I stumbled upon those Sexpert videos and I watched a few. OK, more than a few. All of them. Because she's funny and she's cool and, frankly, she's kind of who I wish I could be. And I…. I took notes. I took lots of notes. And committed them to memory. So I'm sorry I used another woman's repertoire on you, it wasn't right. Maybe a little bit dishonest because it's a teeny bit like wearing one of those magic bras that make your cupcakes… I mean, boobies… look great. And then your guy takes your bra off and just looks at them like, 'What the fuck just happened?' You know? It's a little bit like that. And so… well, I led you on. I'm not a good blow jobber and I cheated."

I gulp air because I used up all my breath with my super-lame excuse, and then huff it back out, making my hair fly up over my glasses.

He just looks at me.

He's never gonna believe this.

I shift from one foot to another. Then cross my arms. Uncross them and shift my feet again. Push my glasses up my nose. "I'm sorry. OK? What else can I say?"

Really? What else *can* I say?

Believe me, I pray.

Please, please, please…

CHAPTER TWENTY-TWO

What. A. Load. Of. Horseshit.

I grew up on a horse farm. I know.

I sigh. Because this whole thing is going to end badly. Son of a bitch.

And while it won't end badly in the cruel and sometimes empty ways all my other relationships have ended badly, it's still gonna be awful. Maybe this is going

213

to be even worse. It's not even a proper relationship yet. It's just...whatever it is. But I liked where it was headed and now... Now, it's gonna end with the probable devastation of someone who's cute and sweet and who pouts when she gets frustrated. And devastating a cute, sweet, pouty person is just the worst kind of devastation. It's like flattening a field of flowers with a steamroller.

Well, that's a bummer.

So I know what I need to do. I need to just say, "OK," and then step away from her. I need to climb down off this wall, let her figure out how to get down on her own—because she's not my problem—and then go back to the office so that I can run the app, pull the conclusive match, so that there's no more denial and debate, and get this whole thing over with.

Yeah. That's exactly what I need to do.

But.

My arms reach out and I grab her around the waist, drawing her into me tightly. Her hands immediately come up to grab hold of my exposed shoulders and slide under the fabric of the tank top I have on. Her fingers grip into the muscles along my back and her nails scratch the flesh.

My tongue lances in between her teeth and she duels in kind with hers. Suddenly, I find my hands on her ass, drawing her to me, and as I do, she stumbles forward, kind of biting my lip, her nails digging even harder into me and scraping the skin, causing me to yelp in pain and let go of her. And as I'm pulling back, she drags her teeth along the skin of my bottom lip and now I'm bleeding from my mouth and my back all at once. Which is no small achievement for a five-second make-out session.

"Ow! Fuck!"

"I'm sorry, I'm sorry, I'm sorry," she cries, waving her hands in front of her and hopping in place from foot to foot. "Oh, shit, I didn't mean to do that!"

"Ach," I breathe out, trying to walk off the sting from having been slapped, scratched and bitten. "It's fine," I say through clenched teeth. "Don't worry about it. But those nails are the reason you couldn't get a grip on the wall. You need to cut those fuckers."

"Fuck, I'm sorry. I don't—Why'd you kiss me?"

"What? I dunno! I like you! Why'd you slap me?"

"Why? Because you're accusing me of something I didn't do! I did NOT STEAL PIERCE CHEVALIER'S GODDAMN IDEA!"

"Eden... I'm going to ask very simply, one last time: are you the Sexpert?"

There's loud music playing downstairs. Really loud. I think Leo must've gotten into the DJ booth. I don't think anyone just heard our little outburst, and now we're silent. Just staring at each other. Again.

"Look, I'm gonna be able to pinpoint the voice and match it. I get it. Pierce is an asshole and you work for him and the guy can't even remember your name and... I get it. But, I mean, look. This is not gonna go great for you, but if you tell me *why*, I can help. I really can. Dude listens to me. And I know you think I'm just a rich, selfish asshole, but I promise that I really strive to see to it that only one of those things is true. And I like you. OK? I know we don't know each other really, but I like you. And I can help. I can make it be OK. Hey, I could've stolen a charger from anyone sitting on the freeway that day, but I picked you. And there's gotta be a reason for that. So just let me give you a hand. OK? Please?"

Once more, she's not meeting my eyes. She's looking everywhere but at me. Finally, after long moments of avoiding eye contact, she says, "Borrowed."

"What?"

"You didn't steal my charger. You borrowed it. You gave it back."

I smile. "Yeah. Borrowed."

There's another long moment and just as I'm opening my mouth, she speaks first. "It's not me."

She says it so quietly, I can barely hear her.

"What?"

"It's not me." She says it only slightly louder than before, but I make it out this time.

"Eden—"

"It's not, OK? It's not."

I look down at her. She pushes her glasses up the bridge of her nose, sniffs, rubs the back of her hand across her runny nostrils again, and looks at me like she's trying very hard not to cry. And I am reminded of something I once heard. It may have been in an art theory class, or it may have been with those guys on the peyote excursion, or it may have been somewhere else entirely, I don't really remember. But the gist of it was:

Facts are just some shit that we all agree on.

So. I take a moment. I nod my head. And I say, "OK."

"OK?"

"OK."

I want to agree with her on the shit she's telling me. And I want to believe her.

Because I really, really, *really* like her.

"I'm sorry I got weird," she says in her still-small voice.

"No, hey, look, look at me." She does. "It's OK. The whole thing was weird. The whole first couple of days that I was here were weird. Don't sweat it." She nods. "Listen," I say, "I, uh… I feel like I need to get some Band-Aids and maybe some Bactine or something. You wanna, I dunno, get out of here?"

"I have to be here. It's mandatory team-building."

"Well, I mean, first of all, I'm still not sure Pierce knows you work for him." She laughs. "And second, it wasn't specified *which* team you're supposed to be working on building, was it?"

She gets a teeny smile that makes my dick jump and shakes her head. Her hair kind of shakes in front of her face with the shaking of her head. I push the strands back from her cheeks and she looks up at me. Slowly, I take her glasses off, breathe on them, wipe the lenses with the hem of my tank top, and then put them back on her face. She smiles wider.

"Do you…?" she starts, then cuts herself off, nibbling at her bottom lip. She slays me. She absolutely slays me.

"Do I what?"

"There's this art gallery thing."

"What art gallery thing?"

"I dunno. Some art gallery that's supposed to be opening this week. I heard about it. I was gonna go, but I don't really know anything about art and figured… I dunno. You're an artist and stuff, and that maybe you'd wanna go and, like, explain stuff. Or something? And I was gonna ask you, I really was, but then I got freaked out because I like you too, I really do, and I was worried that like, maybe because I'm bad at, y'know, the stuff, the sex stuff, I mean not all of it, but the sexy mouth stuff that it would be weird and you'd be thinking about that, and then

217

I got weird, because I think I might be weird, and... Do you think I'm weird? Know what? Don't answer. Doesn't matter. But so, so then, when I saw you here I got embarrassed or nervous or something, which—I know! Hard to believe! Haha. – But, so, but yeah, so anyway. So the art thing. Do you wanna go and like, teach me about, you know, art? 'Cause...? No. Never mind. But, yes. Do you?"

She takes a deep breath and holds it, squinting her eyes tightly and smiling with a lot of teeth. I look at her and a smirk overtakes me.

She's being half-flirty, half-coy, half-flibberty-gibbet, and half-little-lost-lamb-oh-won't-you-show-me-things-big-strong-man. Which I realize I just made up and also that four halves equal two things, but I'm starting to think that she's maybe five or six things all rolled into one.

I tilt my head and say, "Are you asking me out on a date?"

"... Am I?"

"Are you?"

"I dunno."

"Think you might be."

"What? Asking you out on a date?

"Sounds like you are."

"Oh. Well then, yeah, I guess I am."

A beat. Then we both start laughing.

To hell with it.

"Yeah," I say. "Sure. I'd like... Yes. I will go out on a date to an art gallery thing with you. It's Colorado, so it'll probably just be a bunch of Ansel Adams wannabes, but why not?"

She closes her eyes and then looks up at me through her lenses.

"Andrew?"

"Yeah."

"I would never steal anything from anybody."

"... Yeah, I believe that. It's OK. Sorry I got in your face about it. Let's get out of here."

She leans up, gives me a kiss on my lip where she bit me, then turns and walks out of the studio. At the edge of the wall, she trips and almost goes careening down the side, but she catches herself and looks back at me and grins, nervously.

"Do you think you can get down on your own?" I ask.

She looks down, looks back at me, looks down again, back at me. "I dunno. I mean, probably. I think so."

"Do you want my help?"

She gets a momentarily pained expression and then, after a second, she nods quickly.

I shouldn't be doing this. I shouldn't be helping her. I shouldn't be going on a date with her. I shouldn't be engaging with her. I'm going to burn her. Not because I want to. It's the last thing I want to do. But when it does turn out to be her, I have to tell Pierce the truth. I have to. I just... I have to.

Don't I?

"Yes, please," she says in a tiny voice.

I smile because she makes me smile and I say, "You got it," before placing myself in position on the side of the wall so she can brace herself against me, knowing that if she does happen to lose her grip on the way down, I'll be there to catch her.

HOW TO NIBBLE
HER KIT-KAT

She knows it's coming. You know it's coming. And we want
this first time to be perfect. Nibling her Kit-Kat means you
eat the chocolate first and save the cookie for later. You take
your time with the kissing. You're not just after the cherry
on top, you want the center of the Tootsie Roll Pop.

CHAPTER TWENTY-THREE

"*Ticket?*"

I'm at the dry cleaners picking up my best black silk dress for my date with Andrew tonight. "Hi!" I say to the woman behind the counter. Svetlana is her name. I introduced myself when I dropped the dress off the other day. And even though she's not wearing a lick of makeup and her face is shiny with sweat since it's hot as hell in here, she's beautiful.

223

I think every girl called Svetlana is probably beautiful. I wish I was called Svetlana. It's definitely a Sexpert name. Maybe in the next video I'll tell everyone my name is Svetlana?

Would Andrew buy that? Would it throw him off the trail? I mean, I think I did a pretty good job of convincing him I'm definitely not the Sexpert. I think he bought it.

He did. He has to. Because if he didn't, then this date might be a setup and I don't want it to be a setup. I kinda like him. And if he could just make Pierce let this stupid obsession with the Sexpert go, maybe we'd have a chance?

"Lady," Svetlana says. "Give me ticket." She drawls that out in her most do-not-fuck-with-me-I'm-Russian Russian accent.

"Eden," I say. Because she doesn't recognize me. "Remember? I introduced myself the other day?"

Svetlana glares at me.

I hand the ticket over.

"Wait here," she growls, as if I have a choice, then scoots off to go find my dress.

I glance around to see if I know anyone behind me. That's the cool thing about living in the TDH. Your neighbors are everywhere. But nope. I don't. And everyone is too busy checking their phones to make eye contact with me, so I can't even make a new friend while I wait.

"Here," Svetlana says, hanging my dress on the little rack to my right. "Forty-one fifteen."

"Wow," I say. "OK. Forty-one dollars to dry clean a dress." I go fishing for my credit card.

"You want pretty dress for sexy date so you can hook rich TDH billionaire, sexy girl? You pay for it."

Right. I shove my credit card into the chip reader. That's one bad thing about living in a super-trendy neighborhood that isn't close to anything else. You pay a premium for services. I mean this is the only dry cleaners in the whole neighborhood. It's like the Russian mob has paid someone off so they can inflate prices. So if I want to clean a silk dress on the cheap, I gotta take it somewhere else. And that involves getting in my car and driving places. And if I add up the cost of gas and effort, it's really not worth it.

So yeah. It sucks. And Zoey has already explained that we won't get any money from this month's killer take for about two months. That sucks too. Because I feel very much like I'm living outside my means right now.

"You want receipt?" Svetlana asks.

"Yes," I say. "Business expense." And then I smile, feeling a little bit proud that next year I might get to itemize my taxes because I'm a legit business owner.

Svetlana just rips the little piece of paper off the cash register printer and hands it to me. "Next!"

I take my receipt and tuck it away so I can give it to Zoey later. I'm pretty sure this date is a tax write-off because it really is business. I mean, I have to convince Andrew I'm not the Sexpert. That qualifies.

So here's my plan for that.

One. Distract him with the dress, but not the cupcakes. Hide the cupcakes. And this dress is perfect because it's all sexy in the back and goes all the way up to my neck in the front. I'm talking *Baby Got Back* kinda back.

Wait. I think that means ass. Well, I'm pretty sure my ass will look good too.

Two. Go someplace quiet and peaceful. Which is what I was thinking when I had that crazy art gallery monologue moment at the end of our rock climbing date. Well, that wasn't a date. Not really. Even though it kinda felt like one. There's flyers all over the TDH for this stupid art gallery thing. Like, it's a Big Deal. So, good call, Eden. Art gallery is the perfect place to have a serious I-swear-to-God-I'm-not-the-Sexpert talk that will end all talk of me being the Sexpert.

Three. Kiss him.

I actually sigh when I think that. Andrew is a great kisser. God, his lips… So I'm gonna kiss him. I'm gonna give him my very best kissing ever. I even rewatched my Sexpert video on kissing so I'm all brushed up on how to do it right. That's a gem that never got much attention, so even if he's watching my videos, he probably didn't see *How to Nibble Her Kit-Kat*. Get it? Nibble her Kit-Kat? You always eat the chocolate off first. Everyone knows that. At least I thought they did. Maybe not. Maybe that's why that video was a dud?

Anyway, eating the chocolate off is the first thing you do. Just like kissing. So I'm ready for the kissing.

But… four. Four is new. Because four is all about going all the way. Like I'm talking *How to Have Your Cake and Eat It Too* video. We've had several sexy encounters but we've never actually done it.

Oh, we're gonna do it tonight. For sure.

So, that's my plan. Dress up sexy, but only in the back. Go to the art gallery thingy and have a nice, long quiet chat about how I am not the Sexpert while we look at paintings and eat fancy finger-foods off silver trays, and then go back to his place and do it.

Nothing will go wrong.

I've got this in the bag.

OK, SNAFU in the dress department.

I didn't properly think this through because I realized too late that backless dresses require special bras. Like those sticky things you paste on your skin to hold your girls up in proper position.

Which I do not have. So I have no bra on.

I'm checking this out in the bathroom mirror, trying to decide if it makes me more or less sexy.

I decide more. Because my girls are perky with a capital P. And he's only gonna be looking at the back of the dress anyway.

Plus, it's the best dress I have. And I spent forty-one dollars getting it cleaned, not to mention putting up with Svetlana's bad attitude. I'm not changing it.

Besides, the whole point is to take off my clothes, right? So braless means one less pesky article of underwear to deal with.

At eight o'clock, right on time, my doorbell chimes. I'm walking towards it, pretty proud of the fact that I have this whole night planned to perfection, when I realize he's never seen my apartment.

I look around and take it all in from a new perspective.

It came furnished, so everything was here when I moved in. But of course, I put my little touches on it.

Touches that happen to all be in shades of pink and white, I realize.

Andrew's apartment is all shades of muted blue and yellow, but mine came in like three shades of gray. Which is so blah and made it look like a prison. So I had to pop it up and pink and white go perfect with drab gray. I have fuzzy pink throw pillows—Zoey and I love those—and a pink and white comforter on the bed, and a pink rug on the bathroom and kitchenette floor. The bed is super whimsical too. Because I have white mosquito netting hanging over it. It's like a princess bed.

And then my gaze falls on the one picture I have hanging on the wall over the bed. I'm a terrible picture hanger so this one was all I had the energy for.

It's a giant cupcake. A pink cupcake with white frosting and pink sprinkles that I bought in the mall with my babysitting money when I was sixteen.

Holy shit. I almost fucked the whole night up before it even started! *That* picture above *that* bed in *this* apartment is a big flashing sign that says Sexpert.

The doorbell chimes again.

"One second!" I call, then rush over to the picture, take it off the wall, and… where the fuck can I hide this thing? It's huge!

I could shove it in the bathroom, but what if he wants to use the bathroom?

"Eden?" Andrew calls from the other side of the door. He chimes the doorbell again. "What are you doing?"

I hang the picture back up and decide he just can't come in. That's all there is to it.

I grab my purse and swipe the hair out of my eyes (I always forget how long my hair is because it's usually up in a ponytail, but tonight with it down and me not wearing my glasses, I remember. Maybe I should put it in a bun, or... Oh, hell, no time) as I walk over to the door and pull it open, just enough to slip my body through and start to close it behind me.

I have to squish past him because he starts forward, thinking he's going inside, just as I'm scooting out before he can see my place, so we're stuck there. Kinda wedged in the partially opened door, my magnificent breasts pushed up against his rock-hard chest.

"Uh... what are you doing?" He laughs.

"I'm ready," I say. "We can go now."

"You're not gonna invite me in?"

"Nope. I think we're late for the artsy thing so we'd better get a move on."

"I'm pretty sure there's no set time to be there. Here," he says, holding up a bottle of what looks like champagne. "It's non-alcoholic, semi-effervescent, sparkling cider, made from the finest Granny Smith apples. It's pretty terrible. Let's have a drink!" He starts to push his way into my place.

"Oh, wow. That's super thoughtful to bring me a gift." I hold him back, grab the bottle, turn my back, slip it through the door, set it on the floor, and close the door behind me, making sure it clicks. When I turn to look at him he's... "What?" I ask.

"Do you have another guy in there?"

"What? No! Of course not."

"Then why are you hiding your place?"

I take a deep breath. OK. I'm being weird. I'm so not good at this covert shit. "It's just... I'm not terribly sophisticated, OK? And my apartment looks like a sixteen-year-old girl lives here."

He chews on his lip like he thinks this is super sexy or something. "Is it fucked up that I think that's super sexy?"

I knew it!

"Yes. Yes, it is. Just... You'll see it later. K? Promise." Which is an empty promise, because we will be going back to his place later. Then tomorrow I will get rid of all the pink and replace it with navy blue. Yup. Navy blue.

And then, because he's not buying this *at all*, and this seems to be my *modus operandi* when I need a distraction, I kiss him.

CHAPTER TWENTY-FOUR

I find this girl very confusing.

But I also don't care because when I kiss her I feel good. And it's probably that feeling that's causing me to do certain things I wouldn't otherwise do.

Like avoid Pierce's calls and texts for the last couple of days. Because the only thing that continues to be on his mind is this goddamn Sexpert thing. He's more and more convinced by the day that it's Myrtle. And he wants me to confirm it.

The avoidance of Pierce dominoes straight into my avoidance of Dev, who is telling me that the app is ready. But I keep blowing him off and telling him I have other important stuff to take care of. And that dominoes into my avoidance of Carrie at Justice, who keeps reaching out to ask if we're ready with the app. Because some splinter cell of... Yeah. I don't even really want to know if I'm being honest.

Jesus. Who would've thought that a crush on a girl I met on the freeway would result in my tacit abetment of criminal and possibly terrorist activity?

Meanwhile, my dick isn't asking any such questions. It's just noticing that her mouth tastes like salt water taffy.

"What kind of lipstick are you wearing?" I mutter out.

"It's called Salt Water Taffy. Is it OK?"

"It's great," I say as we keep kissing.

My hands now find themselves sliding down her hips, tracing the fabric of the dress she's wearing and causing the fabric of the blue, gabardine pants I'm wearing to feel tight around the crotch. To make sure I'm not getting myself worked up too far too fast, I pull my hands up to her back, but that's not helping because now my hands are touching her actual back. As opposed to the back of her dress. Because the dress has no back. Oh, my God.

"Um," I say on a swallow, "I like your dress."

"Thanks," she says and smiles. "I wasn't sure..."

"Wasn't sure what?"

"Nothing. Just. I wasn't sure it was the right...fit."

I step back and twirl her around by the fingers. She obliges by allowing my hand to turn her in a pirouette. I stop her when her rear side lands facing my front side.

"Oh. Well. No, it's the right fit. Can I give you a compliment?"

"Please don't. Girls hate compliments on how they look."

Kill. Ing. Me.

"I just..." I say. "Well, to quote the great poet and, I think, knight, Sir Mix-A-Lot, 'Baby got back.'"

She pulls her shoulder to her chin and looks back at me. "Really?"

I nod as I turn her back around to face me head on.

"And front," I say.

She giggles and looks down at my crotch. Pulling me toward her by the lapels of my jacket, she says, "Your front's not so bad either."

"Thanks." I smile, my mouth close to hers. "I work out when I can."

And just as her mouth and mine are about to connect again, I hear, "Oh..."

Turning my head, I see our pal Cheryl.

"Oh, hi, Cheryl."

"Andrew. Eden. Um, I was just heading to... How are you both enjoying the building?"

"It's got its perks," I say, grinning.

"Indeed," she says. "Very good. I'll let you..." And she scurries off past us.

Watching her go, I say, "Oh, shit."

"What?" asks Eden.

"I meant to ask her if she still has my pants."

And as Eden's murderously sexy giggle lands in my ear, we take our leave.

"OK, so... Ansel Adams it is not."

Like, it's really not. I just figured, at the least, it'd be some boring, traditional gallery with a bunch of bourgeois assholes oohing and ahhing over stuff that's not really all that great. And then I'd be the bourgeois asshole *explaining* how it's not, in fact, all that great.

But this is most decidedly not that.

First of all, it's dark. Not pitch black but certainly dusky. In the middle of the room is a giant spool of barbed wire. And half-dancing, half-slithering around it are a half-dozen naked people. They're climbing all over each other, occasionally bumping into the barbs and retreating. Some of them are bleeding.

A low, thrumming drone hums throughout the space, plodding and tribal in its groaning bass. I can feel the vibrations in my chest.

The pieces hanging on the walls are all sculptures and for the most part are fairly macabre representations of people in perverse sexual positions. Compelling and occasionally exquisite three-dimensional grotesqueries. Some bordering on genius.

"Oh, no," Eden mumbles over the hum.

"Oh, no, what?"

"This... I'm so sorry. This is not at all what I thought it was going to be."

I bend my head to her and lift her chin to make sure she's looking at me. "Are you kidding? This. Is. Amazing."

"What? Seriously? It is?"

"Yeah. Honestly, if anything, it makes me a little jealous."

"Why?"

"This"—I wave all around me—"is what I wanted to do. It's kind of what I thought I would be doing. It's like...

It's like... Marina Abramović meets Karen Finley with a touch of Andres Serrano thrown in."

"Totally." She looks around. "Who are they, then?"

I laugh. "Later. Come here." I pull her over into a corner where a piece has caught my attention. "Look at this."

She does. I can see that she's having a hard time processing what she's looking at. She stares hard and then goes to touch it. I pull her hand back.

"Probably shouldn't touch the art. Unless you plan to buy it."

"Oh. Shit. Sorry."

"No apology necessary. It's just one of those things. I've always thought it's stupid. To my mind, the greatest compliment you can give an artist is to be so drawn to their work that you want to get closer to it. That's what it should do. It should draw you in. Instinctually."

"Yeah," she says, staring at it.

I watch her looking at it and it fills me up. "What do you think?"

"Huh?"

"What do you think of it?"

"I mean, I think it's ... incredible."

"Why?"

"Why?"

"Yeah, why do you think it's incredible?"

"Oh, I dunno. I'm not an art critic—"

"No," I say, putting my fingers around her lips to stop her talking. It makes her look like a sexy duck. "No, that's bullshit. Art critics are idiots anyway. I'm not asking you to critique it. Just tell me how it makes you *feel*."

I let her mouth go and she steps back to look at it. I step back with her.

"I dunno," she says. "It's just... Well, at first glance, it just looked like kind of a piece of stone. Just, y'know, rock."

"Uh-huh."

"But then I noticed that there"—she points—"there it looks like people. Like two people climbing their way out of something. Like out of the rock, maybe."

"Like maybe they've been trapped and they're struggling to get free."

"Yeah. That's... Yeah. And then it looks like ... are they having sex, I think?"

"Sure seems that way."

"Yeah. But it's so twisted together that you can't tell where one of them ends and the other begins. Like they're intertwined, and they're also intertwined with the rock, and like, just like all of it has become one. Or something."

I don't say anything. Just stare at her with a dopey grin on my face.

"What?" she asks, self-conscious. "Is that wrong? Is it stupid?"

"It's your impression. So it's not wrong. And since it's your impression, I'm also inclined to say it's not stupid." I wink.

She grins. "What do you see?"

Nodding, I say, "Pretty much what you do."

"Really?"

"Yeah. Really."

There's a long beat where we just stare at each other and finally she says, "That's cool."

The dark. The thrumming. The gyrating, naked people. The art on the walls.

She almost leaps into me and kisses me again, her hand straining for my crotch.

"You wanna get out of here?" she asks.

I laugh. "We just got here."

"I know, but..."

"I mean, yeah. We can get out of here. I know it's here. I can always come back. Wanna go to your place? There's some shitty sparkling cider for us to drink."

"Oh." And suddenly she doesn't seem so eager.

"What? What is it? Seriously. What's the deal? Do you have a dead body in your apartment?"

"No. No. Nothing like that, it's just—"

"Mon ami! Where the fuck have you been?"

I know that voice.

Turning, I see Pierce approaching with a wisp of a girl in tunic. Not a tunic dress or a tunic-like thing. A tunic. Hair so black it blends into the background of the gallery. Skin so pale she almost looks like a floating face.

She seems fun.

"Hey, dude," I say as he steps to us. "Sorry, I've been... My bad for being MIA." He gives me a hug. I hug him back. Pulling away, I offer my hand to tunic lady. "Hi. Andrew Hawthorne." She just stares at my hand.

"Oh, sorry," Pierce says. "Andrew, Serilda. Serilda, Andrew. This is Serilda's place."

"Oh, well, congratulations. This is. Uh. It's fucking incredible, actually."

"Thank you," she utters sleepily in an approximately Teutonic accent.

"Andrew used to be an artist," says Pierce.

"Oh?" Serilda... not exactly asks. Because to say 'asks' means that someone might give a shit about the answer.

"Yeah. Yeah. I was."

"And what do you do now? Used-to-be-artist?"

Most people might take issue with being scoffed at so brazenly, but I've been around enough artists in my life to have become inured to it. I know exactly who this chick is. So I offer the only answer that makes sense and will change the dynamic appropriately.

"I'm a billionaire."

The hum continues in the background.

Serilda stands about an inch taller now. "Oh?" I nod. She looks at Pierce. He nods. Serilda follows with, "How?"

"Eh, you know, little of this, little of that. Hey, who's the artist?"

She re-gathers her comportment of priggishness and says, "His name is unpronounceable in human language, but he is very gifted."

"Yeah?" I say, unable to stop my smile from spreading. "Is he here?"

"He is here, and he is not here. He is everywhere, and he is nowhere."

I have to admit, of all the things I miss about art, conversations like these are not one of them.

"Cool. Well if you talk to Insert Name Here when you're next on Pluto, tell him I'm a fan."

I smile. Pierce kind of laughs. Eden kind of laughs. Serilda does not. Then Pierce extends his hand to Eden and says, "I'm sorry. Pierce Chevalier. Enchanté."

I close my eyes and sigh. "Pierce, this is Eden. She works for you. I helped her up a rock wall the other day. We all had dinner the night I got into town. She runs your social media department. You sit a floor above her."

Pierce nods and squints at Eden as if he's trying to place her. Then he goes ahead and kisses her hand.

"Well, I'll surely not forget again. My apologies." Then, "I thought Gretchen ran the social media stuff."

"Oh," says Eden. "She does, technically. I just do most of the actual formatting and stuff like that."

"Are you the one handling the offsetting of the Sexpert travesty?"

Eden looks at me nervously out of the side of her eye. "Um, yes."

"Ah, yes. Well, then I'll *certainly* not forget again. I do apologize. The whole thing has had me very distracted."

"Yes," I say. "Also, he's kind of a dick."

"Are we close, And?" Pierce says, staying on his favorite topic.

"Uh, yeah. Yeah. We're close. Any day now we should be able to pinpoint..." Now it's my turn to glance at Eden who looks at the floor. I step in so only Pierce can hear me. "You still convinced it's Myrtle?"

He nods. "She's been acting very weird."

"Yeah? Weird how?"

"She's kind of avoiding me."

"How? She's your secretary."

"Executive assistant. Jesus, man. Stay woke." Seriously, sometimes I don't understand the guy at all. "She just," he goes on, "she used to stay late, poke her head into my office to check in during the day, all that kind of thing. Lately, I dunno. She's just been getting... Weird. So. You tell me what I'm supposed to think."

I nod slowly and glance over at Eden once more. She's trying to avoid our conversation and staring at the sculpture again.

"How soon can I nail her?"

"Nail her?"

"Myrtle. How soon before we can prove it?"

"Oh. Well, have you even confronted her about it?"

"Aw, come on, man." He leans in conspiratorially. "Do you think she'd just come out and admit it? That she's trying to eat off my idea? No way someone would just cop to that. We have to prove it."

I nod yet again. Yeah. He's a hundred percent right.

"You're not gonna let me down, are you, mon frère?" he asks. I get a thousand-yard stare, looking nowhere in particular. "And?" he says.

"Sorry. Uh, no, no, of course not. No way. We'll get her, man. OK? Don't worry. You and Serilda just go off tonight and ... do ... I don't care. And within a week we'll have this sorted. Don't sweat it. I got you."

"Je t'aime," he says, kissing me on the cheek.

"Yeah, yeah, moi aussi."

"Eden," he says, taking her hand and kissing it once again. "Eden," he repeats.

"Yes?" she says, hesitantly.

"Just locking it in." He points at his head and winks. He and Serilda take off. I don't tell Serilda it was a pleasure. Because it wasn't. She's got good taste in nameless, faceless geniuses though. I'll give her that.

"So," I say, reaching for Eden's hand. "You still good to get out of here and go pop the cork on that grown-up juice box?"

She sighs, heavily, says, "Yeah. Sure," and starts to walk.

"Hey." I pull her back to me, "What's up? No bullshit. What's wrong?"

"Nothing. I just. I dunno."

"Eden... I'm not gonna make a thing out of this. I'm really not. K? I promised myself I wouldn't and I'm not gonna. But... is there *anything* you need to tell me?"

I bear down into her eyes with mine. She gets a little teary. Shit.

And then she says, "No. No. Just... I think maybe being around all this art has made me emotional." I let out a breath and hang my head. "Is that weird?" she adds.

I take a long, long inward breath now, stroke a hair from her face, and finally, I tell her, "No, cupcake. It's not weird. Art is an expression of the artist's truth."

I give her a small kiss on the forehead, pull her into a hug, and whisper over the thrumming heartbeat-like drone in the space...

"And the truth can do that to people."

CHAPTER TWENTY-FIVE

My perfect night is blown. First the apartment mistake. Wow, how did I not see that coming? And my reaction at the door earlier? Totally batshit crazy.

Then the gallery. That was not the quiet evening I envisioned. Don't get me wrong, it was super fun. But now Andrew is even more suspicious of me than he was before we went out.

Why is this happening to me?

Seriously? Why does my perfect guy have to be my sworn enemy out to destroy me?

It's not fair.

"Well," I say, unable to hide the fact that I'm now depressed. "This is me." I fish around in my purse and find my key card, then look over my shoulder at Andrew one more time. It might be the last time I ever get to gaze at his beautiful face because I'm pretty sure my pink apartment covered in frosting is a dead giveaway that I'm the Sexpert.

The lock flashes green, but I hesitate.

"Allow me," Andrew says, turning the handle and pushing the door open. But then he waits, waves his hand, and says, "After you."

I sigh and enter, flipping the lights on as I throw my arms up and say, "Here you go. Me in all my teenage glory."

Andrew enters, walks to the center of the room, then spins in place. It's so small he can see everything in this one spin.

"That's the kitchen," I say. "The bathroom is behind that door. My closet. My living room," I say, pointing to my mini loveseat and the coffee table in front of it. "And... bedroom."

He takes it all in, slowly studying everything. The couch, the pink fuzzy pillows, the bed and princess mosquito netting. And then... yup, he sees the cupcake picture and walks over to it to get a closer look. Like he can't see the four-foot-by-four-foot dessert from six feet away.

"Interesting choice of art," he says, looking at me over his shoulder. "And it's the only thing you have on the wall."

"I have more," I say.

"Yeah? Where?"

"In my closet."

"Let me guess. Is it a picture of strawberry shortcake with whip cream on top?"

"No," I say, getting irritated with him. I want to scream at him. I mean, he knows it's me. He knows! And right now this whole night feels like… like he's just waiting for me to admit it.

But I don't scream at him. I don't have the energy? Fight? Whatever. I just walk over to the closet and pull out the small picture frames I didn't have the time or patience to hang up. "See?"

He takes the stack of small frames from my outstretched hands and laughs. "Kittens?"

"Yeah, so? I like kittens. I was like, fourteen when I bought these, OK? This is my first apartment! I was living with my father a week and a half ago. And I had to save up for two years to afford to move to the TDH. I didn't want to dip into my savings to redecorate so I just brought my childhood bedroom with me. Sorry if I'm not up to your level of sophistication."

He softens a little because that was harsh. Then hands the pictures back. I tuck them away in the closet and close the door.

When I turn to face him again, he's looking at me weird, his head tilted to the side a little. "What?" I ask.

"Where's your office?"

"Office," I huff. "It's a studio apartment. There's no office."

245

"Where do you keep your computer?"

I point to my tote bag on the floor. "In there."

"There?" he asks.

"I mean... when I want to use it, I put it on the coffee table. Or prop a pillow on my lap and sit it on top of that."

"Hmmm," he says.

"What's that mean? Hmmm."

He rubs his hand over his face, absently feeling the delicious shadow of stubble on his jaw. "OK."

"OK?" I ask.

He shrugs. "It's not you."

"I told you it wasn't me!" I say that too loud. And I'm pointing my finger at him.

He walks across the room towards me. It's such a small apartment, it only takes him a few steps. He reaches for my pointing finger, wraps it up in his warm hand, and says, "I'm sorry. It's just... you're just so..."

"So what?" I ask, moving towards him. Into him. Because he smells good, and he's so handsome, and I really, really, really like him.

"So fucking Sexperty sexy."

"I'm really not. I'm just..." I shrug. "I'm just a simple girl, Andrew. That's all. I like pink, and kittens, and cupcakes."

"You're killing me."

I pout a little, kinda confused. "I don't get it."

He leans in and kisses me. He's warm and his soft lips are like a gentle touch. I get lost in them as I open my mouth and our tongues do that sweet little dance I've come to love. And then he whispers, "The fact that you don't get it makes it so much sexier," right into my mouth.

And then I stop caring about what he's talking about. I don't care about cupcakes or kittens or how I turned a trendy TDH apartment into a pink princess palace, because his fingertips are playing with the string tied at the back of my neck.

I shudder a little as the soft silk tendrils brush against my bare back, and then his hands come around to squeeze my perfect, perky, braless breasts.

He lets out the sexiest breath of air, so soft and filled with desire, I want to die.

"Jesus," he says, his hands squeezing tightly. He places his mouth on one of them, over the fabric, and bites at the erect nipple that's been stimulated to attention, making itself known.

I run my fingertips through his hair. And my heart is beating so fast right now, I think he probably hears it.

He lifts his head up but I can't bring myself to stop playing with his hair, so my arms lift up, stretching my breasts into their fullest, most perky position, the sides of my boobs peeking out from the curve of the dress where it arcs its way down my body, and he just... shakes his head as he gazes down at them.

"You kill me," he says, walking me backwards, his hands lifting my hem, his fingers tracing the seam of my black stockings and the garters holding them up. He nibbles on my earlobe and whispers softly, "Kill me dead," as he bites at the flesh and I groan from deep in my throat.

I am also sorta thinking about how wearing stockings and garters was in the Have Your Cake video and I really nailed that tip. But then again... sorta not.

Because who gives a fuck?

I take one more step backwards, kneel down a little, and look up at him.

I know that's a tip in some video I've made as well, but that's not why I do it.

I just want to look up at him as I unbuckle his belt, pop the button on his pants, slide the zipper down, and take out his cock.

CHAPTER TWENTY-SIX

"Oh, my God."

"What?" she asks. "Is this OK?"

"Yeah, cupcake. It's more than OK. I was just thinking... You actually should take up rock climbing. You've got the grip strength for it."

She giggles, and I grab her by the ass, lifting her back up and pulling her to me. I want my mouth on hers. She begins pumping on my shaft as we kiss. I want to take her hard, in exactly the same way you want to tear into some kind of delicious dessert, but I also want to savor every bite of her. I decide quickly that both things are achievable.

I let my tongue land on her pouty lips and trace them in full, sliding inside her mouth once I've completed a perfect 'O.' Something about the hardness of her teeth juxtaposed against the softness of her lips reminds me of the sculpture that we saw. Soft sensuality and sharp edges blended together and becoming a part of each other. Dichotomy incarnate.

She continues stroking my cock and my hands reach down, grabbing folds of her dress and lifting until my hands land on her ass. My fingers slide under the lacy fabric of her panties so that I can tease her asshole. I have no idea how she'll react, but I'm not thinking a lot about it. Like scaling a mountain or painting a picture, I'm just reaching out, throwing caution somewhat to the wind, and trusting that the end result will be something glorious.

The moan she makes into my mouth lets me know I'm on the right path to the summit.

I pull on the dress more to lift it up over her torso. Up. Up. Up. And those breasts are in front of my eyes again. They are a sculpture themselves. A perfectly rendered example of living art.

I tug the dress up over her head and...

I tug the dress up...

I tug the...

I tug...

Shit. I think I needed to, like, unsnap something around the back of her neck. It's stuck over her head.

"Um," she says, muffled by the fabric.

I'm standing three feet away from her, tugging at the dress, my cock sticking out through the zipper hole in my pants; she's bent forward, black, backless dress pulled up around her head, wearing nothing else but a thong and heels.

We're like a living version of a Chinese finger trap.

"Andrew...?"

"I know. I... Hold on."

For whatever reason, I choose not to do the logical thing and pull the dress down her body. Not sure why. I just walk it toward her, inside out, and toss it over the back of her head like a cape.

For a second, seeing her faceless, naked body distracts me for a couple of reasons and I just kind of stare at her.

"Are you still there?"

"Shit, sorry." I swing around behind her to see if I can undo the clasp in the back.

When I get back there and step in to reach her dress, my cock kind of... Well... It kind of pokes her in the ass.

"Oh!" she yelps.

"Yeah, sorry, it's just... There."

And then suddenly she gets very still, turns her still covered head, and muffles out, "I don't mind."

Fuck unclasping.

I grab the neckline with both hands and rip it at the seam, tearing it off her. It falls off her head and to the ground. She looks down at it pooled around her ankles and then looks at me and says, "I just got that cleaned."

"I'll buy you a new one." And then my hands are fisting her hair, pressing her mouth against mine again and she's fumbling for my belt.

I have the thought, instantly, that there's a very good chance that she'll manage to catch her finger in the buckle, snap it back, breaking her wrist, and at the same time somehow succeed in tightening my open zipper with the torque of her pull and wind up chopping my dick off. Yes, it's crazy, and yes, it's implausible, but then again...

"Hold on, hold on," I mutter into her kiss. Stroking her arms to gently pull her away from my belt, I step back and look at her.

"What?" she asks, nervously, rubbing her knees together shyly. "Did I do something wrong?"

It breaks my heart and turns me on at the same time.

"No," I whisper. "No. You didn't."

Slowing things down, I unbuckle my own belt. Sliding it out of the belt loops, I keep both eyes on her only. I toss off my jacket and kick my shoes off at once. I pull off my socks, still staying focused on her, then begin unbuttoning my shirt. She bites at her bottom lip in the way she does that makes my dick jump. And my dick jumps.

I discard the shirt, tuck my cock back into my boxers long enough to slip my pants and underwear off, and then stand in front of her, naked. Her legs twist a bit at the knees and she kind of shimmies in place. I don't even think she knows she's shimmying. In fact, I realize now that she hasn't been kidding or playing coy even a little bit. She has genuinely no idea how sexy she is. Which is also part of what makes her so goddamn sexy.

She goes to kick off her shoes and unfasten her garters, but I stop her. "Leave 'em on."

She glances down at her feet and then lifts her eyes to meet mine again. "OK."

I take two steps to reach her, lift her hands, and kiss the backs of both of them. She places them on my chest and steps in closer to me so that our bodies are tight together, my cock pressed between our stomachs.

"What now?" she asks.

In my mind I think to say, *I dunno. What would the Sexpert do?* But I don't. I don't want to fuck this up. And in not asking the question, I think this is the moment I decide that this girl means something to me. Something special. Or, at the least, she could. She stands the chance of being. I wasn't looking for her at all and she fell into my life like an avalanche. I want to see what that brings with it.

I'm not sure how I'm going to avoid getting crushed by the next avalanche that I'm certain is going to come, but I'll figure that out when it happens.

"Now?" I respond. "Do you have a condom somewhere?"

"I... Yes. I mean. I think so. They're the same ones I've had for a while, but I don't think they have an expiration date. They're in my nightstand. Why?"

Why? "I wanna make balloon animals." She furrows her brow. "I wanna have sex with you! Is that something you'd be into? Because I'm usually pretty good at reading signals and *this*"—I make a circular gesture, encompassing our bodies—"feels like a pretty clear signal."

She gets a small smile, nods, and says, "Yes, I'd like that very much, please, thank you."

Kills.

I grab her up in the air. She wraps her high-heeled ankles around my waist and I carry her to her nightstand. My cock presses against the ornately patterned silk of her panties as we step over. She feels warm. Damp. And that's when I realize for the first time that the panties aren't sewn completely shut in the front. There's a slit. A point of entry. A convenient opening in the wrapper covering her milky sweetness. Fuck me.

"Condom, condom, condom," I say three or four times, a little loudly.

She giggles, reaches down, opens a drawer, and inside are about a hundred condoms. My eyes widen.

"The fuck are you planning?" I ask.

"I didn't buy them all. Some were, like, party favors. Some my friend Zoey gave me. A few were on sale when I was buying orange juice, and I'm always looking for a deal... I dunno."

I shake my head. Then, "Do you have any magnums?"

Her lips press together tightly, trying to stifle a grin. She nods. "Uh-huh. I think so. I bought some one time because I had it on my vision board."

"You had 'guy with a big dick' on your vision board? You *had a vision board?*"

She nods again. "I guess that manifesting shit works, huh?" She fishes around until she finds a magnum, pulls it out, rips open the packaging with her teeth, and then I lower her to the floor so that she can slide it on me.

She drops to her knees and kisses the tip of my cock. It sends something like electric ice through my spine.

"I'm... I'm not sure it's gonna fit," she says.

"You mean the condom?"

"Yeah. Did you think I meant...?"

"I didn't wanna presume."

"No, I mean, I'm not sure about the other thing either, but we'll make it work."

I laugh a little and the muscles in my stomach tighten, causing my dick to jump again. And as she stretches the condom out to fit around me, she says...

"Oh, yeah. We'll definitely make it work."

"Do... you... want... some water?" she gasps out, flopping off me and landing on her back next to me in the bed.

"Are you OK?"

"I'm fine... I just... Water."

"I'll get it. Stay here." I lean over and give her a kiss, which she kind of can't return because she's so out of breath. She makes an attempt, but then just gives me a thumbs up.

It takes about two seconds to get to the kitchen in the small apartment. I look around, surveying the space, and think...

No.

Anyway.

She has the same fridge with the same water dispenser I do. For whatever it's worth, they do outfit all the places in this building pretty well. When I had them set me up here, I didn't bother to consider whether or not I'd "like it." Honestly, I didn't have much of an intention of staying. Figured I'd get things up and running, maybe even cash out in the next year or so, and then go seek another adventure. But now... I dunno. Maybe I'll stay a little longer than I planned.

"Here you go," I say, handing the water to her as I get back into the bed.

"How are you... not... winded?" she asks, between gulps.

I shrug. "Climbing. Best exercise you can get. You should come with me in the real world. I think you'd be good at it."

She shakes her head. "Heights," she manages to get out.

She has the sheets pulled in between her legs, covering her nakedness just up the middle. I rub her exposed thigh. "Sorry," I say. "It just takes me a long time when I'm wearing a condom."

"No, no, it's fine," she says, her breathing returning to normal. "I'm sorry I couldn't stop coming."

"Yeah. Guys hate it when they make girls come a bunch of times."

She looks at me to see if I'm serious, then starts giggling. She sets down her water. A more serious look parks itself on her face. "Can I ask you something?"

"Of course."

"Do you miss it?"

"Do I miss what?"

"Art."

"You mean do I miss making art?" She nods. "Nah. I mean I love beautiful things. And I love making beautiful things, so in that regard sure, but not really. Besides, I feel like what I do now has its own artistic value. Kind of. Maybe that's a justification, but with the art world especially... I dunno. Like everything, there's just so much bullshit involved that it starts to feel... I mean, it's my *art*. Y'know? Which sounds redundant, but it is. I *care* about it. So, like, I could never figure out how to get OK with turning it into a money-making thing. It would've felt... not good. And, of course, the art world is filled with Serildas, so..." Her skin feels good under my fingers. "Why do you ask?"

"Just wondering. Were you good at it? Making art?"

"Well... Subjective. But... Yeah. Not bad."

"You're kind of good at everything, aren't you?"

"No, not really. I just don't really pursue things I'm not good at. There's a difference. If I have one strength, it's knowing my strengths. What about you?"

"What about me?"

"I dunno. Like, how long you been at *Le Man?*"

"Couple years."

"You like it?"

She shrugs. "It's a job. I mean, I think I'm OK at the stuff I do, but... I dunno. It's certainly not my *art*."

"Sure. Do you have an art? Something you feel passionately about?"

She thinks about this like it's the first time anyone has ever asked her the question. After a long moment, she says, "Being a good person, I guess."

A puff of breath escapes me. "Yeah?"

"Yeah. Why? Is that dumb?"

I get a sad but totally content smile. "No, no, cupcake. It is the opposite of dumb."

I lean down and kiss her thigh. Then I run my nose under the sheet and start inching toward her inner thigh. She pushes me back.

"What?" I ask. "What's wrong?"

"I just... I have to work in the morning."

"So do I."

"Yeah, but not really. You run the place. You can do whatever you want. Also, you have a different kind of stamina. Apparently."

I pull back. Unhappily. But I do. "OK."

"Soooo... Are you gonna go?"

"Go? Where?"

"Back to your apartment."

"Now?"

She nods.

"Do you want me to go?"

"Where? Back to your apartment?"

"Yes."

"Now?"

"Yes."

"I mean... If you want to. Do you want to?"

"Go back to my apartment? Not particularly."

"So... You wanna... Stay?"

"Here?"

She nods.

"With you?"

She nods.

"Yes."

She smiles.

"So... OK."

"OK."

There's a brief silence where we both grin at each other. Then she starts to get out of bed.

"Where are you going?" I ask. "Are *you* leaving?"

"No." She slaps at me as if to say, *You silly Billy*. "I wanna lay out my clothes for tomorrow so that I can sleep an extra five minutes in the morning."

"It's two A.M."

"*Later* in the morning."

She walks over to her closet and the silhouette of her body in the dim light coming only from the Hello Kitty night light by the bed (amazing) freezes my breath for a second.

"Your body is so incredible," I tell her.

"Noooo," she starts to protest.

"It is. It took me a minute to fully grasp just how incredible it is. You're working with a loaded clip, kid."

I can't see her blush, but I can feel it. "Well... Thank you."

She tosses a shirt and skirt onto the edge of the bed. I can't help but notice that they're kind of exactly the same as the ones I see her in all the time.

"Hey." That's me. "Why do you hide?"

"Excuse me?"

"No, no, not an accusation, just... It only took me a minute to see it because you do a pretty good job of covering up your... assets. But why? I mean, it's fine, just... Where does that come from?"

She turns to look at me. Again, like no one's ever asked her these kinds of questions before.

"No one's ever asked me these kinds of questions before."

"That's fine," I say. "You don't have to answer. Just curious."

"No. It's OK. I just... I don't know. I mean, I guess I was always kind of a nerd. Like, I read Philip K. Dick books when all the other girls were reading Judy Blume. And I dressed in *Star Wars* t-shirts and played volleyball, so I got the reputation as maybe being a lesbian..."

"Thought that was softball."

"It's both." I nod. "So, I dunno, y'know? The world sees you one way long enough and you kind of *become* that thing. So I guess the way I dress, especially for work and stuff, it's like... a uniform. You know? A way to be identified. Or, in my case, not be identified. Like, 'Don't look at me. Nothin' to see here.' Right? Like it just kind of makes me ignorable. Is that a word?" I nod again.

259

"Thought it was. So. Maybe that's why? Also, boring clothes are affordable." She shrugs and smiles.

"OK," I say, jumping up off the bed.

"What are you doing?"

"Cupcake, you are in no way ignorable. Totally a word," I say, fanning through her closet. "And it's time you stopped trying to hide."

"Seriously. What are you doing?" She reaches for my hand to stop. "You're gonna mess it up. I have all my stuff color-coded."

I take her hand, hold her wrist, and look her in the eye. "Hey. Trust me." She draws her chin back into her neck. "Do you trust me?" She nods, slightly and warily. "Good. Will you let me pick out what you're gonna wear tomorrow?"

"Why do you want to?"

I take a beat, stroke her cheek, and tell her, "Because. I love beautiful things."

CHAPTER TWENTY-SEVEN

"Good morning, ladies!" I sing out to Charlotte and Lynn at reception when I step off the elevator.

"Good morning, Eden!" they both chime back. But then Charlotte does a double-take and says, "Eden, what are you wearing?"

I twirl for her. Well, not quite twirl. This black pencil skirt Andrew chose for me is so tight at the knees, I have to take ridiculous little baby steps. It's more of a hop than a twirl. "Do you like it?" I ask, pushing my glasses up my nose. "My boyfriend picked it out this morning."

I feel justified in calling Andrew my boyfriend. I mean he stayed the night. We had ridiculously hot sex, and he was still there in the morning when I woke up.

Plus, picking an outfit from my closet... that's reserved for boyfriends only. Casual hook-ups don't do that.

"Oh, my God, girl," Lynn says. "You are the sexiest librarian ever."

"Thank you!" I say.

And it's not even that far off my usual outfit, either. I mean, OK. The skirt is a bit much. But I have the curves to pull off a pencil skirt, that's why I bought it in the first place. I just never had the nerve to wear it before. And I'm wearing a crisp, white, button-down shirt, just like I usually do. Except this one is just a little low-cut in the cupcake department.

I don't normally wear heels but today I'm rocking those babies. They might not be Prada, but they are four inches high and make my calves look fantastic.

Today... I *feel* like a Sexpert.

I baby-step my way down the hallway, calling out my usual hellos. Sylvia is at the printer and does a double-take too. In fact, everyone is looking at me, and normally that would make me very self-conscious, but ya know what? Doing these Sexpert videos has really upped my self-confidence. I mean, none of it seems so scary anymore. I've always been outgoing but I never liked to flaunt my body. I think it goes back to middle school. I developed early, so I had perfect cupcakes by the time I was fourteen. And it was a real bummer back then. I was an athletic child. I did all those years of gymnastics and volleyball. I even ran track for a year. But then, of course, these ginormous mounds on my chest got in the way of everything. And all the boys made rude comments about them.

Until the Sexpert came along my breasts were always something I wanted to hide.

Not anymore.

I don't want to show them off, exactly, but tastefully accentuating them doesn't hurt.

I stow away my purse when I get to my desk, then log on and open my email.

"Oh," I say, noticing I have something from Zoey. *Reminder! Stevie Is Turning One!* the headline reads.

Oh, shit! I almost forgot about that. She sent out invitations weeks ago, so I wasn't expecting another one in this reminder, but there's a link to click.

When I do, a fabulous animation begins to play. With upbeat country music, and a little boy wearing cowboy boots line-dancing with a little cowgirl, and a whole bunch of confetti spilling across my screen.

And at the end there's a message from Zoey. *I know I already sent out those boring plain-text email invitations, but so many good things have happened to us since then, I wanted to resend and make it all spectacular! Please come to our party tomorrow at noon to celebrate Stevie's first birthday!*

Wow. She's right. So many good things have happened to us. The Sexpert is going crazy. And the numbers haven't stopped climbing. They just keep going up. Even the Kit-Kat video has almost half a million views now.

Hmmmm. I wonder… maybe Andrew would like to go to the party with me? I mean, Zoey is my BFF. If we're going to be a thing, he should meet her. So I forward it to him and add a little message asking if he'd like to come along.

I don't expect a quick answer, but less than five minutes later, he replies. Like he's been waiting for me to email, or call, or text or something.

And it's a yes!

My phone dings a text.

Andrew: *I'd love to go. Thanks for the invite. I'm real busy today with work, but I'll pick you up tomorrow at noon.*

I send back a whole line of red hearts.

Then he messages again. *You look fantastic this morning. God, I'm killing myself for having to work. I want to eat you for lunch!*

My mouth drops open in unexpected glee.

"What are you doing?"

"What?" I say, hiding my phone as I look up to find Gretchen looming over my desk.

"This isn't personal time, Eden. We're still in the middle of a crisis. I need repurposed articles for this weekend on my desk by noon."

"No problem, Gretchen. I'm working on two right now."

"No, right now you're flirting with someone on your phone. And what is with this… this…" She points her finger up and down my body. "This new look? It's not work-appropriate."

"What?" I ask, looking down at myself then pushing my glasses up my nose as I meet her gaze. "It's a long skirt and a button-down shirt."

"Well… it makes you look… sexy."

I smile. "Thank you. I think so too."

"That wasn't a compliment, Eden. Go back to your old outfits."

And then she turns on her heel and walks off.

Janet, the girl on the other side of my cubicle partition who does website maintenance, peeks her head over and says, "Fuck her, Eden. You look great. She's just jealous. And if I were you, I'd tell Pierce that she's taking credit for your ideas. Because that's bullshit too."

She disappears behind the blue upholstery partition before I can even say anything back.

But I think about that for a moment.

Because I do look great. And my ideas are the ones that are keeping this stupid magazine in the spotlight right now. I didn't rewrite anything, but I did send all my suggested edits and graphics up to the blog department and they're using them. And we're getting hits. Not Sexpert numbers, of course. But more people have been visiting *Le Man* online since I started repurposing articles than they were before.

So yeah. F-you, Gretchen.

Myrtle texts me just before noon, asking me to meet her for lunch. So I package up my weekend articles for Gretchen, send them over to her, and then grab my purse and baby-step my way over to the elevator.

Myrtle is already there, looking down at her phone.

"What's up?" I ask.

She looks up at me, opens her mouth to say something, and then stops. She blinks. Three times fast. "Holy. Shit. Eden."

265

"What?" I ask "What's wrong?"

"You look hot, sister." And then she holds up a finger. "Oh, my God. You and Andrew are totally a thing, aren't you?"

How does she do that? Read my innermost thoughts and come up with the right deduction every single time? It's like Myrtle has her finger on my pulse. But not just my pulse. The pulse of the world. She's... worldly. And ever since I met her two years ago, I've wanted to be just like her. Have what she has. Command men the way she does.

But maybe not anymore. I mean the way Andrew sees me, it's almost the way I see Myrtle. He thinks I'm sexy. And when I'm with him I *feel* sexy.

And old me might think he's making me feel that way. But new me thinks I'm feeling sexy because... well, the Sexpert has given me confidence I never had before. It changed me.

I didn't think it would. Not in a positive way. But it did.

I think that's what Myrtle is picking up on. Maybe? My growing self-esteem?

That and... well, she just happened to be there when the whole Andrew thing started so she's probably been taking secret notes about us.

"We seem to be," I reply back, nodding excitedly, as we get into the elevator, she uses her magic card to skip all the stops on the way down, and we descend. "We just... we just click. And bump into each other in the most unexpected ways. And yeah..." I tell her everything that happened these past few days. The date last night, and the outfit picking this morning.

And just as the elevator doors open to the lobby, she whisper-yells, "You're dating a billionaire!"

"Holy shit," I say. "I never even thought of that before. I guess I am."

Weird.

And even though I think Myrtle is probably the most interesting person I've ever met and hang on every word she says, I tune her out this time.

Because she's right. Andrew is a billionaire. And if he's now my boyfriend... wow. Talk about dating up.

Can something like that work?

I mean... why would he want to date me?

Is it because he still thinks I'm the Sexpert so he's trying to trap me?

God, I really hope that's not it. I will die of sadness if that's why he's going out with me because... because I think I'm falling for this guy. I think I really, really like him a lot. I caught myself daydreaming about what our kids would look like earlier this morning. And I even scribbled Eden Hawthorne on a piece of paper on my desk as I did it, just to see if I like the way it looks.

I do. It looks fabulous.

My heart will be broken if this is all a setup.

The next morning, I wake up early so I can plan my Stevie's First Birthday outfit. I want to make Andrew's head turn, but still keep it G-rated at the same time. So I choose a bright yellow sundress, a light cropped red sweater, and a pair of red wedge-heeled sandals.

I feel like a bright ray of sunshine.

Then I walk over to the local bakery and pick up Stevie's cake. I got a little welcome-to-the-neighborhood

267

coupon when I moved in, so I gave that to Zoey to use, since we're still so strapped for cash until we finally get paid. The cake's got a whole cowboy theme going on.

Right at noon, my doorbell chimes.

I take a deep breath and straighten my dress as I walk to the door and pull it open.

Andrew stands there, one hand propped up on the doorjamb, grinning at me.

"Hey," I say, kinda nervous.

"Hey yourself," he says, leaning in to kiss me.

God. I want to melt right into him.

"Jesus, you smell like frosting."

"Oh." I laugh, twirling my hair in my fingers. "I picked up Stevie's cake earlier. That must be why."

"That's not why," he says, leaning in to kiss me again. "I think you're just naturally delicious."

I want to wrap my legs around his middle and kiss him forever. Never let him go. Just… wow. I might be falling in love with this man.

"So…" he says, pulling away. "Meeting the best friend? We're there already, huh?"

"Does it bother you?" I ask. "Too much, too fast? Do you not want to go? You don't have to come with me if you don't want to, I just—"

"Hey," he says, cutting me off. "I am thrilled that *you* asked *me* on a date."

I smile. Nod. "It is a date, right?"

"Do you think it's a date?"

"Do you not?"

"I do."

"Then I guess it's a date."

I smile again. "And we're… we're kinda liking this, right?"

"Yeah. We're kinda liking this," he says, his hand dropping to my hip.

I bite my lip. "You're going to love her. Zoey, I mean. She's so cool. We've been BFF's forever. And she's going to love you back."

"Well, good. Because my best friend can't remember you."

I laugh.

"So I guess after this"—he holds his hands out, palms up—"the only thing left is to meet the parents."

Holy shit. We're at the meet-the-parents stage. "I'd love to meet your parents," I say.

"It's just my mom. And I assure you, you wouldn't. But I'd be happy to meet yours."

"Yeah?" He nods. "Cool. My dad is really going to like you."

"Yeah? Good."

And then we just kinda stand there, staring stupidly at each other for a few moments.

Wow. This is real, I say to myself.

We have something real.

CHAPTER TWENTY-EIGHT

"Oh, thank you," says Eden's friend, Zoey, accepting the gift I hand her.

"Of course. I remember what it was like to be one. Everybody treating you like you're still a baby when all you wanna do is spread your wings and fly. It's a kid-sized hang-glider by the way."

Zoey nods at Eden. "He's funny."

"He tries," I say. I look around at the cowboy motif Zoey has going for the party. "I like your place. Nice design eye. Who's your decorator? Eden needs an upgrade."

Eden giggles and now Zoey's looking at us the way a single mom with a one-year-old looks at kid-less people who've only just started seeing each other. In other words: slight annoyance ringed with contempt.

"Make yourselves at home. Can I get you anything to drink?"

"Do you have any ginger ale?" I ask.

"I have water, punch, and maybe some old breast milk in the back of the fridge."

"Water's great. Thanks."

"Eden?"

"I'm good," she says.

"Yeah," says Zoey, walking away. "You look good."

"I like her," I say, kissing Eden on the head. "She seems kind of mean."

"She's not. She's just... I mean, she's raising a kid on her own without any help."

"Where's the dad?"

Eden gets quiet and then says, "Another time. OK?"

"Sure." I nod. As we wander into the apartment, I nod and smile at all the people. Pretty much all of them have kids. That's what I hear happens. You become friends with the parents you meet at pre-school or at the playground or wherever. I've never really given much thought to having kids myself. Not that I wouldn't, just with my relationship history it's always seemed like a far-fetched possibility. Not only would I never have wanted to have kids with the women I was with, they all would've been pretty mean mothers, I have a feeling.

I grew up with kind of a mean mom, so I know how much fun it isn't. Not really fair. She wasn't mean so much as not terribly present. And kind of judgmental. And a little snobby. And sorta rude. And, yeah, pretty mean.

It always just kinda glanced off me. I mean she wasn't mean to *me*. Just most everybody else. But the thing I appreciated is that at least she was open about it. Usually with Southern women you get smiles to the front and daggers to the back. But my mom has always been good about stabbing people right in the eye. God love her.

It doesn't take a lot of digging in my brain to realize that the women I've been with before now were some sort of version of my mom. Like I've always said about me and Pierce. Our Oedipal wounds run deep. It also doesn't take a Carl Jung to figure out that's why I'm so smitten with Eden. She is, in every way possible, the opposite of that.

She's one of the only genuinely kind people I've met in my life. Not like Cheryl the leasing agent who's "polite" and "nice." Eden is a legitimately and deeply kind person.

I hope, hope, hope she hasn't been lying to me and that I'm wrong about this Sexpert thing. Because with the women in my life before now, I at least knew that I was going to be disappointed right from the start. It would suck to feel this good, trust this much, and go in this hard to have the rug fucking pulled out.

But hell, I've chosen to stand dead in the middle of that carpet, so if and when it happens, it's nobody's fault but my own.

It's so goddamn stupid anyway. If the magazine is failing, this Sexpert idea is not going to save it. The whole thing is now so far out of proportion to its actual value that it's almost laughable.

Except.

It's not to Pierce.

And it's probably not to whoever this Sexpert girl is (please don't be Eden, please don't be Eden, please don't be Eden...).

Jesus. If the government knew I was using their secret spying app to figure out the identity of a pair of talking boobies on the internet...

Like I said. Laughable.

Ha. Ha.

"Wow," I say looking over at Zoey's home computer setup. "That's no joke." She's got a twenty-seven-inch screen, a stand-alone processing tower, and what looks like a supermicro personal cloud server.

"Oh, yeah, Zoey's a nerd too," says Eden.

"Clearly. Is she, like, a gamer? Because all that video game violence is gonna have a real deleterious effect on young master Stevie." I glance over at baby Stevie in his cowboy hat, throwing Cheerios all over the place. "If it hasn't already."

"No, no." Eden laughs. "She's not a gamer. She's a..."

She stops short and trails off.

"She's what?"

"Nothing."

"Eden? What? Is she ... a hacker? A day trader? Is she running a Ponzi scheme? What?"

"No. Nothing. She just. She does, like, web design and like... video production. And stuff."

She takes a deep breath, bites her lip, and looks at me through the top rims of her glasses like she does when she's nervous. And it strikes me that we've now spent enough time together that I can officially tell when she looks at me in a way that's recognizable. I think it's cool as hell that that's happened so fast. But it makes me really

274

uneasy that it seems to have a negative and surreptitious undertone.

And then a series of thoughts begin ricocheting around my brain the way they do when I've solved a problem or cracked a code. The same way they used to when I would stare at a canvas and suddenly what I wanted to create would just appear there in front of my eyes. Or the way I can stare at a pitch on a rock wall and suddenly see the route to the top.

Zoey is a web designer and does video production.

She likely understands how to maximize production values and mise en scène.

She'd also have the tools at her disposal to create content.

Eden would have reservations about telling me this stuff if she, in any way, was engaged with her friend in the process of creating content that might run afoul of my current raison d'être with Pierce.

And speaking of Pierce, how is it that I've been around the guy again for less than a month and I'm already using a shitload of French phrases in my internal musings?

"Andrew?" Eden's voice pulls me back.

"Yeah, sorry, what?"

"Is... Is everything...?"

"Oh. Oh, uh, yeah, yeah, everything's fine. I just got distracted for a second."

She gets a look of resignation on her face. "About what?"

"Nothing. Seriously, nothing. Hey, look at me." She does. "OK. Honestly?" She nods. "I was just... You said video production and that started me thinking about videos and that started me thinking about Sexpert and Pierce and... That's all."

She lets out a long breath and looks at the ground.

"But," I continue. "So what? We've already established that it's not you, right?" She doesn't say anything. "Right?" I ask, a little more forcefully. She looks up at me, makes eye contact and says...

"Right."

I let out a breath. I'm not sure what feeling I'm letting out with it. "OK. So, y'know... It's probably Myrtle, like Pierce thinks, and this week I'll be able to do the voice test and tell him for sure."

She nods a little. I can feel her getting hot. Physically. It's radiating off her.

"Or, shit," I say. "Who knows? Maybe Pierce will get over it by tomorrow and be on to some new folly. He's like a dog with a bone, but when he finds a newer, bigger bone, he'll drop the one he's chomping down on. He's mercurial."

She shrugs. "Yeah."

It's awkward now and I know why and I don't wanna know why and I wanna forget the whole thing has come up and just eat cake and enjoy a round of pin the tail on the whatever-the-fuck. I decide a reset is necessary.

"Hey." I take her by the shoulders and give her a kiss on the forehead. "You wanna get out of here? Go... I dunno. Get our trucks oil changes? Or something?"

She grins and says, "Yeah," in her small voice.

"Cool. Lemme just run to the restroom and we'll jet. K?" She nods again. "Be right back," I say, giving her another kiss. On the lips this time.

On my way to the bathroom I try not to think about all the things that want to weasel their way in. Instead I focus on not stepping on the kid toys that are all over the place and the kids who are also all over the place.

"'Scuse me. Is the restroom in there?" I ask the two tattooed moms playing with their kid in the hall. They're making goo-goo ga-ga sounds and blowing bubbles on his tummy and stuff and he's laughing.

"Yeah," the one mom says.

"But we did just change him in there, so you may wanna wait," says the other.

"Thanks for the heads up. I'll see if I can handle it."

I smile, they smile, and we all have a good titter over how filthy children are.

Walking into Zoey's bedroom, I notice that the Old West design aesthetic may not just be for the party. Must be a Colorado thing. There's wood paneling on the walls and the door to the bathroom isn't a regular door. It's a sliding barn door. As Cheryl the leasing agent might say, "How rustic."

I slide the door to the bathroom open and...

I blink.

I look to the left.

I blink.

I look to the right.

I blink.

It's not the bathroom.

It's the closet.

Except it's not just the closet.

It's also the set for the Sexpert video channel.

It's immediately recognizable.

OK.

OK.

OK.

Fuck!!

Fuck fucking fuck!

She fucking lied to me! She lied to me twice! She's lying to me right now!

Fucking fucking fucking fuck!

OK. OK. It's not the end of the world. Don't blow it out of proportion. She's scared because Pierce is crazy, and I totally get that and that's justified and maybe now we can just talk about it and she can explain and it'll all be fine.

Don't get pissed. Don't freak out.

Don't overreact.

"I gotta go."

Eden turns to look at me and the smile that was on her face disappears.

"What? Why?" she asks.

"I just... Work. Dev texted me and there's a thing and... I gotta go in."

"But—"

"Look, I gotta go, OK? I'll call you."

I start past her and she grabs my arm.

"Andrew, wait."

I stop, take a breath and look at her. I know my eyes are cold, but I can't help it. "Yeah?"

"Do you really have to go to work?"

I take a beat to look at her. I want to touch her. I want to kiss her. I want to stroke her cheek. But I don't. Because I can't. Like I said, the one thing you could always count on with my mom... At least when she stuck the blade in, she'd do it to your face.

"Do you?" she asks again. "Do you have to go to work?"

I close my eyes. I open them. "Yeah," I say.

And with that I pull my arm free and take off to see if I can figure out any way to outrun this avalanche that's now starting to come tumbling down.

CHAPTER TWENTY-NINE

"So I should call him?" Zoey and I are talking in circles. We've been going back and forth about the merits and demerits of playing hard to get for the last five minutes as I walk to work.

"Well…" Zoey hesitates, trying to be thoughtful. Which I appreciate. Because I'm still trying to wrap my head around what happened on Saturday. "I don't know,

281

Eden. I mean… if he's going to be a flake like this, should you bother with him?"

It's a valid question. And as my best friend, Zoey is obligated to ask it. Because Andrew just left me at the party. I had to get a ride home from Zoey after everyone left. And then he didn't return my calls or anything.

"But I like him so much," I say.

"I know you do, babe. But he's making you unhappy and you know he's trying to out us. So maybe this is for the best? You did say he believes you're not the Sexpert, right?"

"Yeah, but…"

"Then maybe you should leave well enough alone. I mean, if he calls you, that's one thing. But don't go to him. If he likes you he'll get in touch. He already knows you like him. You weren't the one being weird on Saturday."

"That's true," I say, sighing heavily. "OK. Well, I'm walking into work, so…"

"OK," she says. I know she's making her BFF pouty face for me. And I appreciate that too. "Call me at lunch if you need to. I'm here all day."

"Thanks," I say, ending the call.

I just don't understand what's happening. We were at meet-the-parents stage on Saturday morning. He wanted to eat my frosting.

And that excuse was lame. Come on, work? On Saturday?

Except I think I used that same excuse on him.

And I was lying, see?

So what is going on?

Unless… unless he found out something about the Sexpert and—

"No," I say out loud. I'm standing at the elevator now, so six people look over at me with curious glances.

I sigh again, then just look at my feet as we all pile in.

It takes like ten minutes to get up to the fiftieth floor, the elevator stops so often. It's weird, because usually the view when I step out is enough to lift my mood. But this morning everything about this elevator ride is annoying.

"Happy Monday, Eden!" the girls call from the reception desk.

I force a smile, once again understanding why people hate it when I say that. "Happy Monday," I say, passing them by.

"We got éclairs," Sylvia says as I pass the printer. "Go grab one before they're gone, Eden!"

But not even dessert for breakfast can up my mood today.

I am heartsick. And I hate it.

I put my purse away, sit down, and log on to find out what fresh hell is waiting for me today.

"Eden!"

Well, there's the Devil's mistress now. "Yes, Gretchen?" I say, popping my head up over my cubicle partition to see her office.

"Get in here now."

Shit. I make eye contact with Janet, who gives me an exaggerated eye roll, and then call back, "Coming!"

I grab my tablet and reluctantly make my way to Gretchen's office. "What's up?" I ask. My upbeat tone is totally fake, but who cares? It's not like Gretchen gives a crap about my mood.

"What's up?" she huffs. "Why did you disobey me?"

"Excuse me?" I ask, kinda bewildered because I don't recall disobeying her, but mostly annoyed. Because it sounds like something a parent says to a child. "I don't understand what you're referring to, Gretchen. Please explain."

She narrows her eyes at me, totally catching on to my passive-aggressive response. "You changed those articles. They are all about dessert now."

"No," I say, pushing my glasses up my nose. "I gave the bloggers some suggestions so they can maximize traffic. That's all. I didn't tell them to use it, I just provided them with options."

There's nothing Gretchen can say about this. Not really. Not without coming off as a total bitch. So she looks me up and down, like she's studying my outfit.

I'm in the clear there. Because I'm back to my usual uniform of drab skirt and button-down shirt.

"Much better," she says, nodding to my clothes. "You looked ridiculous on Friday. I was just trying to save you from humiliation."

Do. Not. React.

That's what I tell myself. I was, after all, passive-aggressive first, right? This is her earned retort. I should just say, "Mmmhmm," bob my ponytail yes, and move on.

That's what I *should* say.

"Well, I'm surprised you noticed me at all, *Gretchen*. Since you blatantly pretend I don't even work here when you steal my ideas and present them to Pierce as your own."

She gasps.

Yup. Probably not the right response. But for like two seconds, it makes me happy.

"Is that what you think? That your childish ideas about sex and dessert are what will save this magazine? And"— she huffs out a laugh—"I suppose you think you're the clever, scrappy everygirl who will have all the answers and get some big promotion at the end of your delusional fantasy?"

Oh, yeah. We're on. Big-league bitch fest coming in three, two, one…

"Attention! Attention!"

"What the hell?" Gretchen says.

We both look up at the ceiling where Pierce's voice is blaring though a speaker.

"Attention, please!" he says again. This time there's a whine of feedback and everyone collectively groans and holds their ears. "Please give me your full attention!"

I look at Gretchen, trying to decide if our 'meeting' is over and I should go back to my desk, or stay here and listen to the announcement.

"We're not done yet," she snaps.

"Fine." I nod and turn my head away as Pierce begins to speak.

"I have an announcement to make. As you all know, our top priority right now is finding that harlot who stole the *Le Man* Sexpert idea. And we've made significant progress. We have that little cupcake in our sights and we're about to go in for the kill because she is one of us!"

Oh, shit. Does he know? I look around nervously. I can see almost everyone through the floor-to-ceiling windows of Gretchen's office. But no one is looking for me, so I force myself to calm down and take a deep breath.

"Was that too much?" Pierce asks someone.

"Just… just keep going."

Wait, was that Andrew? Is he up in Pierce's office right now?

"But in the spirit of benevolence," Pierce bellows in a deep voice that might actually be an imitation of a—

king?—"we are going to give her one. More. Chance. To come clean. Sexpert, we know you're here. So listen carefully, shortcake. One chance. Come up to my office right now and out yourself, or we will be forced to—what?" There's mumbled whispering. Like Andrew is giving him pointers. "Oh, right, right, right. Got it. We're here to make an offer, Sexpert. A very generous one. You see... I respect what you've done." His tone turns a lot more conciliatory. "Because... because it was genius. We think you are the perfect partner for *Le Man* magazine and we want to make you our next superstar!"

"Since when do we have superstars?" Gretchen asks.

I'm thinking the same thing, but I keep my mouth shut. I don't need any extra attention right now.

"So... Sexpert. What do you think? Can we work together? Come see me. Quickly. Because this offer expires at the end of the day and after that we'll be forced to take more deliberate measures." There's more screeching feedback and then we hear Pierce say, "That went well, right?" before the speakers go dead.

Everyone's chattering and laughing out in the cubicles, looking around, trying to figure out who the Sexpert is.

I turn back to Gretchen, very much wanting to get back to business, so I push my glasses up my nose and say, "OK, so where were we?"

But Gretchen is lost in thought. "Who do you think it is?" she asks.

"Umm... Myrtle?"

Shit! Why the fuck did I just say that?

"Myrtle!" Gretchen practically guffaws. "No way. If she were a Sexpert she'd compare everything to pain and death, not cupcakes and frosting."

I do not move. Because Gretchen suddenly gets an idea. And it's about me. I can see that little lightbulb going off over her head.

But then she shakes it off and says, "Go back to work."

"Cool," I say. "Good talk."

"And Eden," she snaps.

"Yes?"

"Do. Not. Disobey me. Again."

"No problem," I say, closing her door on my way out with the hope she will just stay in there and never come out.

I go back to my desk and do simple mindless things like disobey Gretchen's last direct order. I find new scrumptious graphics to send up to the bloggers. And come up with new titles. But I'm just on autopilot. Because all I can think about is that offer.

Maybe I should do it? Maybe I should just go up there and tell him it's me?

I mean... he said superstar, right? He'd give me a promotion. He'd get me out from under Gretchen's thumb.

But what about Zoey? We're on the verge of some real financial independence and she'd never want to stick Stevie in daycare to join the rat race again.

I mull that over all morning and then someone yells, "Eden! Eden Presley?"

I pop my head up to find a delivery woman standing near the reception door looking around like she's lost. "That's me!" I say. "Over here."

The woman smiles and weaves her way through cubicles, relieved to have found her target. "Delivery. Sign here."

"Oh," I say, instantly happy. Because it's a very glossy pink box with a black satin ribbon. "What's this?" I ask as I sign her slip.

"There's a card." And then she just stands there and smiles at me.

"Right!" I say. "Tip. One second." I fish through my purse, come up with five dollars I can't really afford to give her, and hand it over.

"Thanks so much, Eden. Enjoy your surprise!"

I make one of those teeth-clenched grins and turn back to the pink box that is now atop my desk, then take the little card out of the little envelope and read it.

Welcome home. This will look perfect in your new place.

But there's no name.

"What is it?" Janet asks, popping her head over the partition wall.

"I dunno," I say, pulling on the slick satin ribbon. It comes loose like chocolate melting in your mouth. I lift the lid off, pull the layers of tissue paper apart, and...
"Oh."

"Wow," Janet says, blinking at my sculpture. "That's... sexy."

"It really is," I say, breathing those words out in a low whisper.

It's the sculpture from the gallery last week. The people entwined and most definitely having sex.

"Who's it from?" she asks.

"Andrew," I say dreamily. "Andrew Hawthorne. We're dating."

"Wow," she says again. "Score, Eden. He must really like you. Because my friend works at that gallery and I know how much the pieces start at."

"How much?" I ask. "No, don't tell me. It doesn't matter."

And it really doesn't. Because my world has been righted again. OK. Yeah. He was totally weird over the weekend. But this is Monday now. And he sent me a gift. He probably had some emergency and had to… I dunno, leave town or something. Or he was on a deadline. Something very important like that because he's a very important guy.

"Attention! Attention!"

Oh, for fuck's sake. Pierce is back.

"The hours are ticking down, Sexpert. It's lunch time, sweets. And your offer is going to expire in—what?" he says to someone. "I'm not being aggressive!" Andrew is up there still, giving him, what? Suggestions on how to handle this? Why is he up there and not down here asking if I like his gift? "You have five hours, Sexpert. After that, we're calling in the lawyers."

The speakers go dead again and I just look at Janet.

"He's fucking lost his mind," Janet says, bobbing back down into her chair and disappearing.

"Right?" I try to laugh it off. But… lawyers. It scares the fuck out of me. Because Zoey and I are both broke. And we won't have any money from this Sexpert stuff for months. How will we fight back if he sues us?

We won't be able to. We'll just have to give in, I guess. Hand over our idea and let him have it. And I'll probably get fired. No. I will *definitely* get fired. And that totally sucks. Because we didn't steal anything. It's just a weird misunderstanding. It's not even anyone's fault. Just… a weird misunderstanding.

I grab my phone to call Zoey and tell her what's going on, but it rings in my hand.

And it's Zoey. "Holy shit," I say, answering. "I was just calling you."

"Oh, my God! Oh, my God! Oh, my, God!"

"What?"

"We got a corporate sponsor!"

"What?" But she's talking so fast, I can't even understand her. "Zoey, slow down. What's going on?"

"I got an email a couple hours ago from Pink Lady Media—"

"Yeah?"

"And they want us to work for them! This is huge, Eden! They said we could work from home, just keep doing what we're doing and... and... they love us! We even get benefits!"

"How'd they find us! Like... hello? We're anonymous!"

"Oh, it came into the Sexpert email. And I used a proxy to email them back. Then I went out and spent my diaper money on a burner phone so I could have a conference call with them. And oh, my God! We did it! Oh, shit! She's calling me back on the other phone. Later."

"Wow," I say, breathing out. "Now what do I do?"

"Hey, cupcake."

I look up and see Andrew staring down at me. "What was all that about?"

CHAPTER THIRTY

"What do you want?" She's pretty cold. I can't necessarily blame her. For being cold that is. I get it. I bailed on her and then disappeared for thirty-six hours. And she doesn't know why.

Although, I must say, I'm having less of an easy-breezy time getting OK with the fact that after repeated attempts to get her to just be honest with me, she made the choice to continue to lie. So, in that regard, her righteous indignation sits a little less well.

I suppose I also made the choice to be lied to and go along for the ride, so there is an argument that I'm complicit in my own disappointment. But fuck it. I'm trying to get everyone out of this situation clean right now, so I'm gonna go ahead and cut myself some slack.

"What's wrong?" I ask her, playing naïve.

"You ghosted on me out the blue for no reason."

"Yeah? Was it more or less ghostly than the way you ghosted on me when you did?"

"Don't—That's—You—"

"Hey, I'm sorry. OK? I am. I had... I had an emergency and it couldn't be helped and, honestly, it's still kind of fucked up and I'm dealing with it. But you know what? You're right. It was a bad move to just ditch out, and I'm sorry." All of that is true.

"Well," she says, meekly, pushing at her glasses in the most Edenly way possible, "OK. But just... It made me... sad."

There's the pout. That pout could cause a man to do things he wouldn't normally do. Forget things he wouldn't normally forget. And deny that the sky is blue, water is wet, and she's the goddamn Sexpert.

"Well, I am sorry. I did not want to make you sad." I bend down and force her to look up at me. She catches my eye and she shrugs.

"What are you doing on my floor?" she asks.

"I was up with Pierce. You hear the announcement?" She nods. "I convinced him that being conciliatory is way better than being litigious." She shrinks back in her chair.

"I wondered if that was you."

"Whattayou mean?"

"It sounded like somebody was coaching him on what to say. Figure you're the only one he listens to, so..."

She trails off. I see the sculpture on her desk.

"Oh, good. It came."

"Oh," she says, looking at it. "Yeah. Just now. Andrew, I don't—"

I put up my hand to stop her. "I want you to have it. It meant something to you. It touched you when you saw it. Well, now you can touch it." She looks like she's stuck in between smiling and crying. "Besides, you need an interior décor upgrade, and this feels like a good start. Enjoy."

She reaches out tentatively and touches the piece. Her fingers trace the lines of the bodies emerging from the granite.

"Thank you."

"You're welcome." I watch her for a second, then say, "What do you think is going to happen?"

"What do you mean?"

"You think anybody is going to come forward to Pierce?" She stops touching the piece and sinks back into her chair again. "To, y'know, claim a partnership deal with *Le Man*? I dunno, seems like a pretty sweet deal to me." *Your honor, leading the witness. Yeah, I know.*

"How...? How can he be so sure that it's someone here? I mean seriously? Have you...?"

"Have I what?"

"Have you done your voice...thing?"

"Well, no. If I had done that already then Pierce wouldn't be making the offer. But even I have to admit that the evidence is starting to look pretty solid that whoever stole the idea stole it from within."

293

"What? Stole? What evidence? What are you talking about?"

"Know what? Don't worry about it. It's not your problem." God, this sucks. "What was that on the phone when I came up?"

"What?"

"The phone. You said, 'Now what do I do?' What do you do about what?"

"About what?"

"Yeah. About what?"

"Who?"

"You."

"Me?"

"Yeah."

"What do I do?"

"Uh-huh."

"About what?"

"That's what I'm asking."

"What—?"

"Yeah. Pop-Tart? I enjoy Abbott and Costello as much as the next guy, but I'm not sure our version of Who's On First is that crisp."

She lets out a nervous laugh and says, "Oh, uh, it's just..." She looks around like the answer is down the hall somewhere. "Uh, my boss. I'm just having a hard time with my boss."

"Gretchen?"

She looks up at me. "Yeah..."

"Yeah, she just popped into Pierce's office as I was leaving."

"She did?"

I nod. "Yep. Came in to say that she thinks she knows who it is."

"Knows who what is?"

"The Sexpert."

"She did?" I've never seen Eden's nostrils flare before. It's cute. I like it.

"Why?" I ask her. "What's up?"

"Did you hear her say who she thinks it is?"

She opens a bottle of water on her desk and drinks down the whole thing in one gulp.

"Good. It's hot outside. Important to stay hydrated."

"Did she say *who* she thinks it is?"

I nod slowly, my lips pursed. "She did."

She swallows. "Who?"

"She said she thinks it's Myrtle."

I swear to God her eyes go bigger than the frames of her glasses. "She what?"

"She said that at first she couldn't be sure, but then she started thinking about it, and that it has to be someone ... how did she say it? Oh. 'Playing against type.' And that that's what led her to Myrtle. Because she said no one would think to suspect Myrtle since she's all leather and chains and the Sexpert is all frosting and ... y'know ... cupcakes."

I let it hang in the air.

Here's the thing: It's not even about Eden being the Sexpert anymore. Honestly, apart from the fact that it's making Pierce an insane obsessive, I could give a shit. This is not my fight. Or at least it wasn't. But now it's about this girl that I really like—like, really, *really* like—lying to me. Repeatedly. To my face.

And all I want—*all* I want—is for her to just cop to it and make it go away so that I can understand why she lied, hope to get over it, and keep on hanging out with her and putting my penis inside her. It's that simple. That's all I'm after.

But trust, man. Fuckin' trust. I need it.

I've tee'd her up perfectly. If she's been worried about the repercussions, I have taken that away. I've gotten Pierce to agree to not only not be a lunatic but to reward her. I mean, I did that partially because it's the right thing to do, but mostly because it'll actually help Eden. It's a win/win. Or technically, a win/win/win. Because this way I don't have to choose between lying to my best friend or torpedoing any chance I have with this girl who just... She's moved into my heart, man. Like, real, real fast and real, real hard. And if she's gonna be living there, I want her to let me help decorate the space.

I watch her carefully. I can almost see the gears turning. Finally, after her brain has done a couple of full rotations, she looks at me apologetically and says...

"Well... Pierce thought it was Myrtle anyway, huh?"

Damn you, Eden.

"Yeah." I sigh. "He did."

"So... maybe it is."

"Yeah. Yeah... Maybe."

She looks at me like there's more I should be saying. There isn't. But I go along anyway.

"You think," I say, "if it is her... That she'll take Pierce up on his offer?"

"I dunno. Do you think she should?"

"Yeah. Yeah. I very much think she should. I talked him into this fragile peace, but it won't last. He already feels like he's showing weakness by even making the offer. If she doesn't take it and he feels like there's egg on his face... Well, to quote from Iron Maiden's *Number of the Beast*, 'Woe to you, o earth and sea, for the devil sends the beast with wrath.' That may actually be in the Bible, but I dunno. I'm no biblical scholar, but I do know that Pierce is likely to *go* biblical."

And, I mean, that's it. I've done all I can do. It's up to her now.

"Yeah," she says. She just repeats it half-a-dozen times. "Yeah, yeah, yeah, yeah, yeah... Yeah."

"Yeah," I echo, giving her a look.

"Well," she says. "Thank you again for the piece. I love it."

I sigh. Internally.

"You're welcome. And, look, again, I'm sorry for going MIA. I promise, there was a reason."

"I know."

No, she doesn't. But she's gonna find out.

"Hey, do you want to come to my place later?" I ask.

"Really?" she responds, hopefully.

"Yeah. I've got one other thing for you." I don't want to lie to her, but I also don't want to tip her off. Not here. Not at her job which she kind of doesn't like in the first place. I don't wanna do it here.

"Honestly, you don't have to get me anything else."

"No, I really kind of do. Swing by after work? Six? Six-thirty?"

"Can we say seven? I'll wanna run to my place and change."

"Sure. Seven's fine. Just come on in when you get there. I'll leave the door open."

"OK," she says, a small smile finally on her lips.

"OK," I say, a probably sad smile on mine.

I give her a tiny, tiny kiss. It's only tiny because she's at work, otherwise I'd really lay one on her.

Because that's what you do before you kill someone, right? Really plant one on 'em? A kiss before dying.

"See you tonight," I say, and then turn and walk away.

I make bad choices! That's what she said to me on the rock wall. *I make bad choices.*

I know, cupcake, I know. But you've got four hours and fifteen minutes to correct that pattern.

Please do, I think, as the clock keeps ticking.

HER SECRET
CREAMY FILLING

OK, it's not a secret but it can be harder to find than the missing cookies in the cookie jar. First rule of finding her secret creamy filling is... you never find yours before she finds hers. There is no expection to this rule, guys.
Ever.

CHAPTER THIRTY-ONE

"So why were you calling me earlier?" Zoey asks. I have her on speaker phone while I put on my makeup because I've been telling her all about my upcoming date with Andrew.

"When?"

"When I called you and told you about Pink Lady Media. You said you were just about to call me. What was that all about?"

"Oh," I grumble. And then I tell her the whole story about Pierce and his offer. Which you wouldn't think I'd have forgotten about after how panicked I was earlier, but Andrew asking me out on another date—this is a date, right? It is—kinda made all my worries disappear. Plus, we did get that offer from Pink Lady Media. So yeah. My world was righted again. Andrew and I are still a thing and Zoey and I have a new opportunity.

Things are actually perfect. No need whatsoever to out myself to Pierce. Pierce who? And that makes me chuckle. I don't need him anymore. He can take his offer and shove it up—

"Huh," Zoey says. "Actually, wow. How did you keep that to yourself all day? I mean, why didn't you call me back and tell me?"

"Oh, well. Sorry. I was distracted this afternoon. And I figured you didn't want to take the offer anyway."

"Right. We don't want that offer." But then she goes silent for a few seconds, and I don't say anything either because I'm curling my eyelashes and I have to do weird things with my mouth when I do that.

When I finish, I blink quickly six times and say, "So yay for us, right? We got exactly what we wanted and I didn't have to go crawling up to Pierce's office like a puppy begging for scraps. *And* Gretchen can suck it, because she steals all my ideas. *And* Andrew is definitely interested in me. He sent me that gift and he asked me over to his place tonight. Things are really falling into place. Everything is perfect. I'm probably gonna marry him."

Silence.

"Zoey? Shit," I say, picking up my phone. "Did I lose you?"

"No," she says. "No, I'm still here."

"Oh, my God, what's wrong?"

"That's kind of a great offer Pierce made us. Don't you think?"

"Is it?" I say. "I mean, Pink Lady said you could work from home, right?"

"I know, but Pink Lady is independent media and you know how those are. Here one day, gone the next. *Le Man... Le Man* is legitimate."

"You're not seriously thinking I should—well, I can't now. The deal is over, Zoey. It ended at five o'clock! Besides, I already lied to Andrew about this. So many times. If we take Pierce's offer, he's gonna know I was lying and it's going to ruin everything!"

"I'm sorry. I didn't know about the offer. I might've told you to just... do it."

I take deep breaths. Steeple my fingers. Place them against my chin. And say, "Pink Lady is perfect."

"But *Le Man*—"

"No. Jesus. You know how much I want to get out of there, Zoey. Pink Lady is perfect."

She sighs.

"Pink Lady—"

"I get it," Zoey says. "But you should've told me about the offer while it was still in effect, Eden. Why didn't you tell me? We could've discussed it."

I want to get mad at her right now and I never get mad at Zoey. But... I take a deep breath and calm myself down, then say, in a low and even tone, "We started this because we wanted independence. We wanted things a corporation like *Le Man* and Corporate Solutions couldn't give us, remember?"

"I remember, but Eden. God. Shit. I dunno. I mean… what I really want is stability. Ya know? I have a baby to take care of. And maybe we'd have talked it all through and said no anyway, but now… now I kinda feel like… you took that decision away from me."

"I cannot believe you just said that."

"Well, I can't believe you didn't even bother to mention this offer to me. Eden! That was a fabulous offer! And I didn't even get a say. We're partners. You should've told me!"

I don't know what to say. I am… mad? Sad? I'm not sure.

"I think," Zoey says, "that what you did… was a little bit selfish. Because… because maybe you just sold out our best opportunity to make this work because you wanted to keep your stupid boyfriend who, in my opinion, isn't even your boyfriend. You sold me out for a *fling*. And I'm upset about it."

"Oh, my God! How can you even think that? I put everything on the line for this Sexpert stuff. I've been lying to everyone to keep our secret. And Andrew is not a fling! He's a serious prospect!"

She stays silent for a few moments. Then she says, "Stevie is crying. I need to go."

And then I get three quick beeps.

And Stevie was not crying. She just lied to me!

I huff at my reflection in the bathroom mirror. "What the hell?"

Because I don't get it. Every time I have a great day something goes wrong.

Sexpert goes viral, my boss accuses us of stealing his idea.

We get a fabulous career opportunity and my best friend gets angry about a lost one.

Just... what the hell?

I blink at myself. Take another deep, deep breath. And say, "Pull yourself together, Presley. You can fix things with Zoey tomorrow. Tonight... tonight is the first night of your new future."

And because I'm someone who ravels myself up in the face of adversity, I do that.

I put on my shimmery light blue summer dress, my most sparkling earrings and necklace, and fluff my blonde hair until it looks just fucked.

Because this is my night and I'm gonna make it count.

At five minutes to seven I leave my apartment, take the elevator up to the penthouse—trying not to hyperventilate with excitement—and find the door cracked open.

Just like he said it would be.

I knock anyway. "Knock, knock!" I call out. "I'm here!"

And then I smooth an imaginary wrinkle out of my dress and step into his apartment looking and feeling like a million bucks.

"Andrew?" And then I see him. Standing out on the terrace with his back to me. Hands in his pockets as he looks towards the sun just starting to dip below the mountains off in the distance.

He turns, his body backlit by the sunset, his face hidden, and we walk towards each other.

"Wow," I say. "That's some view."

"Yes," he says, his hand reaching for mine as we close the distance between us. "It's pretty spectacular."

I take his hand and let him pull me in for a kiss... on the cheek.

That makes me giggle. "Just a cheek kiss?" I ask, grinning up at him. "That's all I get?"

"We'll see," he says.

I laugh again, but this time it's smaller. "Um... is something wrong?"

"I don't know. Is something wrong with you?"

"Uh. Nope," I say, starting to feel odd. "Nope. Everything's pretty good with me."

He nods his head and then points to something behind me. "I wanna show you something. Come have a seat."

"Wow," I say, taking in his huge outdoor television. "I didn't notice this last time. Pretty cool. Are we watching a movie?"

He sighs. "Sorta. Have a seat. Let me find the remote."

I do... because I don't know what else I *can* do.

But suddenly everything feels wrong here.

The way it felt on the phone just before Zoey got angry with me.

I watch him cross the terrace, pick up the remote, and then point it at the TV.

And that's when an eighty-inch Sexpert appears.

My cupcakes, in all their glory.

And my voice.

My voice.

Explaining to my audience how to give a blowjob.

306

*"**What the hell is this?**"* she asks, standing back up and turning to face me.

And I'm sad. Because she looks beautiful. Her blue dress is catching the light from the setting sun, sparkling in a way that makes her look like something out of a dream. And her golden hair is ruffled, just like her personality. Looking just-fucked. And she's wearing jewelry, and makeup, and...

She thinks this is a date.

And it's not.

"I didn't want to do it this way. But I gave you *all* the chances to come clean. And you just… you just kept lying to me."

"What? You asked me up here to… to… *ambush* me?"

"If your man has a delicious cock, it's easy to lick him like a lollipop," the Sexpert says on the TV as she—as Eden—demonstrates with a banana.

"No. Not to ambush you. To ask you… why? Why the hell didn't you just own up to this? You knew I was going to figure it out. Hell, I don't even need the new app to ID you. I can hear you sitting right here."

"Take him in your hand and give him a few pumps to let him know you're ready," the Sexpert whispers.

"Jesus Christ! Can you turn that off, please?"

"Then slide your tongue up and down his shaft to whet your appetite for the banana cream pie he's about to serve up—"

"Is this uncomfortable for you? Yeah. That's tough. Well, as awkward as this is for you, for me… for me it's painful. Because I like you—"

"I like you too!"

"But I can't be lied to. I just… I can't."

"But listen, Andrew. This Sexpert stuff. It was a secret, OK? I mean it's got nothing to do with you."

"And then, when you're both good and ready, slip him into your mouth and…"

"Turn it off!" she yells, coming at me. She snatches the remote from my hand and clicks a button. But instead of turning off, the footage switches to another video.

"A sprinkle of nuts," the Sexpert says, *"is a more appetizing way to think of tea-bagging."*

"Oh, my God!" Eden says, pushing another button on the remote.

But it just switches to another video. Because I knew she'd do this and so I set it up. Yes, it's a mean thing to do. Whatever.

She clicks again, and again—but each time it's a new version of her as the Sexpert. Her cupcakes. Her hands demonstrating sex toys, and props. Her words spilling out of her mouth—in her voice—as she describes... well. Sex.

Finally, after several agonizing seconds of this, she finds the pause button and the videos stop, her cupcakes frozen in the act as she shows viewers how to titty-fuck a cannoli, the cream center spilling out the end.

She looks at the screen. Then at me.

And she is horrified. Humiliated. Paralyzed.

I shrug but shake my head at the same time. Because it's got everything to do with me. "I asked you, over and over again, if you were her. And you said no."

"What else could I say? It was a secret!"

"I told you. I was on your side."

"Well, clearly you're not now, are you? What exactly are you doing here? Trying to ruin my life?"

"Looking out for my best friend. Like he asked me to." I shrug again. "Sorry, cupcake. That's who I am."

She says nothing.

"I asked you what was wrong the first night I got here. You know? The one where Pierce told you all about his plans on how to find the Sexpert and you just sat there listening? And then you got weird and had to go to work, remember that?"

She just stares at me. Saying nothing.

"Lie number one. So you could what? Go call your partner in crime, Zoey, and tell her everything Pierce just told you? Was that why you got weird and had to leave that night? So you and Zoey could come up with a plan?"

Still. Nothing.

"Lie number two was after we had our sexy time up there." I point at the pool up on the roof. "When you used all your little Sexpert secrets to…." And then I have to laugh and shake my head. "And your excuse when I asked you—point blank, on the rock wall—if you were the Sexpert—your excuse was… 'I'm not very good at this. So I watched her videos for pointers.' Right?"

She clenches her jaw and crosses her arms. Still saying nothing.

"You slapped me in the face for accusing you, for fuck's sake."

And now I'm starting to get pissed off. Because this girl has some nerve.

"Lie number three. After the art gallery. You said the reason you had cupcakes on your wall was because all that stuff came from your childhood bedroom. And I, like a fool, said 'OK.' And it really was OK. It really was. I was on board with the lies. I bought into them. Because I like you. I like you *a lot*. And I was willing to forget all about my silly Sexpert accusations because you *told me* it wasn't true."

She blinks at me. Three times slowly. And says nothing.

"And you invite me on a date to meet your best friend. It's a big step and you were very excited and blah, blah, blah. But then… but then I get there and I go looking for the bathroom and accidentally find something else instead. Evidence I didn't need because I already knew. But by that time I was lying to myself just as much as you were lying to me."

She lets out a long breath of air. She didn't know this part.

"And look, this is... I mean this is not really a big deal. Y'know? I mean, not really. I mean it's a big deal insofar as it's a big deal to Pierce and it's clearly a big deal to you, but in the grand scheme of things... Eh."

She's starting to tear up a little.

"I mean, hell, we were really only just getting to know each other. It's a good thing we didn't get too far down the path and I started telling you anything *real*, because God knows what would have happened then. I mean I'm working on some shit at work that... Well, it's the kind of thing you can only share with people you trust. So..."

A single tear falls now. It hurts, but I can't stop. I wish I could. But I can't.

"But I kept hoping and hoping and hoping. And no, you didn't hurt *me*. Per se. Not really. But I'm not gonna lie, I really, really thought that you'd make the right move. The solid move. You can see where this is going, right? How, when I came to you today, practically begging you to tell me the truth and take Pierce up on his offer, I had high hopes that you'd come through. That you wouldn't turn out to be *that* girl. The liar that it turns out you are."

I pause. Wanting her to tell me anything. Wanting her to defend herself and say... I dunno. That she made a mistake? That she wasn't thinking clearly? That she panicked, and she takes it all back?

I dunno.

But it doesn't matter. Because she says none of that.

She just nods her head. Breathes through her nose several times. Then nods her head again and...

Walks out.

CHAPTER THIRTY-THREE

You know you've been a terrible friend to someone when bad things happen and you can't bring yourself to call them and cry about it. Because they needed you to be there for them once, and you weren't.

And maybe you are a bad friend and a liar, but you're not a hypocrite so you know that you don't deserve the sympathetic ear of that friend.

313

That's why I don't call Zoey when I get home from Andrew's intervention.

I don't deserve her.

I was a bad friend. I was only thinking of myself. And I don't deserve to be consoled over the absolutely humiliating experience I just went through.

It's my own fault, anyway.

So I cry. I take off my pretty dress. I take off my jewelry and wash the makeup off my face. And I pull my perfectly mussed-up, just-fucked hair into a ponytail.

I change into shorts and a t-shirt and lie down on my bed face first hugging my pillow.

And I cry.

Alone.

Not because I was humiliated. Not because I have no one to talk to.

But because I was a bad friend to both of them.

And I have no one to blame for my sadness but myself.

I get up in the morning like it's just another day because I have to.

I take a shower. Put my hair up in a ponytail. Slide my glasses on. And put on my uniform.

Wait.

I stare at my reflection the mirror and ask myself an honest question.

"Why the fuck do you wear this ugly-ass outfit every goddamned day, Eden?"

I don't really know. Partly it's because I'm trying to hide my breasts. It's always the first thing people notice when they meet me, which makes me super self-aware and uncomfortable, and I figure button-downs are just one step up from baggy sweatshirts in the conceal-the-cupcakes department.

It's a good enough answer for me, so I move on and ask another question.

"Why did you change your outfit when a man asked you to and not before?"

This is much harder to deal with.

Because even though I'm a strong, smart, capable woman trying to make her own way through life—Sexpert equals Example A—the answer to this question is because I... I need validation and I felt like Andrew gave me that.

Because I'm ashamed of my body. I wish I looked different. I wish my breasts were smaller, and my hips narrower, and I hate my double chin and... yeah.

Fine.

I have self-esteem issues. I can admit that.

Moving on.

"So then... Eden... *why* did you start a video channel centered around your cupcakes?"

I don't know. Because it seems like a really stupid, humiliating idea right about now.

And I have go in to work and face up to it. Andrew has probably already told Pierce and there's gonna be another one of those screeching PA announcements about the whole thing, and I'm gonna be humiliated all over again.

Everyone I know at work is going to watch those videos and know it's me.

And... Fuck it. Fine.

But if that's gonna happen, I'm gonna go in there wearing something that is not a button-down shirt and drab skirt. "Because life goes on, Eden. This day will end and tomorrow will come, and I will have to find a way to survive."

My walk to work is way too quick and a part of me wishes that I never moved to the TDH. That I still lived back in my dad's house in the crappy part of Lakewood and I had to drive my old truck to work every day and get stuck in traffic like I used to. I wish I was still sixteen and my pink and white bedroom was age-appropriate instead of ridiculous. I wish I had never started this stupid Sexpert thing. I wish I had never met Andrew Hawthorne or even gone to work at *Le Man* in the first place.

But I did. I did all those things and now… now it's time to face the consequences.

So I hold my chin up as I walk towards the TDH building and go inside to find a huge crowd of people all waiting to walk up the stairs to the second floor.

I stop and look around. "What the hell is going in here?"

"Oh, hey, Eden." It's Sylvia from the printer. "Pierce just made an announcement—"

"Attention! Attention!" Pierce's voice booms from the ceiling. "All *Le Man* employees, please report to the auditorium on the second floor. There is a mandatory meeting. Your attendance is required."

"Oh," I say, deflating even more than I was before I came in here. "Well, that's just great."

"Do you have any idea what this is about?" Sylvia asks.

"Yup." I sigh. "And I guess I shouldn't be late so I better get up there."

She walks with me, chatting the whole time about some cheesecake at a new local bakery, oblivious that my demise is underway and I'm the star of the show this morning.

The second floor of the TDH building is convention space, I guess. There's lots of conference rooms along the perimeter and then at the end is the giant auditorium where everyone from *Le Man* is waiting to file in for the big reveal.

"Eden! Eden! Over here!"

I look to see Myrtle waving her hands at me. "I'll see you later, huh, Sylvia?"

"Sure, Eden," she says, moving forward with the crowd.

I make my way over to Myrtle, who is smirking at me. "Well, don't you look nice today?"

"Thanks," I say.

"What's wrong?"

"Oh… nothing," I say, sighing heavily.

"You look like you're going on a job interview. You're not quitting, are you?"

"Quitting?" I laugh. It's a real laugh too. Because that's not what's happening today. "No. I'm not quitting."

"Good," Myrtle says, smiling at me. "Because you're like my best friend here and I'd be super upset if you left. Come on, there's a back way in. Pierce showed it to me earlier. He's saving me a seat right up front. That man," she titters.

Which makes me look at her funny, but I don't have time to unpack that comment, because she leads me over to a door, and we slip inside the auditorium right up at the front, like she said.

Pierce is there. Up on stage already, standing in front of a microphone.

And so is Andrew.

He looks right at me, his eyes narrowing as I take my seat next to Myrtle, and I want to look away. I really do. I want to act brave, and stoic, and unaffected by what's about to happen.

But I can't. I don't look away. I'm not brave, I'm scared. And I'm not stoic, I'm emotional. I can feel the tears welling up in my eyes as reality sinks in.

He's told Pierce and by the end of this meeting, everyone I know at *Le Man* will think differently of me.

Andrew looks away first. Pierce is looking over at me now. His eyes... his eyes... I look over at Myrtle, who has this weird smile on her face as she gazes up at Pierce.

What the hell?

Is she looking at him weird?

And... wait. Is he looking at her weird too?

Andrew leans in to whisper something to Pierce and Pierce takes his attention to the microphone in front of him. He nods to someone off stage and then taps it, making the room boom with loud thuds.

"Looks like we're ready," he says.

And does he sound... sad?

Jesus. I sigh. I didn't care what Pierce was feeling before now, but seeing him so affected by what's happening... I feel so guilty. For all of it.

"I'm very sad to bring you all here this morning. But..." He looks at Myrtle and me again. "But we have a traitor in our midst. A traitor of the highest order. Because she took advantage of my trust."

There's an audible gasp from my co-workers.

"Yes, this is about the Sexpert. This is about one of my employees—someone I counted on to help me run this business efficiently—taking advantage of private information and using it for her own benefit."

I slink down in my chair. That's not how it happened. That's just *not* how it happened.

"I made a generous offer with the hope that this whole mess could be avoided. But she refused to come forward. So yes, Le Manians, I suppose we could just... let it go. Or perhaps she could be sent an injunction or there's some other legal recourse. But honestly, I'm beyond all that. This is no longer about who did what to whom in a legal sense. This is about loyalty. This is about trust. This is about *Le Man*. The envelope, please."

Pierce holds out his hand and Andrew, rolling his eyes, hands Pierce a pink envelope, which Pierce opens with a loud rip.

He takes out a black card, stares poignantly right at me, and says, "And the Sexpert is... Myrtle Rothschild."

"What?" I say. And so does Myrtle. But I say it with surprise and she says it with laughter.

"Oh, that is too much," she cackles. "Me?" She looks up at Pierce, her hand over her heart. "I'm flattered, but—"

"Security!" Pierce bellows with a wave of his hand. "Escort Ms. Rothschild from the building!"

Myrtle stands up now, because two gigantic goons in black suits are coming toward her like she's about to be whisked away to some top-secret *Le Man* rendition protocol. Even with all the other ways Pierce can be insane, this is in. Sane.

"Pierce!" Myrtle yells over the commotion that has erupted. Everyone is on their feet, talking loudly, as the goons grab her by the arms and start dragging her away. "Pierce!" she yells again. "You cannot be serious! I'm not the Sexpert!"

I look at Andrew. He looks at me and shrugs. And even though I can't hear him, I read his lips loud and clear.

He mouths, "Ball's in your court, cupcake."

"Wait!" I yell. But no one is listening to me. "Wait!" I try again, louder. "It's not her!"

Still, no one is listening. Everyone is talking too loud and now Myrtle is being dragged up the center aisle, resisting like a sacrificial virgin about to be thrown into a volcano.

And then Myrtle's last words echo in my head. *"You're like my best friend here and I'd be super upset if you left."*

I panic. And run up the stairs that lead to the stage. But I'm blocked by a security guard who spreads his arms out wide, dodging left when I dodge right, then right when I dodge left, because he thinks I'm about to assassinate Pierce.

But I'm an athlete. Was. Once. And I know how to body-check a goon. So I rush forward right at him, and his eyes go wide like he's not sure what to do with an insane blonde woman in a professional suit, and I check him with the full weight of my cupcakes behind me. He goes reeling off to the side long enough for me to dash behind the podium and yell into the microphone, "Stop!"

And you'd think it would take more than one "Stop!" to quiet this room down so I could… you know, gather my thoughts and figure out what the hell I'm doing.

But it doesn't.

Because that's how my day is going.

"Stop," I say again, only much softer now because the room has gone quiet. Myrtle and the goons have gone still up at the top of the aisle. Pierce is off to my right, in mid-escape. And Andrew… Andrew is staring at me with a very smug look on his face.

Fucker.

"Eden?" asks Pierce. Then he looks at Andrew and mumbles, "It is Eden, right?"

"Yes, it's fucking Eden," I say, annoyed. "Eden Presley. And Myrtle is not the Sexpert," I say now. Loudly. Calmly. Confidently. "I am."

Gasps erupt and the whole room is commotion again.

"I'm the Sexpert, Pierce. Me. Not her. So let her go."

"What? You!" Pierce bellows. And then he looks at Andrew. "You're—you're… cupcake girl?"

"Yes," I say. Too loudly. Because the microphone screeches and people cover their ears. "Me. And my cupcakes. We're the Sexpert. And I'd just like to go on record that…"

Shit. I have no speech to give. I don't know what to say. But I have to say something because two hundred sets of eyeballs are now focused right on mine.

"I and my business partner, Zoey Cooper, absolutely did *not* steal your idea."

And that's when I notice the cameramen. Stalking up the middle aisle of the auditorium towards me, little blinking red lights letting me know that this is being recorded.

"You did!" Pierce yells. "That was *my* idea! I'd been percolating it for a year and then you came along—"

"I came along and made it up myself," I say, sounding very lame. But I have no choice. I've started something here and now I have to finish it. "And my business partner and I had to do something to make ends meet, OK? Because… because my job is shit, and she's a single mom who gets no child support, and I was tired of living at home and she needs a backyard. So yeah. We invented the Sexpert. And I put myself out there and made those videos. And for one year nothing happened. Nothing. All that work and no payout. And then one day we're on the radio, and we go viral, and then you come out of nowhere, Pierce. *You*. Not *me*. I was already here. And you accuse us of stealing. Well, it's not right! We did this on our own."

I stop to catch my breath.

"We did it to survive. And…"

Everyone is quiet now. And I suddenly realize what I've just done.

"And I only have one more thing to say." Everyone is looking and it's dead quiet. "I quit."

I take a deep breath. Hold my head up high. Straighten my professional jacket. Walk down the stairs silently chanting, *Do not fall. Do not fall. Do not fall.*

And I do not fall.

I walk out.

And as I'm making my way back to Sunset Towers, crying, I pull out my phone and call Zoey.

And I don't care if I'm a hypocrite, because she picks up on the first ring and lets me cry all the way back to my apartment, saying nothing except, "It's OK, Eden. Whatever it is, we'll fix it."

And that's how you know you have a good friend.

Because they're there for you.

Even when you weren't there for them.

CHAPTER THIRTY-FOUR

I thought I knew what I was feeling, but it turns out I don't.

Last night it was anger. Just the thought of being lied to was enough to ignite a small fury inside me. That's how I got through the reveal. That's what kept me going even though her feelings were painted plainly on her face as I exposed her.

That little rage was enough fuel.

But then… after she walked out on me it kinda burned itself out. Or changed states or something. Like heat turning water into steam.

It became indignation. Maybe a little bit of self-righteousness.

After all, *I* wasn't the one who lied.

"What the fuck?" Pierce says.

I look over at him. He's stuck in some position that is half turning, half walking away, like a statue. But then he completes the turn and stands facing me.

"Yeah. What the fuck?" I mutter to myself, glancing back at the door through which Eden disappeared a few seconds ago.

Myrtle is shrugging off Pierce's goons, trying to gather up her usual comportment of mystery. She shoots us a look. Or rather, she shoots Pierce a look. Daggers actually.

I glance at Pierce and see him automatically recoil. Like her gaze is a laser beam that burns. "How did we get this so wrong?" he asks.

"We?" I laugh. "We didn't get anything wrong. I knew."

"You knew? Since when?" Pierce says.

"Um… I mean… well, last night is when I found out for sure. But—"

"Last night?" Pierce says. "Last night? You knew it was Eden last night?"

The irony of him getting her name correct now isn't lost on me. "Well, yeah, but—"

"And you let me embarrass Myrtle like that? Dude? Andrew, mon frère. My ami. You know I love you. Would do anything for you. But my God! Why the fuck would you let me do this, then?"

"Uh… well…" I sigh..

"You… You lied to me?"

"No," I say, looking Pierce dead in the eye. "No. I was trying to make everyone happy. I was trying to get her to admit... I mean, I knew, but I kept quiet because…"

But then it kinda clicks into place.

That whole puzzle-solving thing I like to do.

"She was lying," I say. Because I'm reaching. "She was keeping a secret, man. And you know."

Suddenly I remember that we are standing in front of a room of mumbling, confused people. Myrtle has been hauled off somewhere. And I am starting to get the sneaking suspicion that this whole circumstance *may* constitute an overreaction on my part.

Pierce remembers as well because he turns to the Le Maniacs and says, "OK! Back to work!" It's a thing he does. If you pretend something didn't happen, maybe it didn't. As everyone is filing out, more confused and mumbly than before, he looks back at me, smiles, huffs out a laugh, and says, "Did she owe you her secret, man?"

"What do you mean? Why's it feel like I'm suddenly in the hot seat?"

"Did she. Owe you. Her secret?"

I think about that for a beat. "Owe." Did she *owe* me? Then I decide, "Yes!"

"How long have you known this chick?"

"I dunno. Two weeks. Why?

"Two weeks?"

"Almost three."

"And when did you start suspecting her?"

"I dunno? Like day two."

"Day...?" He sighs. "So you thought... you really thought she *owed* you her most private secret after two days?"

How is Pierce the rational one all of the sudden? "What are you asking me right now? What do you want?"

"I'm just trying to get my head around it. Because this whole morning is now a goddamn nightmare. I have camera crews here, for the love of fuck."

I look at the camera guys filming people walking out, presumably trying to get footage they can piece into something. "Yes, I see that. What the hell is that?"

"PR, my friend. Don't change the subject."

"Change the...? Wha—? Who—? Wha—?" I'm getting, I dunno, ruffled now. Or something. I'm sort of waving my arms around more than usual. I don't typically find myself in a state of flustration (is that a word? I dunno. I'm ruffled), but here I am.

Pierce slaps me.

"What the fuck?" That's me.

He grips my shoulders. "Look at me." I do. "You like her. Yes?"

"Sure." I shrug. "Yes. I like her."

"And you did this to her?"

"I didn't... this isn't even my fucking fight, OK?"

"No, it's mine." And then he sighs. "And I get what you were doing. But... what you did to her... dude." He's shaking his head at me.

"What?"

"Jesus, friend. C'mon. This wasn't about helping me." I open my mouth to protest, but he goes on. "Yes, obviously I asked you for help. Yes, obviously you commenced wanting to help me. But this, all this"—he gestures sort of generally to the air—"you were just testing her. I mean… in what world does a virtual stranger up and admit their deepest, darkest secret? Especially when the consequences of such a thing will result in her being sued, or fired, or both? Does that sound like a reasonable thing to do?"

My eyes go wide and my jaw goes slack. "*You're* lecturing *me* about what is and what isn't reasonable behavior? Fuck you, man! I can't believe you're taking her side! After she stole your idea!"

He sighs and lowers his head, as if somehow my craziness has sucked all his craziness right out of him. "Did she?" he asks.

"Don't," I say, pointing my finger at him. "Do not even go there. I'm the one who was the voice of reason in this whole debacle! I'm the one who said you were overreacting. I'm the one who said it was probably just a stupid coincidence!"

"Oui." He sighs again. "You were. Listen, I'm fine with it. I mean, I suppose we have to hire another social media whatever-she-was, and I have to see where in the world I can find another executive assistant like Myrtle, probably. Spoiler: I can't. But other than that, I'm cool with it. And I mean…" He bows his head a little. "Your loyalty is awe-inspiring. Completely fucked up, really messy, and kind of selfish, actually. But awe-inspiring." And then he smiles, crosses the distance between us, and pulls me into a hug. "Sturdy and chaotic at the same time. Fuckin' rock-climbing artist freak," he says into my ear. Then he claps me on the back, pulls away, and says, "I gotta go find Myrtle. If she quits…" He shakes his head at me. "No. I can't have her quitting."

One last clap on the shoulder, and he's gone.

So... Like I said... I thought I knew how I was feeling about all this.

But I don't.

Because he's right. That puzzle I was solving wasn't the one I thought I was.

I was looking for my secrets, not hers.

I practically jog over to Sunset Towers. Don't even bother waiting for the elevator, just take the stairs up to the second floor and knock on her door. "Eden?" I say. "It's me. Can you please open the door?"

No answer.

"Eden?" I say, knocking again. "Please?"

I take out my phone, find her contact—which says Cupcake and seeing that word kinda makes my heart hurt—and press send.

It rings, then goes to voicemail. No. Wait. It's not voicemail. It's a message.

And it says... *This number is not accepting calls at this time.*

Because she blocked me.

CHAPTER THIRTY-FIVE

Zoey hugs me hard the moment I step into her apartment. I've stopped crying. I cried the whole way back to my apartment to pack up a bag, and then all the way over here in my truck.

So now… I'm just tired.

She still doesn't know what happened and she doesn't ask, either. Doesn't need to ask. Doesn't even need to know. All she needs to know is that I need her and all I need to know is that she's here for me.

I drop my overnight bag on the floor in her front foyer and then flop onto her couch and pull a pillow into my lap as I stare mindlessly out the window.

She goes about her day, leaving me alone, but still paying attention. She makes me a grilled cheese sandwich and I pick at it as she feeds baby Stevie his pureed sweet potatoes. Then she does laundry and plays patty-cake, and does some web design.

I just sit and run the past twenty-four hours through my head over and over again.

How he embarrassed me last night.

How he put me on the spot this morning.

How I humiliated myself by making a stupid speech in front of two hundred people and then quit my job.

"I quit my job," I say softly.

"What?" Zoey is washing sippy cups in the sink, which faces the living room, so she's looking right at me when I say it.

"Yup." I nod. And then the whole story spills out. And when I get to the part where I walk out of the auditorium, she smiles. "Why are you smiling?" I ask. "This is horrible!"

She shrugs. "I dunno. Is it? I mean, it's not what we planned, that's for sure. But since when does life go according to plan?"

We both look over at Stevie, who fell asleep in his baby swing. He's sucking his thumb looking very innocent and adorable.

"I can't say my life is on track either but... but it's a nice life."

I smile at her. And it's not even forced. "You're a good mom."

"Shit." She laughs. "I'm adequate. But one day, Eden, one day, if things go as planned, he's gonna be old enough to know about this Sexpert stuff. And then... well, when that day comes all I can say is I did my best, ya know?" She shrugs. "We're just doing our best, that's all. You didn't do anything wrong."

"I lied to him," I say. "He takes that stuff kinda personally."

"Sure. OK. I get it. But that's his deal, Eden. Not yours. You don't owe him anything and if he made you think you did... well, he's wrong, babe. He's just wrong." She sets her half-clean sippy cup down, wipes her hands on a dish towel, and walks over to the couch to plop down beside me. "You're practically strangers, Eden. It was a brand-new relationship that happened on the wrong day, that's all it was. That's all. It's no one's fault. It's just life."

I nod my head, because it makes sense. I mean... everything that happened was just one long weird coincidence.

"But I feel... I feel really, really bad, Zoey. And I have no job." I pout my lips.

"Hey," she says. "You didn't like that job anyway. And we've still got the Pink Lady offer. We're totally on track for success, you'll see."

My phone buzzes on the coffee table, so I reach over, hoping—for just a second—that it's Andrew. But then I remember I blocked him.

"Who is it?"

"Myrtle," I say, reading her text. "She says to turn on Channel 9. Oh, God..." Because I can see where this is going. Those cameras were there for a reason. "Don't," I say.

But Zoey is already reaching for the remote.

Channel 9 is showing the footage. And there's a headline at the bottom that says, *Sexpert reveals herself. Local girl working for* Le Man *magazine.*

"Well, that's just perfect. Now my dad is gonna know."

And then, like life is conspiring against me, my phone rings. And you guessed it, it's my dad.

"I better take this," I say, getting up from the couch and heading for the bedroom. "Hey, Dad," I say, once I accept his call.

"Hey, cupcake," he says. "How's life?"

I start crying immediately and it's like my whole day is on repeat as I recount the story again. My dad, to his credit, just listens patiently. Lets me get it all out. Lets me have all the feelings I'm feeling. And when I'm done talking he says, "Well, your life has gotten quite exciting since you moved out."

"I'm sorry," I say.

"For what?" he asks.

"Um… for being the Sexpert?"

"Shortcake, you don't need to explain your life to me. You're a grown woman. You're smart, beautiful, innovative. Always have been. You don't have to explain your decisions. I'm your dad. I'll be here no matter what you do."

"I might need to move back home," I say, sniffling like crazy.

"No, you won't, pumpkin. You'll figure it out. I know you will. Just take a few days and relax."

"Should I keep being the Sexpert?" I ask, acutely aware that this conversation is weird. But hey, if he's gonna be Mr. Understanding, I'm gonna get his advice.

"Do what makes you happy, Eden. If you do that, I'll be happy too. Now, you wanna come over for dinner tomorrow? I'm making your favorite dessert."

"Chocolate strawberry cake?" I ask.

"With whip cream filling and cherries on top."

"I'll be there."

CHAPTER THIRTY-SIX

"Have you talked to her?" Pierce asks.

"You know I haven't. She blocked me."

"Blocked you?" He kinda laughs. "Lame."

"I know. She's being ridiculous."

"Not her, you."

"Me?"

"Yeah. Blocked you? What are you, fourteen? You can't get around a call block?"

"I stop by her door and knock four times a day. She's not there."

"So go find her," Pierce says, fucking with the TV remote.

I know where she might be. And I could go over there, but I don't think Zoey liked me before, and now? Yeah.

Pierce is in my office today because I just stopped visiting him. Going anywhere, actually. So a couple days ago he started showing up here. Kinda took over and claimed one of the chairs that used to be in front of my desk as his new throne. He's got it pushed it up against the window for effect or something. That's where he's sitting now.

I'm not pissed off at him, even though he thinks I am. I mean… I have no reason to be pissed off at him.

Pierce sighs and then points the remote at the TV. "There she is."

Yup. There she is. In all her cupcake glory.

She and Zoey are on a local morning show trying to explain and come to terms with their newfound celebrity.

Those cameras Pierce had at the Big Reveal last week actually wound up getting a local goldmine of footage and that shit was on TV that night. Since then Eden and Zoey have been lying low, but at some point you gotta make a statement.

Sexpert is booming. Like last I looked they had five million subscribers.

Pierce is unusually calm about that.

I look at him, leaning forward in his new throne, elbows on knees, staring intently at the screen as the morning show introduces the Sexpert. Or Sexperts, since they are partners.

"Why do you torture yourself?" I ask him.

He reluctantly drags his eyes away from the TV. "What do you mean?"

"Watching them succeed? It's gotta hurt. It was your idea and all."

He shrugs and turns the volume up.

"So," the morning host says. She's blonde, young, and perky. "Eden and Zoey, what a difference a week makes! How are you handling your newfound success?"

"Well," Zoey says, taking control. Eden just sits there and smiles, her perfect cupcakes well-hidden underneath a professional blazer. "We're a very young company, but we're making the most of it. We've gotten several job offers since——"

"Several?" Pierce snorts. "No wonder Eden hasn't returned my calls."

Now he knows her name, that's for damn sure. "Why would she?"

Pierce looks at me, brows furrowed. "Why wouldn't she?"

"Uh… because you went insane. And had her outed on camera."

He points his finger at me. "I think that was you, mon petit chou."

"What's that mean?"

"Term of affection. Means, literally, my little cabbage."

I love how I'm getting all the blame for this current shitstorm when all I was trying to do was be loyal. And honest.

I huff. I guess I should probably reconsider my values since loyalty and honesty don't get you far.

"And then, you know"—Zoey is still talking—"I got pregnant and the father wasn't involved, so we just... we needed a way to support ourselves. And yeah, we've seen a lot of nasty comments on the videos. Saying we're exploiting Eden's assets. But..." She pauses to shrug. "Hell, they're hers to exploit if she wants. We're not hurting anyone. So yeah." She smiles. "We're doing this."

"And, Eden, how do you feel about it?"

She's doing one of those teeth-clenched grins, staring right at the camera. She clears her throat and pushes her glasses up her nose, and God, I miss that. "I'm just... you know. Making things up for new videos. And looking forward to the future, of course." She smiles uncomfortably again. "I mean, it's been stressful because I'm running out of desserts to sexify—" Everyone laughs.

Pierce huffs.

"—so that's challenging. There aren't as many phallic desserts as you might think," she says, finding her rhythm. "I mean, aside from the cannoli and the éclair, how many long pastries can you squirt on camera? Am I right?" More laughing on screen.

I crack a smile. Just a little one.

"Well, there's the ladyfinger," the hostess says.

"Oh." Eden points to her. "Good one, Jackie! Can I steal that?"

"Only if I can give you the tip to go with it!" Jackie exclaims, winking for the camera.

"Deal." Eden snorts.

They all laugh more.

She's so. Fucking. Cute.

Pierce points the remote at the TV and turns it off. "Well, a man can only watch his own demise for so long. I mean, the lawyers are still pushing forward so we're not quite done fighting. But it's going to be a bitter win when it comes and—"

"What?" I say. "Are you fucking kidding me right now?"

"What what?"

"You're still going to try to take her to court?"

"Why would I just give in?" Pierce asks. "It was my idea."

"You're the one who was saying maybe it wasn't last week when she walked out."

"I've had a change of heart."

"You mean, you saw the five million subscribers on YouTube and decided to take a piece of her pie."

"Nice." He laughs. "But yes. It's just business."

"You can't win this."

"I think I can. I have money, and power, and the best lawyers in the state. At the very least I have something to negotiate with."

"So you really do want a piece of her pie?"

"Of course," he says. "I'd be stupid to let her get away with this."

"Wow," I say. "You're a dick."

"Me? No. I'm just trying to save my magazine."

"Is that all you think about?"

"What else is there to think about?"

"Um… well, let's start with a healthy dose of human decency for one."

"You know as well as anyone that human decency doesn't go far."

"Fuck you," I say.

"Fuck you back," he says. "Do you have any idea what I had to promise Myrtle to get her to stay on as my assistant?"

I picture long nights of Pierce being handcuffed in Myrtle's secret dungeon lair as she stands over him in thigh-high latex boots holding a whip.

"She now makes more than my VP. And she's hostile."

"She was always hostile."

"No, she was assertive. Now she's just angry. And that's all because of you. You knew it wasn't her and you let me embarrass her in front of the whole company."

I sigh. We've been over this a dozen times and hell, I've done nothing but apologize to him—and Myrtle, and let me tell you, apologizing to Myrtle isn't something I ever want to do again—so what more can I say?

"I'm sorry." I just give in and say it again. Because... whatever.

"So yeah," Pierce continues. "I'm going all in on this little fight. I deserve something out of it."

I just look at him. Like... seriously. How is this guy my best friend? Maybe it's me who makes bad choices?

"They're gonna slaughter you."

"I'm ready."

"You're gonna be the sole reason this magazine goes down."

"At least I'll go down fighting."

"Dude." I laugh. "You can't win this. These are two young women with a solid high-concept idea. One of whom is a single mother with no child support, the other is being attacked by her former employer for *succeeding*. That relationship with your father? Gone. Because this magazine won't recover from a PR nightmare like that.

Not to mention, you're just an asshole for even considering it. Just do the world a favor and accept the fact that she had the idea first and didn't steal it, OK? Because we're all tired of your fake aristocratic attitude. You're not a king. You're just a sad, sad man with daddy problems."

He purses his lips and nods his head. "Yeah, OK. But at least I'm being honest with you. Which is more than you're doing with me."

"What? What the fuck does that mean?"

He shrugs. "*You're* still holding a grudge. So why should I give up mine?"

"She lied to me."

"Whoopty-do! She lied to me too. So we're even."

"We're not even. I'm not the one trying to ruin her life."

"Then why do you feel so guilty about what you did?"

"I don't."

"Well," he says quietly. "Then you're the sad one, Andrew. Because you found a girl you liked. And she liked you back. And talk about a royal fuckup? You're the king of that kingdom. I'm not gonna sue her, asshole. I'm just trying to make a point."

"What point?"

"I wanted to see what side you'd land on."

"Side? What?"

"It was a test."

"A test? What? What the fuck? What are you doing right now?"

"Doesn't feel very good, does it? You are the one who ruined this. And I'm not talking about the magazine. I'm talking about the relationship. And your litmus test just proves that you're the asshole here, not me. I dunno. I'm just doing some shit I read about in one of our articles. Reverse transference, or... something. Some way to make a chick think she's crazy. But I'm just using it on you. Doesn't mean I'm not right."

I laugh. Guffaw, actually.

"You got fucked over by a woman once and now you've got this test to see if people are worthy. Well, good luck with that. Because your standard is impossible to meet. You set them up. Just like I set you up. Beautifully, I'll add."

"Honesty?" I say. "That's an impossible standard?"

"Trust is *earned*. You didn't earn it. You just expected it."

I pause to mull that over. "Say more."

Pierce stands up, buttons his suit coat, and says, "Mon chou, if I've got to explain that part to you, well... watch the video. Take a good look at it. Because that look on your face when she's up there on that stage?" He sighs. "It hurts me to see it. It really hurts me. Because once upon a time you were the far better guy in this friendship and somehow..." He shakes his head. "I dunno. Somehow, we're now equal. And I always figured maybe one day I'd learn to be more like you. Not the other way around."

And then he walks out.

"I'm not the one avoiding *her*!" I yell after him. "She blocked *me*!"

But all I get back is a faint, "Boohoo," as he makes his way out of the Aureality offices.

It's bullshit. I mean... what the actual fuck? I'm not the one who lied. Repeatedly. I'm the one who was trying to help. I'm the one who has his back. I'm the one who got her that deal, a great deal too. And she's the one who refused to take it.

Right?

Right?

I flip the TV on to see if they're still interviewing them on the morning show, but they're not. They're gone.

So I do a search for the Sexpert, and not because Pierce told me to, either. It's just... I haven't seen it yet. I've been avoiding it, actually. The first video is the one about blow jobs, but the one right below it is the footage at the TDH building last week.

I press play and the sound comes on. Pierce and I are on stage. He looks stressed. I look... I lean a little to make sure I'm seeing this right. Because I look...

Smug.

Do I? Or am I making that up?

Oh, no. No. I'm definitely smiling.

Jesus. Was I happy that morning? I honestly don't recall smiling like that.

There's no footage of Eden at this point. No one was looking at her while Pierce was doing his little act up on stage. But as soon as he says Myrtle's name, a camera goes looking for her. Finds her. She's laughing it off while Eden... Eden is horrified.

The goons appear and start dragging Myrtle away, but I catch a glimpse of Eden, who is not watching Myrtle, but staring up at the stage.

At me, I realize.

The angle flashes back to the stage to find Pierce's reaction. He looks... devastated. And I look... holy shit.

Am I laughing? What the fuck is wrong with me?

Eden makes her way up on stage and the whole thing changes, the focus no longer on Myrtle's valiant attempt to beat the shit out of her security detail as she's led up the aisle to be booted from the company, and now it's all directed to Eden's speech on stage.

I'm standing next to her. In the very same spot I started out in next to Pierce. And again… I'm smiling. Like this whole thing is my proudest moment.

I blink at me on the screen.

Unable to recognize myself.

Holy shit. No wonder she blocked me.

My self-righteous gloating is… sad.

Who are you, Andrew Hawthorne?

What have you become?

CHAPTER THIRTY-SEVEN

I go home after the morning-show interview. Which may not sound like a big deal but it is because I've been at Zoey's house since the whole Sexpert débacle happened eleven days ago and aside from the one trip home to my dad's for dinner (and dessert, of course) we've pretty much been hermits. We just put our heads down and forgot all about the threats, nasty comments, and opportunities that were never meant to be.

We put our heads down and we worked. We worked our asses off.

Because we realized something while we were having dinner with my dad.

We make our own opportunities. We don't need permission from anyone to make a new opportunity. And even if Pierce's lawyers rip us apart in court and take the Sexpert away, it won't matter. We're going to make sure of it.

So we've been making a lot of changes. For one, we have a website now—courtesy of her mad design skills. And two—well, the URL of that website *isn't* Sexpert.com.

And ya know, ya'd think that after a whole month of unexpected beginnings and middles, I'd be prepared for the unexpected ending as well.

But it was a very sweet surprise.

I take the elevator up to the second floor because I'm hauling my overnight bag of dirty clothes and a stack of pink bakery boxes filled with sweet, delicious desserts, for research, of course.

The elevator dings and I get out, smiling at the other people in the elevator when I exit. God, what a difference eleven days make. When I was here last I was a broken mess. My heart aching for the love that was never meant to be.

I'm over that now.

I'm focused, hopeful, and one hundred percent ready for the future.

Now if I could only get my key card out of my purse—

"Here. Let me take those for you."

And then the bakery boxes are lifted out of my hands into the waiting ones of… Pierce Chevalier.

"You," I say, all my Zen bullshit flying out the window. "*You*," I seethe again. "What are you doing here? If you think you're gonna threaten me again, well, buddy, let me just school you in what's gonna happen next—"

"Hey, wait a minute. I'm not here to threaten you, Eden."

"Oh, so now you know my name!"

Pierce is a handsome man. And he's got a very charming smile. Which he unleashes on me right now as he shuffles the boxes into one hand and places the other over his heart in a gesture that makes *my* heart ache because I think about Andrew crossing his heart with promises. "You're quite unforgettable. I will never make that mistake again."

I huff out a breath of air that sends my hair flying up and my glasses sliding down my nose. But I'm not in the mood to push them back into place. Because I have *things* to say to this man. "You know what my motto is, Pierce?"

"Uh… Eat dessert first?"

"When things get hard, I work harder." But I kinda like his motto too. I might have to revise.

"Look, I'm here to apologize. And if you'll just invite me in, I swear, you won't regret it."

Now I do push my glasses up my nose. "Don't be so sure, mister. I'm still pretty upset about things." Which is only half true. I mean… I really did find my inner Zen, even if I lost it for a second there. But I feel obliged to play this part with him.

Pierce places a hand over his mouth, trying to hide a chuckle, I think. Which kinda pisses me off all over again, because I get the feeling this guy doesn't take me seriously.

But then he says, "Please. Eden. Five minutes of your time. I promise to make those minutes as sweet as the desserts inside these boxes."

"Five. Minutes," I growl, turning to flash my key card at my door lock. "I'm a very busy businesswoman."

I don't look back at him, but I think he's chuckling again.

I open the door and wave him in, but he says, "After you."

So I go inside and... sigh. I'm kinda glad to be home. I mean hanging out with Zoey and baby Stevie was fun and super productive, but I missed this place.

It's home now. Even though the main reason I moved here is gone, I still feel like my future is in the TDH.

"Should I put these in your kitchen?" Pierce asks. But then he kinda squints his eyes at my tiny kitchenette and looks around for another option.

"Just give them to me," I say, letting my overnight bag thump to the floor next to the bathroom door. "I've got to put them in the fridge so the frosting doesn't go bad."

He looks at my apartment-sized refrigerator, then back at my stack of pink boxes, and spends about five seconds wondering how I'm gonna do that.

I just take the boxes from him and open the fridge door.

It's kinda packed with old take-out containers, and I'm trying to balance the pastries on my hip as I rearrange things, when Pierce comes over and starts clearing space for me.

I watch him sniff the containers, and then unceremoniously throw them in the trash. "So listen," he says, moving on to reorganizing my condiments. "First of all. Andrew——"

"I don't want to talk about him. OK? So if you're here on his behalf, I'm sorry, but I'm gonna ask you to leave. I've moved on, he's moved on…" And then I just get sad, so I shut up and start placing the boxes inside the fridge.

"OK," Pierce says, checking the expiration date on the ranch dressing. "That's not really why I'm here. I'm here to make you an offer."

"No," I say. "I'm not interested."

"You didn't even hear it."

"Doesn't matter. The Sexpert was our idea and we don't care how many threats you throw at us, my dad has a lawyer who said he'd help us for free if we needed it, and we'll use him if we have to. We will."

My dad does have a lawyer friend, and he did say he'd help us for free, but he's like some kind of estate planning guy. Still, it sounds good in the moment.

"There's not going to be any lawsuits."

"There's not?"

"No. I've… I've decided… When did you come up with the idea?"

"When? Like two years ago. I didn't steal your idea, Pierce."

"Yeah. I know."

"You do?"

"I do."

"How?"

"I know."

OK. Fine. He can be mysterious. Just as long as he doesn't sue me.

"I know it was your idea first," he emphasizes again. "And you know what?"

"What?"

"It was a damn good one."

I smile. "It was, wasn't it?"

He nods. "And I think your take on sex is something special."

"You do?" I say, sniffing a little because I must've left the AC on in here when I left and it's freezing.

"Desserts. It's kinda perfect. I mean... yeah. Just perfect."

"Well, thank you," I say. "That part was all me. Well, no. Zoey was all, 'We need a schtick. A thing. And your cupcakes are fantastic.' And she was right. I do have the most fabulous cupcake recipe. So at first—"

"Wait." He laughs. "You came up with this because"—and then he looks over at my giant cupcake picture over my bed—"because you actually bake the perfect cupcakes?"

"Yeah. My dad owns a bakery and I've been working in there since I was six. All those pink boxes? Those are my desserts we sell at our store. As I said. I've moved on. We're keeping the Sexpert because, well... it's just too lucrative to let it go. But we're moving into consulting."

"You are?" Pierce raises an eyebrow. "What kind of consulting?"

"You don't need to know that. And before you make me an offer to take the Sexpert off our hands, my answer is still no. It's ours."

His hand goes to the slight shadow of stubble on his chin. Like he's thinking about this. And then he says, "How many clients do you have?"

"Plenty," I say. Which is a lie. We have my dad's bakery and that's it. But one is better than none. And I don't owe Pierce an answer anyway. "Plenty," I say again.

"Well, I'm only asking because I'm actually in the process of hiring some marketing consultants. Is that what you consult about?"

"Yes," I say. "We're social media experts."

He smiles. And I do admit, that smile is super charming. "You know, you might not've heard, but my social media expert quit last week."

"You don't say?"

"Yup. She did. We kinda pissed her off. We're very sorry about that, by the way. In case you're worried about her. Very sorry. But that means I need to hire someone else—"

"No way. I'm not working for you again. You didn't even know who I was last month. And I'm tired of stupid Gretchen stealing my ideas and then taking them up to you, pretending they're hers. It's bullshit."

"Total bullshit," Pierce says.

"I was the one who came up with the idea to repurpose articles so your stupid magazine could compete with my Sexpert. Did you know that?" I don't wait for an answer, because I've been wanting to say all this to Pierce ever since I started working at *Le Man* and was forced to deal with Gretchen's dictatorship because I had no choice. "And I was the one who retitled all your dumb blog posts and got them delicious graphics. Me. And Gretchen was thwarting me at every step. She actually ordered me not to do that. So. No. I don't want your job. I'm a businesswoman. Not some cheap, entry-level hashtag maker."

"Wow," he says.

"Wow what?"

"I can totally see why Andrew is so devastated about losing you."

"Yeah," I snarl. "He should be! Oh, hey, wait a minute... did you say he's devastated?"

I allow myself a moment of hope. Because after rewatching that day on film... that smile he was smiling as my world was falling apart... Well, that was some real eye-opening shit right there. I'd given up on him. I figured he was just one of those asshole guys.

But that doesn't mean I didn't miss him. Or what I thought we had.

I do.

And if he's devastated, I mean, that's a strong word.

"Devastated," Pierce reiterates.

"But he was so happy about busting me."

"It's my fault," he says. "It's all my fault."

"What do you mean?"

"I'm like a... *king*. And I just unknowingly project this incredible sense of loyalty. Some say it's in my genes. My family history. Or maybe my father's corporate holdings, but I like to think it's just part of my charm."

I think he's serious. So I don't laugh. "And that has what to do with Andrew?"

"First, the offer. Because one has nothing to do with the other. OK? You can take my offer and it's got nothing to do with Andrew. Or you can tell me to fuck off, because God knows, I deserve that. But that will not affect anything you do with Andrew going forward. So hear me out for a second?"

I shrug one shoulder and say, "Fine. Make your offer."

"I need a marketing consultant. And when I say need, Eden, I mean it. I need someone to help me. To partner with me. Because if I don't do something creative, something innovative, something that can capture the attention of men the way you did... well, I'm done. That's all there is to it. This magazine was my one chance to prove to my father that I was capable and worthy. And I'm failing." He throws up his hands and says it again. "I'm failing. And I need help. I need your help."

It's my turn to say, "Wow."

"Dramatic? Maybe. But all true. So... I was gonna offer you your job back—"

"No!"

"—before I came over here and you told me about your new business. But now... Eden... Can I... Will you... let me be one of your clients? Please?" He holds his hand together like he's praying. "Pretty please with sugar on top?"

I scrutinize him. Because this feels too good to be true. And since when do kings say pretty please? "What about the Sexpert?"

"She's yours." And then he laughs. "No, like literally, she's *you*. It doesn't matter if I get the name. The Sexpert is all you. You earned it. And..." He does a little bow, his hand waving around in that little flourish thing hands do when people bow. "And well done, sugar princess. Well done. You win."

I cross my arms over my chest and breathe through my nose as I take this all in. "OK," I say. "You send us an offer in writing and my partner and I will discuss it."

A smile creeps up his face until it's wide and his eyes are sparkling with hope.

Wow. I thought I knew how all this was gonna end, but it just goes to show you... a new day can bring anything.

"Now about Andrew and how that was all my fault."

My heart speeds up again. Because I know I'm gonna lose this battle. No one gets two good things in one day.

353

Example A. The day I met Andrew on the freeway and the Sexpert went viral.

So I'm expecting something pretty terrible to come out of the second half of our conversation.

But I listen to Pierce tell his side of the story anyway. Andrew's side. And hear what he's saying. He tells me of their shared past, and what they mean to each other, and we sit down on my stupid tiny loveseat and have tea and cupcakes.

It's weird, I think. Just so weird how just when you're ready to move on and let the old things go, the old can still surprise you.

And by the time Pierce is done telling his story and he's kissing my hand and thanking me for a lovely afternoon, I'm planning one last Sexpert video.

Because I might just get to have my cake and eat it too.

HOW TO HAVE
YOUR CAKE
AND EAT IT TOO

Hey. It's me. As you can see. Can you? Hold on. OK. Is that better? Can you see me? I think you can. So, uh, hi. Which I just said. But still. Hello. It's me. Eden. The Sexpert. Which is incredibly ironic. Because I'm not. I'm just... **not**.

355

"Andrew, thank you, the Director is very happy." That's Carrie from Justice. I finally stopped dodging her calls and emails and had Dev deliver the app to the government.

"Don't thank me. It's all Dev."

"Is he there?" she asks.

"Yeah, I'm here. Hey, Carrie."

357

"Dev, great job."

"Thanks. Sorry it took a minute. We needed to make certain all the bugs were worked out." He raises his eyebrows at me as if to say, *We didn't really, but my boss was preoccupied with a girl and he didn't want to know the truth about her because he unexpectedly fell for her and didn't want to have to choose between her and his friend, and besides, we weren't going to tell you that we were planning on using taxpayer money to run voice recognition on a pair of boobs on the internet anyway.*

Maybe that's not *exactly* what his raised eyebrows are trying to say to me, but it's along those lines, I feel like.

"So, Carrie," I start.

"Yeah?"

"Maybe I shouldn't be asking, but you guys are just gonna use this for, like, surveillance and to, y'know, ID potential terrorist activity and stuff, right?"

There's a long pause before she says, "What else would we use it for?"

"I dunno. What else *would* you use it for?"

"Andrew, you're not implying that we would spy on US citizens, are you?"

"I dunno. Is that an implication I should be making?"

Another long pause.

Finally, "Don't be silly."

"Ooooo-kay," I say.

"Seriously, Andrew, don't worry. You've done a good thing and you've helped your country. Just go take a swim in your private pool and sleep easy tonight knowing you're one of the good guys."

"How do you know I have a private—?" But she hangs up. And while that should be the most disturbing part of her sentence, the part that actually upsets me is that she called me "one of the good guys." Because, as much as I try to be and as much as I really want to be, I'm not sure I am right now.

"Well, that was fucking creepy," says Dev.

"Yup."

"OK, well, cool. I'm glad that's done. I wanna get back to playing around with Theme-Attack." (It's a thing that takes the rhythms of your own vocal patterns and converts it into musical notes so that you have your own, personalized theme song. It's pretty cool. But...)

"We gotta come up with a new name," I say.

"I like it. Thematic, Theme-Attack, I think it works."

"It's terrible."

"Yeah, is it worse than AVATAR?"

"I wish I had never told you about that."

"Hey, man," he says, rounding my desk and slapping my knee, "I love that you were once a young, idealistic artist. I think it's sweet."

"Like you are now?"

"Nah, man, I'm just young. I've never been an idealist and I'm definitely not an artist. I'm a scientist."

"You think?"

"Yeah. I'm not like you, Andrew. I just like to make stuff. You... You pour your whole heart into everything. Which is cool. I appreciate your passion."

"You do?"

"Sure. It's funny to watch you *care* about stuff. Because at the end of the day, I just don't give that much of a shit."

He's right. I do pour my whole heart into whatever I do. I can't help it. My art, my work, my climbing, my friends, my loves, my losses. It's who I am. I wish it wasn't sometimes. But it is.

I look at him standing there, gangly and wise beyond his years.

"You're not at all like what I expected you to be when I hired you, Dev."

He smiles, his hand on the door to my office. "Sure, man. Nobody ever is." And he leaves.

I laugh to myself a little and stand to look out my window. There the mountains are. Unmoving. Steady. Reliable. Maybe that is why...?

Ahhh. Fuck it. Who gives a shit?

My email dings.

I sit back down at my desk and look. The subject line says, "For Andrew." I open the email and there's a link along with a note that says, "No sugar coating. No frosting. Just what's underneath. The password is CUPCAKES. ~S.P."

I almost hit 'delete' as a reflex, like I'm now conditioned to do when I think something might be spam. But then I read it again.

And I click the link.

It takes me to a private video page.

I enter the password.

A familiar site greets me on the screen. The two most perfect breasts I've seen in my life. And a familiar voice. An *actually* familiar voice. Not Sultry Siren. But still... a sultry siren.

"Hey," she says. And then she pivots the camera so that her face fills the screen instead. "It's me. As you can see. Can you? Hold on." Then her hand covers the lens as she fiddles with adjusting the angle. I shake my head and smile in spite of myself. "OK. Is that better? Can you see me? I think you can. So, uh, hi. Which I just said. But still. Hello."

She takes a breath and I squint my eyes because I dunno... I'm afraid?

I dunno.

She goes on.

"It's me. Eden. The Sexpert. Which is incredibly ironic. Because I'm not. I'm just... not. The Sexpert is an idea. Something that seemed like it might be fun, or funny, or maybe even a stepping stone to something else. Which it was, for a while, until it wasn't. And I'm sorry that it got all confused and messed up and that your friend thought that I stole his idea and..."

She takes a breath and gets a hint of the pout that just about does me in.

"You didn't tell me the whole story. The whole story about you and Pierce."

How the hell does she know?

"You're probably wondering how the hell I know. Pierce came by today. And... oh! And he and I have worked out a deal! I'm going to consult for him. I'd tell you it's because he knows he doesn't have a legal leg to stand on and that I told him I'd bury him in court. But I don't know if he does, actually, and I wouldn't, definitely. So... turns out that your friend, my old boss, is just kind of an OK guy. But you probably knew that."

Depends on the day. But yeah.

"And I know you told me that stuff about him being there for you when you needed him and everything, but you didn't tell me about how you slept with that girl he liked. And you didn't tell me that's how you became sober. And you didn't tell me that Pierce became sober too, just so you wouldn't have to be sober alone. That's... I mean, that's some real, *real* friendship there. So..." She pushes her glasses up her nose. "I get it. I guess. I get why you..." She starts gesturing with her hands like she's trying to summon up the words she wants to use but can't find them.

And she knocks the camera over.

"Shit." She fumbles with the camera for a second and when she gets it set back up, it's pointing at her boobs again. "Dammit." She tries to adjust it, but I guess it's stuck or something. "Shit. It's stuck or something." She bends down so that her face now fills the lens. "OK. I thought this would be a cute, fun idea, but now it seems stupid. Just... Just call me."

And then the screen goes dark.

I can't call her. She blocked me.

Or maybe she didn't anymore. So...

I grab my cell and dial her number.

"Hello?"

"Hey."

"Hi."

There's a long pause. Then she goes on...

"Did you watch it?"

"Obviously."

"Why obviously?"

"Because I wouldn't have called otherwise."

"What? Why not?"

"Because you blocked me."

"Oh. Right."

Another long pause.

"So, what do you want?" she asks.

"I... What do I want? I mean... You told me to call you."

"OK."

"OK."

"So... What did you want me to call you about?"

"Me?"

"Yes."

"Oh..." Pause. "I dunno."

"OK, look, Eden—"

"I'm just sorry, OK? I'm sorry! I'm just... I'm really bad at this stuff. I'm just bad at it. All of it!"

"What? What stuff? What are you talking about?"

"Everything! Just, I dunno. Being a person. I think."

"What? You're like one of the best people I've ever met."

"I lied to you. Like, a lot. And you know why?"

"Of course."

"You do?"

"Yeah. You didn't wanna get sued, or fired, or whatever."

"No. I mean... yes. But, no. It's because I feel like my whole life I've been just trying to fit in, and be normal, and be liked, and be... Whatever. And then I meet you, this cool guy, who seems to have his shit together and all figured out, and... And I just wanted to see if I could drag it out a little longer. Just a little longer before it all came crashing down, like everything always does."

"Eden—"

"No, just lemme finish. And not only that. I mean not just that, but... Also, also I kind of thought if I just stayed away from the truth that the fiction would maybe take over and win. And that I'd win. And that... Shit. I dunno. I just... I was scared. And I'm sorry. OK? I am. I mean, I really, really wanted some cool, awesome speech that explained everything perfectly, but that's not me, so... Yeah."

A really long pause.

"Will you say something now, please?" she finally asks.

"Yes." I take a breath. "So, you don't have anything to apologize for. I mean, no, that's bullshit. You do. Of course you do. You lied to me. A lot."

"I said I was sorry!"

"I know! Yes! Fine! You're forgiven! Jesus. What I'm trying to say is that, I also have to apologize. Because, frankly, I was lying too."

"About what?"

"Same shit. That I know anything about how to be a person. Or that I have my shit together. Or anything. Jesus, I mean I've run from one corner of the country to the next trying to figure out what I wanna do and who I wanna be. Does that sound like a person who has his shit together?"

"Wow. When you put it like that—"

"But mostly... mostly, I knew it was you and I just lied to myself so that I wouldn't have to confront it. Or make a choice. Or... Because... Because I really, really like you. Like. Eden?"

"Yeah?"

"Like... I think I'm falling in love with you."

Silence.

"Hello?"

Silence.

"Eden?"

More silence.

What the fuck? Did she hang up on me?

There's a knock on my office door. I turn around and she's standing there, holding out her phone.

"Hey," I say, shocked.

"Hey," she says.

"I thought you hung up on me."

She shakes her head. "I was here to talk to you in person anyway. I was gonna surprise you in a cool, kind of dramatic way. But then my phone died."

"Seriously?"

She nods.

"Your phone died."

She nods.

"That's... Funny."

She nods. Then she says, "You don't have a charger I can borrow, do you?"

I walk over and stand in front of her. "When did I lose you? On the phone. Just now. What was the last thing you heard?"

"Um... I'm not sure. Maybe you saying that you"—I hold my breath involuntarily—"like me?" I sigh out. "Did you say something else?" I nod. "What?

"I, uh... I dunno. Something about... I dunno."

I feel like a chickenshit. Because I am. And I want to tell her. I absolutely do. But I want it to be right. And now, here, in the middle of what's happening...

I just want to make it right. And special. And I want to take the time. To do it right.

But fuck it.

"I think I'm falling in love with you."

She lowers her head and looks up at me through her lenses.

"What?" she whispers.

"You heard me," I whisper back.

"I know. But will you say it again anyway?"

I smile. "I think I may be falling in love with you."

After a moment she says, "For real?"

I take her chin in my hand and lift it up. "Yeah. For real."

After another moment she says, "That's pretty cool."

"I think so."

"You were smiling," she says, seemingly out of nowhere.

"What?"

"When you and Pierce outed me. Or, I guess, when I outed myself. You were smiling. Like you were enjoying it."

"Jesus. I wasn't. It's... I smile when I get nervous. I... I just... It's something I just do so that nobody gets to see... Jesus. I'm sorry."

"It's OK," she says, pouting again.

"Eden?"

"Yeah."

"That pout fucking kills me."

"Yeah?"

"Yeah."

She does it more. "Sorry," she says. Pouting.

I take her hand in mine.

"What happens now?" she asks.

I shrug. "Honestly? I dunno. You wanna find out together?"

"Do you?"

I nod. "Yeah. I think so."

"You think so?"

"I do."

"You do?"

"I really do."

"And... And that doesn't mess up your zero-tolerance policy about being lied to or whatever?"

"It's a stupid policy."

And at that, I take her face in my hands and I kiss her, long, and hard, on her beautiful, pouty mouth.

"Do you forgive me?" I ask.

"Yeah," she says. "I forgive you."

"Really?" I ask. "I want you to be sure. Because, and I mean this, I don't want to hurt you. I don't. So, when you say that it's OK... You really mean it's OK?"

She takes a long breath, puts her index finger against my lips—I kiss it—then she draws that same finger down to just above her gorgeous cupcakes, and she says, "Cross my heart."

The change of seasons in Colorado is beautiful, I decide. I mean, I don't really decide it. It just is. But I guess I decide to acknowledge it.

I've also decided I'm gonna stay for a while. Which is why I've bought this new place. I'm still in the TDH. Which I will never get tired of making fun of. But I like it here. I like that I can walk places and it feels like, I dunno, a community. That sense of community... It's nice. But I didn't want to stay in the same place I was in, so I bought a place in another building just across the way. I like it. I can still walk to work and I'm actually closer to Eden.

"I'm home," she says, walking in the front door.

I'm *much* closer to Eden. She and I have been in this place for only about a week, but it already kind of feels like home. It's *our* place. I tried to just buy it outright, but she insisted on putting down half the money for a down payment and splitting a mortgage. I told her that I would just pay for it and then she could pay me back half, interest-free, if she really wanted, but she said she wanted her name on the deed too and all that stuff. And I get it. So that's what we did.

And mostly we did it for her. Not me. I mean, I don't need the mortgage money. But Eden and Zoey made a deal with Pierce to be his social media marketing experts. And, for the first time in her life, Eden has the means to do whatever she wants. And apparently what she wants is to pay her share while living with me. Hey... As long as I get the second part, the first part is fine.

And their skill, savvy, and, uh, sexpertise... has turned things around for Pierce. Because Eden and Zoey decided to hire another similar (although not quite as spectacular) pair of boobies to take over for Eden's and they gave the Sexpert a real, proper home on the *Le Man* website. They have a column too. The Sexpert still gives out crazy tips using desserts in the videos, but the Sexpert column in the magazine is more of a Dear Abby type thing. People write to them with sex and relationship questions and then they answer them.

Florent, Pierce's father, is over the moon because it turns out that women like this Sexpert advice column even more than men, and so, yeah. A whole new demographic of print subscribers just kinda appeared out of nowhere. Seems women actually still read. Pierce says it has something to do with them having a better attention span. Or something. I dunno. He kept talking and I stopped listening.

Also, Eden and Zoey really do have their social media consulting thing going. They currently have five clients. *Le Man*, Eden's dad's bakery, and three new TDH businesses have all signed up. They're doing so well that Zoey is in the process of moving into her new TDH home. She put some of her Sexpert money down on a little house in a new-build neighborhood for families so my main man, Stevie, can meet other babies on the local playground and also so that she can be in a secure community. It would seem that Stevie's pop is going to be released from prison soon. (That was the stuff that Eden was "going to tell me about later.") I'm still not sure what he was in for, but it's clear that Zoey wants to make sure there are lots of people around when he resurfaces.

And me? Still climbing. Both literally and not. Figuring out how to trust more. How to just sort of stay in one place, stick with one thing, and know that things are going to be ... okay. I even started playing around with a new idea for an art installation. I want to build a permanent thing on top of one of the range peaks. Something that will welcome anyone who makes the attempt to scale the face and reach the summit.

It's funny. I don't think I considered that a guy who was making vocal software was really struggling to find his own voice. I mean, I don't wanna get all self-exploratory about it; that's what all that time alone in the desert was for. And honestly, I'm not sure I got any closer to finding out anything about myself when I was alone. Not really. Not nearly as much as I feel like I'll be able to discover with someone like Eden.

No. Not someone *like* Eden... Eden.

I remember thinking that she was four or five things rolled up into one sexy, silly, dorky, clever, funny, adorable, perfect package, and every day that we spend together just reveals more and more how true that is.

"Guess what!?" she says, hanging up her jacket and scarf and running to me, jumping in my arms, and giving me a kiss.

"What?" I ask, kissing her back.

"You know Svetlana?"

"Which one's Svetlana?"

"The dry cleaner? The grouchy one?"

"Oh. Yeah. The one who said, 'No, hole was there when you brought them in. Fifty-five-fifty.' Sure. What about her?"

"We're friends now!" she says, beaming.

"Wow. How'd you manage that?"

"I heard her on the phone, yelling at someone in Russian, and when she hung up she started crying."

"No shit."

"No shit. And after some cajoling she told me that some asshole is opening a chain dry-cleaning place across the street."

"Oh. Where the ice-cream place used to be?"

It occurs to me that even though I haven't really been here that long, I've now been here long enough to know where things 'used to be.'

"Yep," she says. "And she's worried about them driving her out of business.

"That sucks."

"I know!" she says.

"You seem exceedingly excited about it all. I mean, she's rude, but..."

"No, silly!" she says, slapping my arm. "I'm not excited that she's being run out of business. I'm excited because I'm going to stop it from happening!"

"You are?"

"I am!" She sticks out her jaw and unconsciously puts her hands on her hips, like Superwoman.

"Great! How!?"

"By doing what I do!"

"You're going to mediate for her? Socially?"

"Yep! I'm gonna build her a campaign and, an online presence, and I'm going to capitalize on her individual... assets, as you would call them."

"She has assets?"

"You haven't noticed?"

"I only have eyes for you, ginger snap."

She curtsies.

"Well," she says, "she does. And I'm gonna help her attract business."

"By using her assets?"

Eden nods.

"Um... How exactly do you plan to do that?"

"What do you mean?"

"I mean... It's a dry cleaner. It's not all that sexy."

"Oh, my sweet, sweet Andrew..." She only ever calls me by my name when she's upset or condescending. "...Everything can be made to be sexy if you know how."

I nod. "And sex sells..."

"Sex does sell."

She shakes her chest and my jeans start to feel snug.

"How much you charging her for this service?" I ask, sliding my arms around her waist.

"Nothing."

"Nothing?"

"Nothing. She's a woman, on her own, struggling to make good things happen for herself in this world. I can't charge her money for helping her."

I smile. Big. And goofy, I have a feeling.

"What?" Eden asks.

I shake my head, "Nothing. Just... I love you."

"I love you too," she says, cocking her head and smiling back. "Oh," she says, looking past my shoulder, "you got it hung."

I turn to look with her.

"Yep. You like it there?"

The sculpture I bought for her is mounted on the wall facing the French doors that open to the patio that has an even more spectacular view of Pikes Peak than my old place had. (Although, to be honest, there is no unspectacular view of Pikes Peak.) We stare at the sculpture for a moment. Two bodies, bound together, growing together, as if borne from the rock itself. The gauzy, Autumn light streaming into the apartment spills over it in a rusty glow.

"Well," she says, "I'm no art expert. But I love it there."

I smile as I turn to face her and put my hands on her ass, "You're no expert?" I ask.

She grins and shakes her head. "Not at art, anyway."

"Yeah...? At what then?"

She shrugs and says, "I dunno. Knowing how many licks it takes to get to the center of a Tootsie Pop?"

"That's a way more valuable skill," I say, placing my mouth on hers as a shadow of lovers bound together in stone expands and spreads across the room.

We all start out as just a piece of rock.

And hopefully, eventually… our shape takes form and we become something.

Sometimes, if you're really lucky, you get to become something together.

END OF BOOK SHIT

Welcome to the End of Book Shit where Johnathan and I get to say anything we want about the book. These are always done last minute and never edited so excuse our typos. :)

J OHNATHAN

Thank you for reading our book. Were you charmed and delighted? We hope you were charmed and delighted. We wanted to do something apart from our first effort together and also pretty substantially apart from what Julie has written, historically.

In short: We wanted to have fun. And we did. So, we hope you did too.

But that's not to say there isn't something else going on inside this story. Of course there is.

On a separate level, beneath the rom and com of it all, this is a story about identity. About perception. Both the perception the world has when they look upon us and the perception we have of ourselves when we glance inward.

And while Julie and I didn't have this conversation when we began working on this book, I don't think it's any coincidence that it's a theme we're both exploring now.

I have spent almost the entire of my life acting. I have been performing in front of audiences since I was eight years old. Acting and being an actor is not just a job or a thing I do, it is very much who I am. My understanding of myself is inexorably bound to the craft and career of acting.

But most of you reading this don't know that. Or maybe, in some passing way, if you see me, you may have some vague recollection of having seen me before in that thing you watched that time. So, for those of you meeting the *idea* of me through reading these books that Julie and I have written (and will be writing), to you I am an author. A romance author at that. And that is something that I am currently learning to embrace and to feel joy in being.

Because I would suggest that the act of feeling joy isn't always something that occurs in a person organically. Sometimes one has to work at it. I certainly do. In part, because I've also spent much of my life occupying the role of a tortured artist. I'm naturally a very moody person, so it was easy, but I also felt like in order to be serious about my work (and to be taken seriously), it was incumbent on me to suffer. But as I've gotten older, what I've come to realize for myself is that the suffering didn't make me a better artist, it just made me a miserable one.

And an unintended side effect of writing these books is that I've discovered my sense of exploration and play again. My sense of wonder at the miracle of discovery. Because every time I sit down to write, I really have only the vaguest of ideas about what's going to spill out. And so, suddenly, I find myself surprised again in ways I didn't know I still could be. And as a result, I find myself eager to do more exploration so that the rush that comes of unearthing new ideas can wash over me again.

I still wouldn't call myself a novelist either, however.

But that's not because I'm not. It's just because I think that I'm deciding I don't intend to call myself anything anymore. Because to be defined or categorized is to limit that notion of exploration I was talking about.

I "am," is something that I don't think can ever be accurate. The next time someone asks me, "What do you do?" I think my answer will just be, "What I can." Because to drill down to a *thing* that I call myself or an idea that is supposed to represent **me** feels disingenuous and like a lie.

I love Eden. Know why? (Of course you don't. I haven't told you yet.) Here's why: Even though Andrew flips his shit on her for lying to him, she never was. Not really.

"Are you The Sexpert?"

She didn't feel she was. I mean, she's not stupid. She knows what he's asking. But part of the reason she never just cops to it isn't simply because she doesn't want to get busted, it's also because on a deep, cellular level, she never felt she was. Not really. Not in any authentic sense. And that made it easy for her to pretend.

She also didn't feel like she was the kind of person who could live in The TDH, or who deserved to be *seen*, or who could have the things she wanted. Again, not really. But, of course, in the end she got kind of everything she dreamed of because – in part – she learned to just sort of follow her own muse. To walk the path that was honest to her.

(Side note: My single favorite thing Eden says in this book is, "...everyone is too busy checking their phones to make eye contact with me, so I can't even make a new friend while I wait." To me that sentence sums up the very core of who Eden Presley is, and I love her for being that way. She kind of breaks my heart. But I digress...)

Andrew has his own issues with identity, obviously. Dev kind of hits at some of Andrew's malfunction, but the real secret to Andrew is found inside the rocks he climbs.

There's this illusion in life that there's a "there" there. That we "become" something, or "grow into" someone. But that's not true. Not that we aren't always becoming or growing, but it's present tense. It's active. There's no plateau. There's always another summit to crest or pitch to throw. And even when you think you've got a grasp, the hold can give away and crumble and then your carefully plotted path has to be reimagined.

Tangential segue: I used to skateboard. I loved it. And the greatest and most influential group of skateboarders from my youth were the Z-Boys of Dogtown out of Santa Monica, California. The Zephyr Skate Team. Progenitors of the art form. There was a movie made about them sometime back called *Lords of Dogtown* starring Emil Hirsch and the late, great Heath Ledger.

But there's an even greater documentary about them called just *Dogtown and Z-Boys*, made by one of the original Zephyr Team members, Stacy Peralta. Skip Engblom, the Captain Hook to these Lost Boys, says in that documentary of the great skater Jay Adams, "He will be in the middle of a maneuver, and have the whole thing collapsing on him, and somehow, in the center of that disaster he'll make something else out of it completely ... which becomes art."

And to me, that's the secret to life. Or one of the secrets anyway. Once you learn to stop fighting the changing, morphing, transitioning evolution of the universe... Once you learn to accept that there's no control to be had... Once you stop trying to conquer the mountain and accept that it's bigger, stronger, and more indelible than you... You can give over to it; and inside what feels like chaos tumbling around you, you can reinvent, readjust, and revive yourself entirely.

And that morphing, twisting, evolving being is who you are.

So, there's no way to classify you... You're constantly a work in progress. You are emerging from the stone, changing and transmogrifying as you stretch and reach and yearn.

I think it's important to look at ourselves. In fact, I think it's crucial. All the greatest assholes I've ever met have one thing in common: They do zero self-exploration. But I think it's equally important not to define ourselves. Not to limit ourselves. And not to be defined or limited by how we're seen by others.

Because we are not one thing. We are everything and we are nothing all at once. We are the vastness of space and we are the inconsequence of ... well ... nothing. I sat here for like five minutes trying to think of something that is truly and utterly without consequence and I came up with nothing.

Which is kind of the point. You are important. You have impact. You matter. If Eden's channel had never taken off and gone viral and launched her into the romantically comedic bedlam it did, she would still have been just as significant. Andrew still would have found her (we believe) and she still would have changed his life just as he changed hers. It would have looked different. It would have felt different. But it would have been no less meaningful.

There were goals I set for myself as a young actor. I've absolutely hit some. Some I don't know if I'll ever hit. One thing I never imagined myself doing was writing romance novels with one of the great and unique voices of the genre. But here I am.

And so, what does that say about my path, my direction in life, my journey?

I'm pretty sure it just says that I'm still on it.

Thanks again for reading this little yarn we spun. There's a whole bunch of inhabitants of The TDH and each one of them has their own tale to tell. We hope you'll keep coming back to find out more about them. We're not yet sure where they'll take all of us, but I have a feeling shit's gonna get wild.

Xo,
-JM
17 July, 2018

JULIE

I have been writing things down on my phone note app about what I wanted to say about this book for over a month and so yeah... I think I have a lot to say.

So when we do these EOBSs I get to cheat a little because Johnathan always turns his in first. Lol Like... I TOTALLY embrace the whole "last minute" thing with these End of Book Shits. So of course he sent his EOBS to me before I sat down to write mine. And I just read it. And I knew his was gonna be about identity because he told me that like a week ago. And I knew mine was gonna be a little bit about identity too. But the thing I really loved about Eden and Zoey was how they got to "their moment" ya know?

Some people get lucky in life. Luck... is sucky. You never want to get where you're going on luck alone because you can't just go grab more luck, right? You can't make luck out of nothing. You can't shape a story into luck. Or a video channel, for that matter.

Just the other day Johnathan and I were talking about the Company TV series. And for some reason we were discussing this whole idea of our executive at MGM being excited about our project and did she just feel that way because her and Johnathan are friends. Because they are. And he was of the opinion that no, that's not why this is happening. Yes, she wants him to be successful. And yes, she wants to support him because they are friends. But she's not gonna waste MGM's time and money on this project for that reason alone. She's a professional, right? And I said, no. Good. I don't want that. Because if that's the case then what we have isn't real. And I need it to be real.

Which brings me back to the Amazon Kindle Unlimited scammers who all just got busted these past few weeks.

I get why people cheat at shit. I get it. They want money, or they want fame, or whatever. They want something and they don't care how they get it.

I am not one of those people. I am not looking for the "result" of success. i.e. Money. i.e. Fame. i.e. Whatever.

I'm looking for personal satisfaction. Much like Johnathan talks about is inner artist and how that dictates his goals and what he wants to do with his time. This is me too. But it's not "art" I'm after. It's just "satisfaction" with what I'm doing, and who I am, and the futures I create for myself.

So this brings me back to Eden and Zoey and their "luck."

Well, it wasn't luck. Their "overnight" success was two years in the making. They hustled out videos and honed their "craft" for a year before anyone took notice. This was me when 321 hit the NYT bestsellers list. It wasn't overnight success at all. I think 321 was my NINETEENTH BOOK! And I had only ever been on one list before that book and that was the Bend Anthology with my Erotica Consortium friends. Hitting NYT for me was WORK. That's it. It was work. I did the work. I wrote the books. I got better at my craft. I kept going. And the stars aligned that winter.

There was no luck involved in what I did. Not really. It was just work.

I like this idea. I hate the idea of luck. People get lucky

all the time. They're called one-hit wonders for a reason.

I've been on the USA Today bestseller's list 21 times. That's not luck. That's WORK.

So yesterday morning Johnathan and I did an interview with Joanna Penn of The Creative Penn podcast. If you're a reader you probably don't know who she is. But if you're an author you definitely know who Joanna Penn is. She's an amazing woman. And I've been on her podcast before a couple years ago and that time I was talking about marketing.

This time Johnathan and I were interviewed together and it was a little bit about the collaborative process and a lot about the whole "journey" we went through from having an author/narrator relationship, to writing a screenplay, to writing a series of novels, to writing this standalone Sexpert book. And how all those things added up to this one moment.

Now, to be clear, we have no clue how the Sexpert is gonna sell. We have no idea if people will enjoy it or whatever. We don't know what's gonna happen in the future.

All we can do—all ANYONE can do—is be true to themselves, do their work, make their "thing" whatever that is, and put it out there.

That's it. That's all you can do.

And some might say the rest is luck.

OK. Fine.

But I don't think it is. Sure, the whole stars align thing seems like luck on the surface, but it's not.

Fate—or whatever you want to call it—is nothing more than preparing for your future. Every time I decide to get up at 4 AM and write so I can meet a deadline I make my future. Maybe that future is big, maybe it's small.

I have no clue. The only thing I know for certain is that if I *didn't* get up and write. If I *didn't* meet that deadline, If I *didn't* put out that book… then sure as shit, *nothing* is gonna happen.

You can't win the game if you're not even playing.

Johnathan and I are most definitely "players" in the game of life. I think we both understand very well that our time here in this world is finite.

Every one of us has an expiration date and none of us know when that's gonna happen. And when you have this perspective you look at life differently. You see all the opportunities to change your life rather than all the things conspiring against you.

Every day is a new opportunity for me. That's how I truly feel. And sometimes I can shift fate just enough to change tomorrow and find the next phase of satisfaction.

If you've read my Junco series you're familiar with this theme. Because through all six of those books that's the goal. To shift fate just enough to change tomorrow.

It can be done, you guys.

One choice can change everything.

The moment Johnathan decided to ask me if I'd like to try and sell The Company as a TV series, he changed his tomorrow. And when I said yes, I changed mine too. And when I asked him to write books I changed it again.

And no, it hasn't been easy. Sometimes it's been really fucking hard. But you know what that's called?

WORK.

But here in this moment I think Johnathan and I both feel satisfaction with what we're trying to do together as a writing team, with the product we put out, with the creative process, with the art.

I don't want success if it's fake. I don't want to cheat

my way to the top of anything. I mean, I guess if I was like... in a life or death Hunger Games world I'd cheat that fucking system to death, OK? Live or die, I'll cheat.

But we're not living the Hunger Games. I'm not gonna die if my book doesn't make the Top 100 on Amazon. I'm not gonna die if The Company doesn't get sold and so I'm not gonna cheat.

Because here's the thing about me... I've got a million stories to tell. If this one doesn't resonate with as many people as I had hoped I got another one in my back pocket. And I'll just take it out and put that out there too. Give myself yet another chance to reach people. And if that one doesn't resonate either, I'll get out another one. And another one. And another one. And I'll keep trying. And I'll keep going.

Because that's how you change your tomorrow.

So I'm sorta glad that Hollywood is so cutthroat. I mean, do people get movies and TV series made simply because of who they are or who they know? Of course. Of course they do.

But that's not the kind of success Johnathan and I are building. We're content to put out a Sexpert video every week for a year with no viewers. We're OK waiting for our moment. Because what we're doing now is getting ready for it.

That's all Eden and Zoey were doing too. They put on their blinders, did their work, and got ready for their moment.

I think I've written about this in another EOBS but I have no idea which one it was. Prepare for success. It might take twenty years for your stars to align, but hear this: If you're not working towards that moment—if you're not on the other side of the door when it opens—

well, that's called ships passing in the night.

You're gonna miss it.

Thank you for reading, thank you for reviewing, and we'll see you in the next book.

Julie
JA Huss
July 17, 2018

Julie & Johnathan
HussMcClain.com

P.S.

If you want to check out our other books you can grab Sin With Me on Amazon, KOBO, Nook, or iBooks.

If you want to try out another JA Huss book that's "sorta" rom com, give Mr. Perfect a go. Buy it at all the same places as Sin. ☺

ABOUT THE AUTHORS

Johnathan McClain's career as a writer and actor spans 25 years and covers the worlds of theatre, film, and television. At the age of 21, Johnathan moved to Chicago where he wrote and began performing his critically acclaimed one-man show, Like It Is. The Chicago Reader proclaimed, "If we're ever to return to a day when theatre matters, we'll need a few hundred more artists with McClain's vision and courage." On the heels of its critical and commercial success, the show subsequently moved to New York where Johnathan was compared favorably to solo performance visionaries such as Eric Bogosian, John Leguizamo, and Anna Deavere Smith.

Johnathan lived for many years in New York, and his work there includes appearing Off-Broadway in the original cast of Jonathan Tolins' The Last Sunday In June at The Century Center, as well as at Lincoln Center Theatre and with the Lincoln Center Director's Lab. Around the country, he has been seen on stage at South Coast Repertory, The American Conservatory Theatre, Florida Stage, Paper Mill Playhouse, and the National Jewish Theatre. Los Angeles stage credits are numerous and include the LA Weekly Award nominated world premiere of Cold/Tender at The Theatre @ Boston Court and the LA Times' Critic's Choice production of The Glass Menagerie at The Colony Theatre for which Johnathan received a Garland Award for his portrayal of Jim O'Connor.

On television, he appeared in a notable turn as Megan Draper's LA agent, Alan Silver, on the final season of AMC's critically acclaimed drama Mad Men, and as the lead of the TV Land comedy series, Retired at 35, starring alongside Hollywood icons George Segal and Jessica Walter. He has also had Series Regular roles on The Bad Girl's Guide starring Jenny McCarthy and Jessica Simpson's sitcom pilot for ABC. His additional television work includes recurring roles on the CBS drama SEAL TEAM and Fox's long-running 24, as well as appearances on Grey's Anatomy, NCIS: Los Angeles, Trial and Error, The Exorcist, Major Crimes, The Glades, Scoundrels, Medium, CSI, Law & Order: SVU, Without a Trace, CSI: Miami, and Happy Family with John Larroquette and Christine Baranski, amongst others. On film, he appeared in the Academy Award nominated Far from Heaven and several independent features.

As an audiobook narrator, he has recorded almost 100 titles. Favorites include the Audie Award winning Illuminae by Amie Kaufman and Jay Kristoff and The Last Days of Night, by Academy Winning Screenwriter Graham Moore (who is also Johnathan's close friend and occasional collaborator). As well as multiple titles by his dear friend and writing partner, JA Huss, with whom he is hard at work making the world a little more romantic.

He lives in Los Angeles with his wife Laura.

JA Huss never wanted to be a writer and she still dreams of that elusive career as an astronaut. She originally went to school to become an equine veterinarian but soon figured out they keep horrible hours and decided to go to grad school instead. That Ph.D wasn't all it was cracked up to be (and she really sucked at the whole scientist thing), so she dropped out and got a M.S. in forensic toxicology just to get the whole thing over with as soon as possible.

After graduation she got a job with the state of Colorado as their one and only hog farm inspector and spent her days wandering the Eastern Plains shooting the shit with farmers.

After a few years of that, she got bored. And since she was a homeschool mom and actually does love science, she decided to write science textbooks and make online classes for other homeschool moms.

She wrote more than two hundred of those workbooks and was the number one publisher at the online homeschool store many times, but eventually she covered every science topic she could think of and ran out of shit to say.

So in 2012 she decided to write fiction instead. That year she released her first three books and started a career that would make her a New York Times bestseller and land her on the USA Today Bestseller's List twenty-one times in the next four years.

Her books have sold millions of copies all over the world, the audio version of her semi-autobiographical book, Eighteen, was nominated for an Audie award in 2016, her audiobook, Mr. Perfect, was nominated for a Voice Arts Award in 2017, and her audiobook, Taking Turns, was nominated for an Audie award in 2018.

Johnathan McClain is her first (and only) writing partner and even though they are worlds apart in just about every way imaginable, it works.

She lives on a ranch in Central Colorado with her family.

If you'd like to learn more about JA Huss and Johnathan McClain you can visit them on their website at www.HussMcClain.com.

You can also join their fan group, Shrike Bikes, on Facebook at www.facebook.com/groups/shrikebikes and you can follow them on Twitter at @JAHuss and @MisterJMcClain.

Printed in Great Britain
by Amazon